CW00504940

THE EXODUS BETRAYAL

N. C. SCRIMGEOUR

ALCRUIX

PRESS

CONTENTS

Prologue   1
Chapter One   3
Chapter Two   17
Chapter Three   35
Chapter Four   45
Chapter Five   57
Chapter Six   67
Chapter Seven   81
Chapter Eight   91
Chapter Nine   103
Chapter Ten   111
Chapter Eleven   121
Chapter Twelve   129
Chapter Thirteen   137
Chapter Fourteen   149
Chapter Fifteen   159
Chapter Sixteen   171
Chapter Seventeen   181
Chapter Eighteen   189
Chapter Nineteen   197
Chapter Twenty   211
Chapter Twenty-One   225
Chapter Twenty-Two   237
Chapter Twenty-Three   249
Chapter Twenty-Four   257

Afterword   263
Read on for a preview of Those Left Behind…   265

Welcome to my head.

I know it's not the most hospitable place, but these things I have to tell you can't be said out loud. They took that from me. Took my words. My mind. They dispossessed me of myself. All I have now are my thoughts, and sometimes I can't help but wonder how many of them are truly my own.

They think they've won. They think they've succeeded in silencing me. But there are pieces of my mind they've never been able to touch. As long as I have a voice in my head that still belongs to me, there's a chance.

That's why you need to know what happened. Even the parts I've been trying to forget. The parts I'll never be able to make right. Because you're the only one who might be able to get me out of this prison they've made my mind into.

No pressure.

CHAPTER ONE

Ryce was going to suspend me.

He'd say it was for ignoring his instructions, but that was only partly true. He'd never admit it, but everyone back at the Spire knew he had no problems looking the other way at the occasional overstep as long as we all got paid at the end of it.

This particular overstep happened to be stealing another warrant from Chase. Maybe it wasn't best practice for a healthy working relationship, but getting one over on her wasn't personal – the most lucrative jobs meant earning more credits, more prestige, more respect. She knew that. So did Ryce.

No, the real reason he was going to suspend me was because his fragile ego couldn't handle the fact that I cut comms on him.

Again.

The last time it happened I'd got off lightly – just a dressing down in front of half the Spire. He'd been red-faced and ranting, spluttering through gritted teeth about my lack of respect and blatant disregard for his authority. I'd taken the public reprimand with as much dignity as I could muster and calmly reminded him about the new ZentaCorp line of anti-stress meds.

As it turned out, neither of us had learned our lesson.

The expletives blowing up my auditory implant were already threatening to give me a cybernetic-induced headache that would last for days. So, just like last time, I fried the connection.

Sphere gave a doleful bleep at my shoulder and I smiled as the translated text flashed in front of my eyes. "Yeah, I know. But the peace and quiet I get now will be worth what comes later."

The little drone whirred in response and zipped forwards, sending images back to my retinal implant as it rounded the next corner. I focused my eyes, zooming in and flicking through the data as quickly as my brain allowed.

"Infrared?"

Sphere obliged. The path looked clear, but that didn't mean anything. I'd been in this job long enough to know there was no such thing as an easy warrant. Anything that looked like it was going to pose no problems usually meant there was something I hadn't seen yet. Still, it wasn't like I had much choice. If I came away empty-handed now, Chase would never let me hear the end of it.

I drew my gun, changing the power output with a flick of my thumb as I edged around the corner. This wasn't the time to be taking chances. In a facility like this, they'd be shooting to kill, not stun.

The hallway was empty. Silent. No alarms triggered, no security. This wasn't right. OriCorp didn't just leave their doors open for anyone to walk in, especially when it came to unregistered research labs.

I kept moving, gun pointed high. Sphere floated back and took up its usual place by my shoulder. Ryce always said I'd be dead by now if it wasn't for my cybernetics but Sphere was as much a part of me as they were. The little drone had saved my ass more times than I could count.

As if it could read my thoughts, Sphere let out a series of urgent beeps. I smacked the helmet release on the shoulder of my suit, not waiting for the translation. The helmet's mask shot up around my jaw and the visor clamped down over my head just as the readout flashed in front of my eyes.

Cyxine. A nasty little nerve agent and one of OriCorp's newest developments. Colourless. Odourless. I'd seen people on the wrong end of it frothing at the mouth and choking on their tongues while they writhed in agony. If it hadn't been for Sphere, it might have been me.

"At least we know we're in the right place."

Sphere hummed, sounding doubtful.

The schematics led down another hall and then to a stairwell. The whole place looked the same. Too bright, too clean and sterile. Almost like it was a government-sanctioned facility and not some shady, off-the-books lab. But who knew with the corporations these days? They were so obsessed with outdoing each other that they sprouted shells and offshoots even they couldn't keep track of.

Warrant hunting was a simpler life. I took a job, I did the job, I got paid. As an arm of the government, most of our assignments were sanctioned. But that didn't mean there weren't other ways we could make money. Running errands for the corporations? Standard fare. Under-the-table credits for rich playboys or jealous wives or violent gangs? No problem, as long as we were getting paid.

My retinal interface flashed. According to the information Ryce had gathered, this was it. There was nowhere else to go at the bottom of the stairwell except through one heavy-set door. That's where my target was.

"Can you scan for what's on the other side? My implants can't get through whatever material they've got in that door."

A light blinked on Sphere's circuits, but it made no reply.

"Never mind, we'll just have to take our chances then. Never hurt us yet."

A short beep.

"That was one time."

I took out a small holochip and held it in front of the door's keypad, waiting for my cybernetics to begin their decryption. If Chase was here, she'd have called it cheating, as if the advantage my cybernetics gave me was somehow more unfair than being blessed with strength or speed or smarts, all because they weren't natural.

Maybe one day she'd finally apply for cyber surgery herself. Then things really would get interesting between us.

A minute passed and then another. The door remained shut. For the first time, a sliver of doubt crept in. This wasn't normal. My cybernetics usually took seconds to break through firewalls, not minutes. Even Felix, who had access to all my protocols and years of practice building defences against them, couldn't keep me out of his programmes for more than an hour. For a standard system to be this defiant was unusual. What kind of tech had OriCorp managed to get their hands on?

I focused harder, ignoring the sudden twinge of pain that shot through my skull at the effort. The system was alive, learning from my attempts to get past it and putting up new walls in place. It was far too intelligent, far too complex. It was beyond me.

The realisation turned me cold. I had never come across something I couldn't break through. Was I losing my touch? Were my cybernetics, so advanced at the time of my surgery, already becoming obsolete thanks to the breakneck speed of the corporations' technological developments?

Then, with no warning, something clicked inside the door and the thick metal frame slid back a few inches with a gentle hiss. I jumped back, caught off-guard. I hadn't been fully concentrating. I'd let myself get distracted while the tech worked away in the background. But somehow, without me at the helm, my cybernetics had intuitively found a way to bypass the system. They had got me in.

I raised my gun and pushed through the door, unsure what I was going to find on the other side.

"Shit. You've got to be kidding me."

Instead of a room with my target waiting, I found myself looking at the inside of an elevator. An empty one.

"That useless son of a – " I shook my head and swallowed the rest of my words, trying to will myself into a calmer state before I opened the comms back up. Ryce had dropped the ball, but matching his temper with my own wasn't going to make anything better.

I could still hear him swearing from somewhere in the control centre when I reopened the connection. It sounded like he was pacing the room, ranting and raving to all the poor techs who couldn't get away from him.

"Alvera, is that you?"

The voice on the other end of the line was soft-spoken and patient, not at all like Ryce. "Felix? Do me a favour and tell our favourite intelligence expert he's in danger of losing the 'intelligence' part of his job title. The information he gave me is off. This whole job could be a bust."

Felix gave a nervous chuckle. "You know I'm not going to tell him that, right? Count yourself lucky I've not opened the channel yet and he didn't hear for himself."

"Do you have to open the channel at all? I don't think I'm his favourite person right now."

Felix groaned. "Please don't give him any more reason to erupt. He's already furious. Chase is threatening to transfer to another team because you pulled another warrant from under her nose."

"She threatens to do that all the time, it's just bluster. Tell your girlfriend the next one is all hers, I promise. I'll even buy her a drink to make up for it. And as for Ryce – "

"As for Ryce what?" His voice was rough and surly as he took over from Felix. "You've got some nerve, Renata. I thought you didn't need our help? You made that quite clear when you cut me off."

He only called me by my last name when he was really pissed off. I was in more trouble than I realised. "I didn't need your help. I still wouldn't if you hadn't given me out-of-date schematics for this place."

"The schematics are fine."

"The fact that I'm staring at an elevator instead of a room with my target waiting for me suggests they're not."

The line went quiet for a moment. "OriCorp must have built another sublevel. I've been monitoring for weeks, never heard any chatter about that. Shit." I could almost hear his teeth grind together. "This is getting ridiculous. How are we supposed to keep track of them without more funding? We can't have eyes and ears everywhere."

"Red tape and bureaucratic bullshit are your problems, not mine. My problem is I'm about to go into a situation absolutely blind, with no idea what's waiting for me down there."

My implant buzzed with static from the sound of his heavy sigh. "Fine, forget it. Head back to the Spire and we'll figure something out. We'll lose out on a score, but sometimes these things happen."

I shook my head. Something was off about this whole job. I meant to find out what it was. "I'm seeing it through."

"The hell you are! I'm not losing my best agent just because you want to prove a point."

"Flatterer. I hope Chase didn't hear you say that." I grinned. "Besides, I wasn't asking for your permission."

"Renata." His voice was dangerously low and silky soft now.

"Make sure my credits are waiting for me when I get back."

"Renata!"

I cut the connection as his roar filled my ear. If I wasn't going to pay for it before, I certainly was now. But I couldn't afford to dwell on it. It was time to find out what was going on.

As soon as the elevator door slid open at the bottom of the shaft, I knew things were about to get worse. There were no lights, so it was only when I heard the water rush in and felt it slosh against my suit that I had any idea the sublevel had been flooded.

I switched on my helmet's torch to get a better look. The water churned angry and black, pouring in from burst pipes in the walls. The only light came from a set of loose wires halfway down the corridor, sparking dangerously close to the water. Even in the few short moments since I stepped out of the elevator, the water level had risen. This was no accident. They knew I was coming.

Some of the rooms were already fully submerged, the

water only contained by the strength of the sealed doors. I tried to peer through the glass, but the only thing I could see was the glare from my torch reflecting back at me.

Thump.

Something thudded off the thick window pane. I switched the torch off and looked for what had made the noise. It was a pale, bloated body with white-blue skin and faraway eyes, tapping against the glass as it rose with the swell of the water. Around its shoulders was a lab coat, floating around like an unravelled shroud.

"Shit. They left their own people to die down here."

Sphere gave a quiet hum.

I should have been more surprised. But when it came to the corporations, especially OriCorp, nothing seemed to cross the line. The government's control was wearing thinner with each advance in technology, each leap in research. Authority couldn't compete with wealth, not outside its base in the Spire. Out in the sectors, the corporations answered to nobody. They could do what they wanted. Even if that meant flooding their own labs to cover their tracks.

There might have been survivors. I didn't have time to check. All I needed was my target. The anonymous benefactor who posted her warrant wanted her alive, but a body would be better than nothing, given the circumstances.

The water rose higher around my legs as I waded through. It wouldn't be long until this whole place was under. That alone wouldn't be a problem – my exosuit was watertight – but who knew what the structural integrity was like? The labs had obviously been built in a rush, designed to be easily destroyed if the wrong people came looking. The last thing I wanted was to be trapped down here, waiting for the oxygen reserves in my exosuit to run out.

"Hello? Is someone there?"

It was a woman's voice. I pointed my gun towards the ventilation shafts running overhead.

"Don't shoot! I'm not armed."

I kept the gun trained at the grate above me. "Why don't you come out and let me see you?"

"I'll come down. Please don't shoot."

The grate slid open and a pair of legs dangled barefoot through the opening. They hovered there for a second before dropping down a notch as the woman they belonged to lowered herself close to the floor. She let go and landed in the water with a splash, the droplets smattering the glasses she was wearing.

"Damn it," she said to herself, wrenching them from her nose and giving them a shake as the holographic interface in the lenses flickered and died.

Sphere bleeped and the warrant picture appeared in front of my eyes. The same pointed nose and sharp cheekbones, the same tightly-fixed blonde hair. Joy Payton. My target.

She pinched her lips together and peered at me through the dark visor of my helmet. "They knew you were coming." The way she said it made it sound like it was my fault. "They started flooding the labs before anyone knew what was happening. They took my research and left me here to drown."

"You were a loose end." I gestured for her to follow me and turned back towards the elevator, the water near my waist now. "You pissed off whoever hired me by running to OriCorp with your research and now you pissed off OriCorp for leading me here."

"Whoever hired you?" Joy Payton didn't sound happy. "You're here on a private contract, not a government-sanctioned rescue?"

"Sorry, lady. Government doesn't have a clue who you

are." I shrugged. "At least whoever hired me wants you alive. Can't say the same for OriCorp."

"That's it? That's all you know?"

"With the number of credits they've fronted for this job, I don't have the luxury of asking questions. Whatever trouble you got yourself into, it's your trouble."

She shot me a look of disgust. "Damn bounty hunters."

"Warrant hunter, actually."

"Do you think a government licence makes you any less of a hired thug?" She curled her lip. "I didn't do anything wrong. This wasn't corporate espionage. I went to OriCorp with my research because I want to help people with it."

"Yeah, the guys who flooded this place and left everyone to die seem real keen on helping people. Nice work."

I tuned out her protestations as we reached the elevator. The door was still open, so I waded in and punched the button. Nothing happened. The lights behind the interface had gone dim. I jabbed my finger into it again, but it made no difference.

Behind me, Joy Payton sniffed. "You don't think I tried that already? They must have rigged it when they left."

"It worked fine on the way down. Maybe it can only be called from the top."

I reached for my gun and shot down one of the panels in the roof of the elevator. Joy screamed and jumped back as it crashed down into the water in front of her.

Without waiting to hear another word, I hauled myself up, shaking the water off my exosuit as I made it onto the roof. It was going to be a long climb. I couldn't see anything above me, not even the slightest crack of light from the reinforced door I knew was up there.

I cursed myself for not thinking to bring cables. There wasn't much to hold on to. The sides of the shaft were smooth and slick, with only the shallowest of handholds and footholds in the form of narrow supports around its perimeter. One had fallen away completely and I had to bridge myself up to the next, trying not to think of the drop below as my legs began to burn and my arms grew heavy.

Sphere circled around me, letting out the occasional beep of encouragement. The readout in front of my eyes showed my heart rate rising, my adrenaline spiking. I ignored it. That information wasn't important to me right now. Getting to the top of this shaft was.

I was about halfway up when fatigue set in. My muscles protested, ignoring what I was telling them to do. They groaned under my weight and cried out when I urged them to stretch that little bit further. I just had to keep going, to reach that little bit more and –

Shit!

My right leg buckled beneath me and I fell, my stomach lurching as I plummeted towards the nothingness below. I reached out blindly and caught my fingers on the edge of one of the supports. Every tendon seemed to swell under the pressure as I hung there, one slip away from falling.

It shouldn't have been Ryce's face I thought of. It should have been someone I cared about. Someone who would miss me when I was gone. But all I could see was the blue of his eyes and the fear of never seeing them again.

Then it was gone.

Sphere bleeped in my ear and I grunted in reply as I pulled myself up. One foot found the wall of the shaft and I flailed about with the other until I wedged myself across, taking some of the pressure off my aching hands. I wanted nothing more than to go back down, but that would have been even more precarious than pushing on. There was only one way to go if I wanted to get out of this alive.

Exhaustion tormented me as I pushed up, one aching movement after another. When the torch on my helmet flashed across a seam in the walls, I thought I was seeing things, afraid my desperate mind was playing tricks on me. But then Sphere gave an excited beep and I looked a little closer. It was the door. I'd made it.

I leaned into the corner of the shaft, bracing myself against the supports, and slid my fingers into the gap. It didn't move.

I tried again, straining my arms as much as I could without knocking myself off balance. The door shuddered but remained closed and I let my arms drop to my sides. "I can't do it. It's too heavy."

Sphere went silent for a moment, hovering in front of the doors. Eventually, it gave a tentative hum.

"A grenade?" I frowned. I always kept a couple of low-tech concussive shells in my belt in case of electronics blackouts. Not devastating enough to cause any real damage, but powerful enough for a shockwave to force open the door. "It might work if I can jam it far enough into the gap, but I'd never be able to climb away fast enough to avoid getting caught in the blast."

Sphere gave a determined beep.

"Too risky. You'll be blasted to pieces if you get hit."

The little drone gave an obstinate whirr and I sighed in defeat. It was right. There was no other way.

I plucked one of the grenades off my belt. It was almost too big to wedge in. My fingers trembled as I pushed it as far through the gap as I could, hoping that the jerky movements wouldn't dislodge me from my perch. After a moment, all that was left of it was the pin sticking out of the end. The pin which Sphere would remove. And after that...

"Get away as quickly as you can," I told it. "Disengage your boosters and let gravity do the rest."

Sphere blinked a light in reply. No promises. It would have to be enough.

I slid back down the shaft to a safe distance, every movement more cautious and laboured than the last. There was barely anything left to give. Even if I was out the blast range, there was no guarantee I'd have the strength to haul myself back up to the doors a second time. Not now. Especially not if–

The impact shuddered through my whole body. A plume of smoke billowed above me, obscuring the doors, and I shielded my head under my arm as debris came raining down.

I waited for it to clear, hardly daring to hope. There it was. Light from above. The doors were open.

"Sphere?"

There was no answer. Had it been too close to escape the blast?

From the darkness came a bleep. Then I heard the familiar whirring of the propulsors powering its anti-gravity field, allowing it to climb back up the shaft.

I let out a puff of breath. "Let's not leave it so close next time."

The last stretch passed in a heavy-headed blur as I clambered back up, determined not to stop until I had hauled myself through the gap in the doors. The interface on the elevator panel at the top was still blinking with life and I punched the call button. It had to work. This couldn't have all been for nothing.

Something inside the shaft whirred and groaned and from the bottom came the sound of rattling steel. The cage was coming, and with it, Joy Payton. With it, my target.

I turned the communications channel back on. "Ryce?

Are you there? I have what I came here for. On my way back to the Spire now."

There was a moment of silence before he responded, and his reply was as brusque as I predicted. "Understood."

"What, no congratulations on a job well done?"

"Congratulations. And Alvera?"

"Yes?"

"You're suspended."

CHAPTER TWO

Most people at the Spire would have you think it was the centre of New Pallas society. It was the closest thing to a capital we had. A bright reminder of civility in the middle of the ever-darkening sprawling city that covered most of the planet.

The Spire was a lie.

Sure, it was sleek and shiny, with glassy skyscraper peaks reflecting the peach-tinged sky. The upper levels were a criss-cross of shuttle lanes and penthouses, sky bridges and rooftop plazas. But compared to the underbelly of New Pallas, it was an anomaly. As if the illusion of it could hide what was going on everywhere else.

There was a reason why what passed for civilisation lived in the sky. We'd used up everywhere else. The few swathes of land that survived the invasion of high-rises and skyscrapers had only done so because they were scarred with unstable mining pits so deep they delved into the planet's core. Pits where we sent people in search of the few natural resources the planet still had to give.

The rest, so far below the city that it was referred to as *the surface* rather than New Pallas, was a cesspit of pollution and overcrowding. People would sleep and shit in the same sad corner of the street they'd managed to claim as their own.

That was the sickness underneath the surface of New Pallas. The dark truth that nobody wanted to admit was down there. And the worst part was how easy it was to forget when you were on top.

I set the shuttle in lane for the judiciary and enforcement complex and turned on the autopilot. Outside, the city whizzed by too quickly to make sense of. One tower blurred into another until they became the same. An endless maze of superstructures, each trying to creep higher than the next. How much further could they go? Worse than that, what would happen when we reached the limit?

The sky was already darkening by the time I got back. Its soft tones had burned into a rich orange sheen across the cityscape, the air shimmering behind silhouettes of dotted lines of traffic.

And there, far above the reach of New Pallas and its spectacular sunset, was the Station.

It had been watching us for as long as we had existed, left behind long ago by someone – or something – else. The lights from the giant, ringed structure blinked from orbit, never acknowledging our existence. Sometimes it descended into darkness and became invisible, as if whatever space it had been occupying was merely a void.

Any expedition to get near it always ended in disaster. Systems malfunctions, hull breaches, explosions in the fuel line. If there was anyone up there, they didn't want to be found. So it just hung there. Watching over us like it was biding its time.

"You know, I expected better than this." A sniff came from the back of the shuttle. "Just because you're a warrant hunter shouldn't mean you lack all sense of common courtesy. It's unbearably cramped in here."

I held my breath. We were almost back. I could see the tall, narrow silhouette of headquarters. If I could last ten more minutes, I'd be handing her over and getting a nice big pile of credits in return. Ten more minutes. That was all.

"I'd be less worried about my courtesy and more about that of whoever put that price on your head." I turned around and saw her mouth scrunch into a line.

Good. She was right to be concerned. Whatever official system of government we had in the Spire, it couldn't control the corporations. They had their own private security and dealt with matters how they saw fit. As long as it didn't do too much to threaten New Pallas, the Spire turned a blind eye.

A plain-clothed security team was there to collect Joy at the landing pad. I still didn't know anything about who sent them, or who was behind the warrant. All Ryce had told me was it was some wealthy benefactor who wanted to remain anonymous. It wasn't my job to question that. The rep confirmed I'd collected the right target and transferred the agreed number of credits.

"What happens to me now?" Joy asked.

I shrugged. "I honestly couldn't say."

"Has it ever crossed your mind that some of these jobs you do enable terrible people to do terrible things? Have you no care what happens next?"

"To you? Not particularly. I'm sure they have their reasons."

She glared. "I suppose that helps you sleep better at night."

It was nothing I hadn't heard before. Targets were all the same. They'd lie, try to tell you there was some mistake. They'd try to escape. They'd try to negotiate, appeal to you to see reason. Then they got angry and resentful. It was easier for them to blame someone like me, trying to do a job, instead of themselves for getting the warrant on their head in the first place. Scorn always came at the end. A last-gasp attempt at retaining some pride in the face of detainment.

I'd seen a hundred Joy Paytons and I'd see a hundred more. Whatever she said, I could rest easy with the knowledge I'd won another successful score for the team.

I only hoped Ryce would appreciate that.

———

"Let's go over this again."

"I don't think there's any – "

"You used your cybernetics to hack into the warrant network. Again. After I expressly told you doing so would get you suspended."

"Chase already had six active warrants on the go. Six! She never stops. I was doing her a favour by taking this one off her hands."

"Then you cut communications despite knowing full well that going into a facility like that without a team at your back is a recipe for disaster."

"I wouldn't have needed to cut communications if you were capable of speaking at a volume that doesn't perforate most human eardrums."

"And above all that, when you found out that we didn't have all the intel, that you'd be going in blind, you ignored orders to fall back and went on regardless. Which again, is – "

"Grounds for suspension, yes. But you're missing one key detail."

"What's that?"

"We got the job done."

It wasn't possible for Ryce's face to get any redder, but the vein popping out of his forehead twitched furiously. He leaned back in his chair and folded his arms across his chest. Even if I didn't have a retinal readout of his vital signs, I'd have been blind not to see the way he was trying to control his breathing. It was his only real flaw. He was a brilliant intelligence expert but a short-tempered one.

Especially when it came to me.

He rubbed a hand across his clean-shaven jaw, not taking his eyes off me for a second. It was never pleasant having his gaze on me like that. The anger, I could take. It was what came after that was more difficult. The way he looked when it had all settled down and all that was left was this raw tension between us, riddled with gaps that had to be filled in one way or another.

It wasn't until he finally looked away that I found myself able to speak. "If I hadn't taken this job, none of us would have got paid today. Chase is one of the best, but I'm telling you, even she wouldn't have been able to see it through this time. The defence system they had was like nothing I've ever come across."

His head snapped up. "What do you mean?"

"It's like it was reacting to my cybernetics. Every time I tried to break through, it had an answer. Like it knew what I was trying to do. Like it was alive."

Ryce's expression was inscrutable. "And you managed to get past it?"

"Like I said, barely."

He didn't say anything for a few moments. His brow was furrowed and he looked deep in thought. Maybe he didn't believe me. Maybe he thought I was trying to make myself seem more indispensable than I actually was.

"You're suspended," he said again, his face hard.

"For how long?"

"Until I say otherwise."

I rolled my tongue in my mouth, trying to keep my own anger in check. "This was a win for us. A win for you."

"You were arrogant and reckless today. It's not just about punishing you, it's about protecting you from yourself."

"Protecting me?" I snorted. "Careful, Ryce. Wouldn't want your personal feelings interfering with the job."

He clenched his jaw. "This isn't about us. This is about me protecting my best asset. My investment."

It stung. It was more than a blow to my pride. It was the suggestion that all I was to him was a tool to bring the credits home. An asset that could be disposed of or replaced as easily as a busted piece of tech.

I scanned his face for a trace of regret. An inkling that he was scrambling to take the words back, that he didn't mean it like that. But he was as stony as ever. I should have known better. Ryce didn't have regrets. He didn't say things he didn't mean. And he never took anything back.

I forced my mouth into a smile. "Nice to know where I stand, at least."

He ignored me. "I'll transfer your share of the credits today. Felix will let you know when we have something for you again."

He turned his back to me and brought up something on one of the holographic interfaces to busy himself with. I could see his reflection. His furrowed brow, the twitch in his jaw as he ground his teeth. Maybe his outburst had bothered him after all. Or maybe I was just imagining it.

I walked out of the office into hushed silence in the main strategy room. It was as if all the tech officers had stopped what they were doing to listen for one of Ryce's infamous rebukes and were now hastily pretending to be working again. Half a dozen sat at their screens, faces illuminated by the glow. Felix glanced over and floated across on his hover-chair, his amusement visible.

"You could just walk, you know," I said, trying to keep the tetchiness from my voice. None of this was his fault. With all the egos on the team, Felix was the one who held us together, who kept us in check. Who reminded us when we forgot that we *were* a team.

Felix shrugged. "Old habit. It was that bad?"

"You know Ryce."

"So do you. Thought you would have learned by now." He grinned. "Any damage?"

I reached to the shoulder of my suit and brought out Sphere from its dock. The drone hummed into life and floated off my palm, blinking its lights in a friendly greeting towards Felix. "It got caught in a blast from one of my concussive grenades. I think it's fine, but I wanted you to give it a check to be sure."

Felix rolled his eyes. "I meant you, not Sphere. You know we've got a case of drones in storage. Brand new, cutting-edge drones."

"Sphere works just fine."

"It's gone way too long without being reprogrammed." He gave me a pointed look. "If it starts thinking for itself, it contravenes AI regulations."

"You don't need to recite the regulations, Felix. I'm well aware of what they say."

He smirked. "So you just disregard them, like you do everything else?"

"I'm not going to reprogramme Sphere. We've been through a lot together. Things wouldn't be the same if you just erased all that."

"It's a drone. It's not like it's… You know what? Never mind. I'll take a look."

"Thank you."

I sank into a chair next to him as he pulled out his diagnostic kit and got to work. There was something soothing about being around him when he had a problem to get stuck into. Felix was a genius with software. Knew exactly how to speak to it, how to make it respond to him.

Beads of moisture gathered on the dark brown skin of his brow and he wiped them away, never taking his eyes from the lines of code flashing on the interface in front of him. He started muttering to himself in unintelligible flurries of miner patois as he so often did when he was concentrating on his work. The dialect was strange and musical to my ears, the words unfamiliar.

"Where is she?"

The easy silence came to an abrupt end as Chase stormed into the room, every inch of her five-foot height bristling. Her eyes narrowed in anger when she saw me and she seemed to swell to twice her size. "You jumped-up, knows-better, warrant-stealing…cyborg!"

"I believe the polite term we're told to use in this office is cybernetically-enhanced." I grinned. "Admit it, you're impressed."

"I'm pissed off." She scowled at me. "I told you last time – get your own damn warrants."

"But you've got such a good eye for the fun ones."

"Fun?" She snorted. "I heard what happened down there. Sounded like a shitshow."

"In that case, you should be grateful for me taking it off your hands."

The side of her mouth twitched begrudgingly. It was almost a smile. "Don't count on it. You owe me, cyborg."

"There you go again with the cyborg thing." I glanced at Felix. "Is she talking to me or you?"

Felix, who had momentarily looked up from his diagnostics, quickly ducked his head back down. "I am not getting involved in this again."

"Having your legs blasted off in a mining accident as a child and getting bionic replacements is not the same as having your brain filled with unstable tech that could fry your insides at any time," Chase said, rolling her eyes. "No offence, but there are cyborgs and there are *cyborgs*. You just happen to be the weird kind. Whatever tech you've got that you think makes you so special, it's not worth the price."

"What price? I'm doing just fine."

"For now. Didn't you hear about the agent on Theta's team last week? Retinal implant overloaded in his sleep. They found him the next day without a face. And he wasn't the first, either. That's what you get when you try to make humans into cyborgs."

"Maybe he just couldn't handle it. My head is full of tech and I've not been fried yet."

Chase curled her lip. "Here it comes. The great Alvera Renata, best warrant hunter in the Spire, never missed a target yet. And look – she's got creepy tech in her head and doesn't get blown to pieces! Don't you think there's something strange about that? Have you ever stopped to think that maybe – "

Felix gave a pointed sigh and closed the lid on his diagnostic toolkit. "I'm done. Your drone is fine." He glanced between us. "Do the two of you mind taking this elsewhere? Some of us still have work to do."

Chase shook her head. "Whatever. I'm off to search the database for a new warrant. Maybe with the cyborg suspended, I'll actually be allowed to do my job."

She turned on her heel and marched out, blowing a kiss to Felix and giving me one last scowl as she disappeared through the sliding doors.

Felix stared after her, tapping his feet off the hoverchair in an offbeat rhythm. Nobody would ever have guessed his legs were bionic. Only the people who knew him picked up on the tell-tale signs. The way he still used his chair to zip across the room. The way he suddenly looked down sometimes, as if to check they were still there.

The mines were no place for anyone, let alone a kid. All the tech in the world couldn't save you from a cave-in or some unstable explosives going off. But that was the corporations for you. Competition was everything, and resources were the way to stay ahead. Even if it meant sending kids to dangerous depths to scrape together what little the world had left.

A slight smile danced across his lips. "I think things went quite well, all things considered."

"Sure, apart from me getting suspended."

"You did steal her warrant. And you knew exactly what you were doing when you pissed off Ryce." He shook his head. "I better get back to it. I've got a lot of work to do."

"Well, that makes one of us at least."

His smile grew wider. "I'm sure you'll find some kind of trouble to get into with your mandatory time off."

"I'll think of a thing or two. But after today, I'm going to start with a drink."

Club Vertigo was far from the most respectable establishment the Spire had to offer, located out on its seedier fringes, but it was still a damn sight better than some of the cesspools outside the capital. Before I became a warrant hunter, I'd had the misfortune of drinking in shitholes where you were as likely to lose an arm as a handful of credits if you pissed off the wrong person. Bars stocked with old-school liquor and bathrooms crowded with glazed-eyed patrons injecting themselves with whatever drug was currently in fashion.

Not that Club Vertigo was perfect. It had its share of dodgy deals going on in the darker corners of the ninth floor, some well-known faces from the underworld around the poker table on level three, a convicted criminal or two behind the bar. But it was clean, for the most part, and I didn't have to worry about picking up some disease or another just by breathing the air.

I ordered the drink of the day and drained my glass in a few minutes before shaking it at the bartender to ask for another. It was far too fruity with nowhere near enough kick, but I didn't have the energy to decide on anything else. I was done with the job and sure as hell done with Ryce.

Even as the alcohol diluted my senses and wrapped itself around my head in a warm embrace, thinking of him still brought a painful twinge to my chest. He always had to make things so difficult. It didn't help that he was as stubborn as I was. Two hard-hitting forces coming straight for each other, neither willing to move. A collision which did neither of us any good. A collision which sent sparks flying, and then *sent sparks flying*.

He'd called it off a dozen times before. Always with some bullshit line about compromising the integrity of the team, putting our future effectiveness in jeopardy. But a few weeks later we'd end up right back where we started, between the sheets of his bed, and we'd never speak of it again. Until the next time.

It was a cyclical dance we'd both learned the steps to,

becoming so familiar that it was almost like going through the motions every time we came together and stormed apart. Trapped in a pattern that neither of us really wanted, but never really wanted to break either. It was how we worked out our problems. It was how we made new ones.

I finished my second glass and gestured for a third. It was going to be a long night.

"I'll get this one for the lovely lady."

It was going to be a *very* long night.

I glanced up to see who the voice belonged to. He was young, with perfectly-coiffed blonde hair and an impish grin. That was what gave him away as someone who didn't belong here. He was too eager, too giddy. His clothes were too carefully chosen. He was just some posh kid who wanted an adventure but was too sensible to see what life was really like outside the relative safety of the Spire. A trip to the outskirts would be enough. He'd go back to his white-collar colleagues the next day and brag about how unseemly it was out here, how edgy he was for hitting the place up.

He already bored me.

"I've got it," I said, looking away and stirring the dregs of my empty glass. "Thanks anyway."

"No, I insist. Besides, you're too beautiful to be drinking alone. Let me join you."

I tightened my jaw, still staring at the glass in front of me. "Not interested."

"Come on, there's no need to be like that. I'm just trying to be friendly. Least I can get is a smile out of you."

"Least I'm going to give you is a bullet between the eyes if you keep going. Piss off."

"I can't believe you're being so rude to someone you just met. Why won't you even make eye contact with me? Can't you just – hey!"

The moment his hand touched my shoulder, my gun was out of its holster and pointed between his legs. "I told you to leave me alone."

His face turned white. "You…you can't do that."

"I'm a warrant hunter. A bit of falsified paperwork and I can do what the fuck I want. Now, do you want to keep harassing me, or do you want to leave here with all your parts intact?"

He stumbled backwards, his eyes flickering around the bar area as if to ask for some help. The bartender just shrugged and a man in a cargo pilot's jacket sitting a couple of seats down smirked, as if to say *good luck with that, kid.* Realising that nobody was coming to his defence, he turned on his heel and headed for the door, only glancing back to cast a final muttered insult in my direction.

"Bitch."

I laughed, strapping the gun back to my leg and sliding over a couple of credits to the bartender for another drink.

"Remind me never to get on your bad side."

I turned to see Ryce at my shoulder. He was smiling to himself, his thin lips illuminated by the electronic glow of a cigarette in his mouth.

"Bit late for that." A sharp realisation jolted through me. "Wait, how did you know I was here?"

"Just wanted to check in."

"Did you track me here?" Rage blossomed in my chest. It was normal for Ryce and Felix to monitor my location and vitals when I was in the field, but that was part of the job. This was something different altogether. He was intruding on my time, my space. The more I thought about it, the more I wanted to throw my next drink in his face. "You are more of an asshole each passing day."

He held up his hands in a gesture of surrender and sat

down across from me, signalling to the bartender for a drink. "I deserve that. But I know how I can make you feel better."

"Not interested."

"Not like that." The light of the cigarette glowed brighter as he sucked in. "I saw what you did to the boy there. I'm not overly keen on getting the same treatment."

"You'll get worse if you keep up your flagrant violation of professional boundaries."

He eyed the gun on my leg. "Government officials aren't really meant to threaten civilians with their weapons when they're off duty."

"Thanks to my boss, I'm likely to remain off duty for a while. Makes me more of a freelancer now, if you ask me."

His lips twisted into a wry smile. "How fortunate. It just so happens I'm in the market for a freelancer."

I narrowed my eyes. "What do you mean?"

"I've got a job for you. A big one. Off the books, though. So off the books I can't have it connected to the Spire in any way."

The weight of his words started to sink in. "Shit. *That's* why you suspended me?"

"That and the fact you know it pisses me off when you cut comms on me."

It was always so strange seeing him like this. The bluster and the tension had faded away, leaving him pleasant and palatable. When he wasn't shouting, he spoke in a slow drawl, his accent from somewhere well to the western reaches of New Pallas. I could hear the light sarcasm, the touch of humour in his voice. It almost made me want to forgive him for earlier.

"What's the job?" I asked.

"I'm not going to go into details here," he said, looking around. "You always do pick the nicest places to get drunk."

"What can I say? Great taste in bars, shit taste in men. Tell me the job, or I walk."

"Not here," he said again. "I can't risk someone overhearing. You're the only person I know who can pull this off. Nobody else can know about it. Not Felix, not Chase, not anyone."

I took a sip of my drink and tried to keep my expression neutral. He'd relax if he knew how easily he'd intrigued me. I didn't want to give him the satisfaction. Not yet, anyway. But it had worked. My earlier anger had evaporated, replaced by something curious and excited.

I watched him as he peeled at the label on his beer. He had a few years on me but not enough to matter. Traces of his brown hair had given way to early silver and he wore the beginnings of faint lines around his eyes that might have been from time or laughter or both. But there was a certain kind of youth to him, a brightness in his piercing blue eyes that the years had not yet dimmed. There was something about him that always drew me back.

"Should I be worried?"

I quickly turned back to my drink. "About what?"

"The way you're staring at me. I don't have a warrant out on me, do I?"

Heat rose in my cheeks. Bastard. He knew. It was too easy for him to reel me back in. But I wasn't going to pretend like he was wrong. Not when we both wanted the same thing.

Emboldened by the alcohol, I looked him up and down, arching an eyebrow. "Why would you of all people be worried about warrants? Carrying something extra in among your cargo?"

He laughed, cigarette bouncing between his lips. "Now that's not the kind of information I'd be likely to divulge to a government agent." He raised his bottle. "Even if she is off duty."

I clinked my glass. "Even off-duty agents have ways of making you talk."

"How do you suppose you'll manage that?" A smile was tugging at the edge of his mouth, like he was humouring me.

This time when the heat rose in my cheeks, it was not from embarrassment.

He looked at me expectantly, his gaze measured and unquestioning. He already knew what was going to happen next. He was just waiting for me to admit it.

I drained my glass and set it back down on the bar with a thud. "Want to go somewhere else?"

It was dark by the time we left Vertigo. Well, as dark as the Spire ever got. The sky might have been cloaked by night, but the streets were still awash with glaring lights more intrusive than the sun could ever be. The Station, wherever it was, must have plunged itself into darkness again. There was no sign of it in the sky tonight.

We walked for a short while, keeping our distance apart from the occasional, accidental brush of clothing when one of us strayed too close to the other. The silence between us was thick and heavy with the weight of expectation, both of us knowing what lay ahead but neither acknowledging it.

At least for a short while.

I felt his eyes on me before I turned to look. They were blue and bright, even in the darkness. Their intensity threw me for a moment. Then I felt stupid. That was the alcohol. Or whatever else it was that was rising in me, warm and insistent. But there was a hunger in the way he was looking at me, a passion that sent warmth to my core and shivers to my spine.

We'd never screwed in an alley before. He'd never seemed like that kind of guy. But a moment later his hands were around my waist and my back was against the wall. He paused for a moment, head tilted to the side. Waiting to see what I'd do next.

I stretched towards him and found his mouth with my own. His lips parted for my tongue and he gave a small grunt as his hands gripped tighter around my waist, pushing me harder against the wall. My head was spinning. Whether it was from the booze or lights or just the sheer unexpectedness of it all, I didn't know. I didn't care.

His mouth worked its way along my jaw and down my neck and I shuddered underneath his firm grasp. The hum of the shuttle lanes below filled my ears. Somewhere above our heads, a neon light flickered on and off, sending shadows across his face when he pulled away to look at me.

I grabbed the collar of his jacket and pulled him back, closing my eyes against the luminous glare and blocking out the sound of traffic with my own heaving breathing. No distractions. Just him and what he was doing to me.

By the time he'd hitched my legs up around his waist, everything else that had happened melted away. I didn't care about being suspended, or earning credits, or my record. None of that mattered right now, not while he was between my legs, giving me a release I hadn't even known I was craving. Everything about him was decisive. As he brought me to the edge, the wall hard at my back and my body trapped close against his, it was as if my mind had been wiped blank of everything but him.

When it was over, he pressed his forehead against mine as I fumbled with my trousers, hoisting them back up around my hips. A sheen of sweat separated his skin from mine, and the warmth of his laboured breaths billowed against my cheek. It was enough.

He took a step back, pulling the folds of his jacket around him and looking at me with a cocked head. There was a twitch at the side of his mouth, the start of a smile that the rest of his face hadn't quite caught up with. "I'll be around tomorrow to go over the job," he said, slipping his hands into his pockets and turning back up the alley.

I watched him leave, his shoulders straight and the silver at the back of his head dancing with colours from the city streetlights. "Seriously? That's it? At least tell me where I'm going."

He didn't turn back, but after a moment, I heard a call through the air so faint I might have imagined it.

"You're going to the Station."

CHAPTER THREE

In the time it took me to sleep off my hangover from the night before, I was already bored. I was good at my job. Without it, I was adrift in New Pallas, like a shuttle cut loose from orbit. I needed a reason for getting out of bed in the morning. I needed a target to track down, a new goal to chase.

Anyone else might have gone to one of the Spire's grand museums or art galleries to waste a few hours, dragging their feet behind them and feigning interest at one display after another. They might have visited one of the giant superstores and spent credits they didn't have on shit they didn't need. They might have gone for a run in one of the rooftop parks that had been artificially constructed after the sprawling city had swallowed up all the green on the surface below.

I wasn't anyone else. That was my problem. Maybe that's why instead of spending my enforced vacation doing something normal, I was attempting to hack into the warrant network.

Ryce had refused to tell me anything else about the job. No details, no clue as to how the hell I was meant to pull this off. Just two barely-whispered words.

The Station.

Waiting for him to arrive and fill me in was torture. I didn't like being kept in the dark. If Ryce wasn't going to give me answers, maybe the warrant network would.

It was a long shot. If the nature of the job was so sensitive that Ryce had to suspend me before he told me anything, there was no way he'd log any details into the system. But that didn't mean there was nothing I could glean from the records. There was a long history of failed expeditions to the Station. Some of them must have been sanctioned by the Spire.

I rubbed my eyes with the heel of my hand, the glare from the interface taking its toll. I wasn't getting anywhere. Felix must have put more safeguards into the system since the last time I hacked in. I didn't know whether to feel grudging admiration that he'd managed to do it so fast or just plain frustration at being shut out.

Sphere gave a timid bleep and I sighed, cracking my neck from side to side. "I'll feel a lot better when we find out exactly why Ryce is sending us up there."

Sphere didn't answer, but its lights blinked in a series of short flashes as a line of code popped up on the interface. I jerked upright, scanning it quickly. This was different. Not one of the usual firewalls. It had Felix's fingerprints all over it, just as I suspected.

"Finally. Let's get rid of you."

Felix might have been good, but there was only so much he could do against my cybernetics, no matter how hard he worked on upgrading security. Others might have taken it personally or refused to work with me over it, but Felix had never muttered a word against me. Instead, he took it as a challenge, proof that there was room for him to do better.

I smiled to myself. He could have been earning serious

credits at any of the corporations, but he was content to be just another tech officer at the Spire. A sharp-minded, inquisitive one, but still just a tech officer. Not that it would ever seem like a waste to him. Not after what he'd been through.

"We're in."

Thoughts of Felix fled my mind as his code disappeared and the warrant database popped up on the interface. It had taken longer than I'd have liked, but I'd done it. Now all that was left to do was scour through the warrant histories.

Most of it was the same old bullshit. A mercenary who'd gone too far in terms of collateral damage. A smuggler who'd skipped bail. A runaway son who was probably chasing drugs and skirts in one of the seedier parts of the city. Nothing interesting. Nothing that caught my eye.

I brought up Chase's file. Her portrait stared back at me with sullen brown-black eyes. She was all cheekbones and chin, her nose and mouth small and pointed. She wore a look of resentment, as if it was me she was glaring at and not the poor admin officer who had the misfortune of taking her picture that day.

"No hard feelings," I said. "At least you'll have your pick of jobs while I'm gone."

I pulled up her active warrants. Blank. That wasn't right. Chase always had at least two or three jobs on the go at once. With me suspended it wasn't like she could afford to be slacking, not if the rest of the team wanted paid. What was going on?

A sharp beep on the holo-terminal snapped me from my thoughts. It was Ryce. He was on his way.

I let out a long breath.

Finally. Time for some answers.

By the time Ryce arrived, the sun had already dipped far beneath the cityscape horizon. I closed the shutters against the glow of the shuttle lanes outside. My stomach had worked itself into a tight knot and my heart contracted painfully in my chest, as if the sheer swell of it might break my ribs.

I'd given up scouring the network for old warrants mentioning the Station. They told me nothing more than I already knew. Many others had tried to dock there before. None of them ever came back. Every now and then, some curious civilian with too many credits to spare would bankroll a mercenary who didn't know better to take a shuttle and see if this time, maybe this time, someone could make it onto the Station. It never worked.

Was Ryce really planning to send me there?

I heard the rumble of his shuttle outside and waited for him to walk through the door. He looked calm and unconcerned, like he wasn't about to ask me to go on a suicide mission. Maybe I really had gone too far this time. Maybe I had pissed him off so much that he was sending me on a one-way trip to the Station as punishment.

I folded my arms, not bothering to waste my breath offering him a seat. He took one anyway, leaning back into the leather and stretching his legs out in front of him. The arrogance of it rankled me. He seemed more comfortable in my home than I did. How could he be so at ease, knowing what he was about to ask me to do?

"If you're waiting for me to beg you for answers, you're going to be disappointed," I said.

He frowned. "You're angry. I thought you'd be pleased."

"Pleased?" Was he really that thick-headed or was he just trying to get under my skin? "You realise nobody has ever made it back from the Station alive, right? If you want me dead, there are easier ways to go about it."

"Alvera, do you really think I'd send you up there if I didn't have a plan?" He smiled, but quickly sobered when he saw my expression. "I give you my word."

"It's not your word that concerns me, it's your ambition. Nobody can get to the Station. It's been tried a hundred times before. Whatever is up there, it's got the means to keep the rest of us out."

"This time will be different. I made a breakthrough." Ryce sat back in the chair, a slow, triumphant smile curling his lips. He was enjoying this. He was savouring it. But I was in no mood to play along.

"In case it isn't already obvious, let me make something clear," I said, hardening my voice. "I'm not going to flatter you into telling me what you know. If you're going to give me the job, then give me it. If not, there are plenty of other places a suspended warrant hunter can get work."

Even as I said the words, I wondered whether I really meant them. Despite myself, I did want to know more. Ryce didn't do things without good reason. If he really had found a way to get to the Station…

He held up his hands in a gesture of defeat. "Fine. Forgive me for getting carried away with the theatrics. It's just…this is huge. Bigger than anything we've ever done before." He took a breath. "I discovered the Station has an extremely advanced identification system. Anything that gets near it without the right clearance codes gets hit by the Station's defences. Approaching shuttles are destroyed without any kind of warning. That's why nobody has ever been able to reach it."

I fought to quell the rising sense of unease in my stomach. My insides were knotted tight. I didn't like where this was going. "How do you know this?"

"A stroke of luck. A few months back, I got a report of a

shuttle crash outside the city, near the mines. I sent a salvage team to recover what they could, but they had no idea what they'd found."

A strange, cold feeling swept over me, like I was listening to him through a dream. "This shuttle…you think it came from there? From the Station?"

"I'm certain of it. The technology was unlike anything I'd seen. Embedded in the navigation console was a line of code. A line of code I'm betting would allow us to get close enough to the Station to dock safely."

The knot inside my stomach pulled tighter and tighter and finally snapped. "You've kept this to yourself for months?"

"I told you this was classified. Off the books. Not another person in the Spire knows. I had to be sure everything was kept secret. There was too much to lose if somebody found out."

"There's too much at stake for *nobody* to find out," I said. "This isn't something you can handle yourself. This could change everything."

"You're right," he said, his voice calm. "Which is why we must act with caution. You know as well as I do how much influence the corporations have. The Spire can't continue to restrain them indefinitely. If this information falls into the wrong hands…"

"The corporations would keep the knowledge for themselves. Keep the rest of us in the dark while they went up there and took the Station and whatever is on it for themselves." I balled my hands into fists. "I'm aware of the danger this information might bring. But that doesn't mean we should keep it to ourselves. Surely there's someone in the Spire you can trust."

"There is," he said, simply. "You."

He took a step towards me and placed his hands around

my cheeks, pulling my face towards his for a fierce, earnest kiss. It was so hungry, so desperate, that I didn't have any words to argue with when his mouth left mine. He'd stolen all my words from me the moment our lips touched.

He pulled away, fixing me with his gaze. "I'm not a field agent. If I was, believe me, I would do it myself. The last thing I want to do is send you up there alone. But you're the only one I trust to do this right. It has to be you."

My throat was dry. I'd never seen him so solemn, so vulnerable. "What's up there that's so important? What is it you're asking me to do?"

"Our future is up there, Alvera. New Pallas is dying. Everyone knows it. Our planet has too many people and not enough resources to sustain them. The balance has already tipped. Right now, it's so slow nobody wants to see it. By the time they do, it will be too late."

His words sent a chill through me, voicing an unspoken truth that so many of us knew but so few wanted to admit. "How does the Station change that?"

"It gives us hope. It gives us a blueprint to move away from New Pallas, to expand into the space beyond our planet. But only if it's in the right hands. Can you imagine if the corporations made it up first and took control?" He clenched his jaw. "It would be a disaster. They already squabble over the little resources left. Give them the Station and they would keep it for themselves. They shouldn't be the ones to benefit from it."

"Benefit from what? We don't know what's up there."

"I know. That's why I need you to find out."

The enormity of his words hit me hard. My mouth ran dry and my breaths came short and shallow. A reconnaissance mission like no other. A venture into a place I knew nothing about. There was no solid intel, no guaranteed reward. If it was any other job, I'd reject it out of hand. The risk was too high.

But it wasn't any other job. It held no guarantees, no promises, but it offered something more. A sliver of hope for a planet that was dying too slowly for anybody to take notice. A chance to make real change instead of chasing credits for petty crimes and the corporations' whims. An opportunity to become something more than a warrant hunter. In the right hands, the Station could change the world.

And I could be the one to make it happen.

Something fluttered in my chest, buried deep beneath the fear and disbelief. I tried to quash it, but it had uncoiled the moment the thought crossed my mind. Ego. Pride. The unsettling sensation reared its dark head, making me doubt whether I would be doing this for the good of New Pallas, or for myself. Maybe it didn't matter, not if the job got done.

I straightened my spine and looked Ryce in the eye. "What kind of backup can I expect if I say yes?"

A strange expression, something almost like relief, flickered over his face. "Not much, I'm afraid. We'll lose contact as soon as your shuttle breaks atmo. I could use one of the orbital satellites to ping you, but there's too much risk someone could intercept it, even with encryptions. For this to work, you have to do it alone."

"Figures." I grunted. "At least you won't be able to suspend me for cutting you off this time."

Ryce smiled. "There is that." He stood and pressed his lips against my cheek. His touch was so light it felt like nothing more than a breath of air. "Alvera. You're going to save us all, you know that?"

I tried to ignore the flush making its way up my neck as he pulled away. When he reached the door, he paused and turned back to me. "I'm not going to wish you luck. I know you don't need it. I'm just going to say I'll see you soon."

The words sounded like a promise. They were all I had. With Ryce gone, I was alone, with only the weight of responsibility to keep me company. It was a burden both terrifying and exhilarating in equal measure.

You're going to save us all, you know that?

His words were a dangerous promise, awakening something in me that was impossible to control. I couldn't back down now, even if I wanted to. Even if it made all the sense in the world.

I cracked open the shutters and peered past the glare of the city below into the darkness of the night. The Station was there, fully illuminated. A beacon, showing me the way.

I stretched my neck to the side, grimacing as it gave a satisfying crack.

It was time to go save the world.

CHAPTER FOUR

The steady growl of the shuttle's engines filled my ears as I pulled away from the skypad. The noisy grumble was a strange sort of comfort, drowning out some of the doubt in my head. I programmed in the Station's coordinates with a trembling hand. If Ryce was wrong about the clearance codes, I was already dead. I just didn't know it yet.

Orbital travel had never bothered me before. The quickest way to some of the more remote sectors on the far side of New Pallas was to break the atmosphere. But this was different. An insistent tug pulled at my insides as the city diminished beneath me, like some invisible anchor begging me to stay. The glaring lights dimmed to faint twinkles far below, a stretching constellation of towers and buildings obscured by distance and perspective. It looked beautiful for a moment, like a shining patchwork of arteries, each sector bleeding into the others in an illuminating glow.

But this was no standard cross-planet shuttle run. It was no exorbitantly-priced sightseeing tour. The overbearing glare of New Pallas had become a distant comfort, faint and far below. Inside the suffocating space of the shuttle, surrounded by the black void of space on the other side of the hull, I was alone.

"You know, I always thought you were a little crazy, but this is possibly the most reckless thing you've done yet."

I spun around. There, crawling out of a container in the back of the shuttle, was Chase.

She hopped upright and dusted herself off before turning to look at me, her hands settling on her hips.

Shit.

"What the hell are you doing here?" I hissed.

"I figured I owed you one for stealing my warrant, so I'm here returning the favour." She glanced out the cockpit window and whistled. "Damn. Looks even bigger this close up."

I tried to ignore the pounding in my chest, the throbbing in my ears. Through the haze of anger, the pieces slowly began to settle into place. The lack of warrants on her roster made sense now. She'd been planning this from the moment I'd stolen the OriCorp job from under her nose.

"Think they're going to blow us out of the sky?" she asked, still peering out the cockpit.

"The plan is for that not to happen," I said, through gritted teeth.

"So there is a plan?" Her eyes gleamed. "I knew something was up. You've pulled worse stunts than that without Ryce suspending you. I figured there was something going on, something neither of you were telling me."

"So you decided to stow away and get in on the action?" I shook my head. "Sorry to disappoint you, but that's not going to happen. I'm turning this shuttle around and dumping your ass back on New Pallas. You can explain yourself to Ryce."

"You break the rules when it suits you, Alvera. Don't get pissed just because I've decided to follow your lead." She glanced at the nav system. "We're too far out of range to send a transmission back to the Spire. Ryce doesn't need to know. Besides, wouldn't you rather have someone at your back?"

A light on the console blinked and I turned my attention away from Chase to look at it. It was a warning, telling me I was approaching the point of no return.

She raised an eyebrow. "Looks like you've got a decision to make."

I was pissed. Pissed she'd figured it out. Pissed she'd managed to sneak aboard the shuttle. Pissed I hadn't realised until it was too late.

More than anything, I was pissed that she was right. I would have done the same if our positions had been reversed. Blaming her for it seemed pointless. Might as well make use of her now she was along for the ride.

I ignored the light and switched the controls to manual, overriding the automated protocols that would turn the shuttle around and guide it back to the safety of New Pallas.

"Right. So we're doing this." Chase let out a breath. "Good."

My mouth curled into a wry smile despite myself. "You were actually hoping I'd turn back?"

"Half-hoping."

"Too late now."

The Station loomed large and unwelcoming. Its central ring stretched so far in both directions I couldn't see where it began to curve back in on itself. It eclipsed any of the planet's orbital stations.

How many others had come this far, thinking they'd be the first to set foot on it?

"You think we'll make it?" Chase asked, a note of wonder in her voice.

I glanced at Sphere. The drone was nestled in its docking

station to interface with the nav console, transmitting what I hoped were the clearance codes. The signal flashed in steady bursts, each the same as the last. There was no sign that it wasn't working. No sign that it was, either.

I let go of the breath I'd been holding and drew another. We were close enough to see the individual airlocks. The clearance codes *must* have worked. If they hadn't, we'd have been blown into space or suffocated as our shuttle turned its systems on us and vented the air. We were too close not to have made it.

Then the cockpit plunged into darkness.

"Shit!"

My retinal implant quickly adjusted to the new lighting and compensated by turning my vision into a palette of green. Sphere floated out from its docking station, blinking in alarm. All the shuttle's interfaces were dead, its systems unresponsive.

I punched in commands through the manual override. Communications were down, navigation was down. Life support...

I thumped the release on the shoulder of my exosuit, prompting my helmet to spring up around my head. I was getting sloppy. I should have been prepared for this.

"Chase?"

I saw her dark eyes peering out from behind the visor of her helmet. "I'm fine."

The readouts in front of my eyes showed the oxygen levels had plummeted. Without our suits, we'd have been unconscious in minutes. But it wouldn't have been enough to kill us. We'd have survived.

Whatever was out there, whatever was on that Station, it wanted us alive.

It took me a moment to realise the shuttle was still

moving. All systems were down, including the engines. The rumbling of the hull had gone silent. But we were still floating along, pulled by some other force. Something from the Station itself. It was reeling us in closer and closer to one of the airlocks.

There were no sounds from the nothingness of space outside, but I felt the tremor in the hull as the shuttle lined up against one of the airlocks. Its docking clamps latched on, securing us in place.

Until now, I hadn't been afraid. But then I looked out and saw the entire Station disappear before my eyes as it plunged into darkness. Every single light emanating from the huge structure snapped out as suddenly as all the systems in the shuttle. It was more than a warning. It was a twisted welcome, a way of telling us it knew we were here.

"What do you think is in there?" Chase asked, a tremor in her voice.

I was asking myself the same thing. Sentient machines, left behind by some long-dead civilisation? An alien race from a far-away galaxy, stationed there to monitor us? Something worse?

"Whatever it is, I doubt it's friendly," I said. "Look at all the failed expeditions over the years. Something didn't want to be found."

A hiss of air escaped from the shuttle door and I jumped back, drawing my gun. Sphere flitted to my shoulder and let out a low, urgent hum as the door slid open. I pointed my pistol into the darkness, finger hovering over the trigger, but there was nobody there. Nothing on the infrared to suggest anything living in the vicinity. No electronic signatures. No movement detected. Nothing.

I stepped out into the darkness and switched on my helmet torch. Its beam illuminated the path in front of me, leaving my peripheral vision to bleed into shadows. The hallway seemed to stretch on forever, disappearing into the gloom. It was empty. It was like the whole place had just been abandoned.

Chase appeared at my side. "We've got gravity." Her voice sounded strange to my ears, like some of it had been lost in a vacuum.

I brought up my retinal implant. She was right. We were moving. The entire inner section of the Station was rotating, just fast enough to mimic the natural gravity on New Pallas.

What the hell was this place?

Each step I took echoed all the way down the hall, as if my boots were made of steel. The sound of my own breathing bounced back at me off the visor of my helmet. Everything else was silent. Whatever was here, it was clear we were the intruders, disturbing the unsettling quiet around us.

"We're not alone," Chase said. "Somebody must have turned those lights off."

"Not necessarily. Maybe whoever lived here left or died long ago, leaving nothing more than automated defences behind."

"We've got New Pallas gravity and my helmet's readout is showing we're getting stable oxygen levels now. You don't pump oxygen around a space station without something needing to breathe it. Or someone."

We continued on. One hallway turned into another. Passageways led to empty rooms with no signs of life. Maintenance corridors, stairwells, ventilation shafts. Whatever we had explored was only a fraction of the Station. There was no way of knowing what was around the next corner, behind the next door.

I kept moving, hoping my torch beam would illuminate nothing more than another empty room, another deserted hallway. The corridors looked like nobody had stepped foot in them in centuries. Thick patches of matted filth hung from rusted air vents. We left footprints in the dust behind us.

Beads of sweat clung to my forehead and I retracted my visor to wipe them away. The atmosphere was still breathable, for now at any rate. The air was musty and dry, but not toxic.

I tried to ignore the shadows in the corners of my eyes. I needed to stay calm. This was just another job.

The next corridor led towards what looked like an abandoned control room. The machines and consoles inside were like nothing I'd seen before. Everything about this place was strange and unfamiliar. Even as curiosity got the better of me and I pressed one of the buttons, nothing happened. The equipment was dead – left to rot under years of dust and grime.

I motioned for Chase to follow as I made my way away from the room as quickly and quietly as I could.

The lights flickered.

It was barely more than a flash, but the darkness had been so constant, so absolute, that I knew I hadn't imagined it. I waited a moment, looking up at the long tubing. It stared back at me, unresponsive. Mocking me for what I thought I saw. No hum of electricity. No fading glow.

Then it crackled into life again. Longer this time, with a low buzzing sound to accompany it.

"What the hell?" Chase said, looking up.

Beside me, Sphere whistled. Then I saw it. The door at the end of the corridor was slowly sliding shut.

"Run!"

All thoughts of caution deserted me. Whatever noise I made, whatever attention I brought to myself, it didn't matter.

The Station was trying to hide something from us. It was trying to keep us out. I had to get through that door.

Chase lunged ahead of me and dashed through. I raced towards her as the gap closed, sliding in front of the door just as the last sliver of space disappeared in front of my eyes and it sealed tightly shut.

I smacked my hand against the solid metal, accomplishing nothing but a jolt of pain down my arm.

"Chase? Are you there? Can you hear me?" I tried to reach her exosuit frequency, but something was blocking the signal.

The lights flickered again and I turned around, the cold grip of dread tugging at my insides. At the far end of the corner, shrouded in shadow, someone was watching me.

I raised my pistol, hands shaking, and fired two shots as quickly as my fingers would allow. The first ricocheted off the walls with a jarring clang. I didn't wait around to see if the second hit its mark. I had to get out of there.

I ducked through another hallway, feet thumping beneath me. There was no time for subtlety now. Whatever noise my boots made was sure to be followed by the footsteps of whoever was in pursuit. I couldn't stop them from coming after me. I could only hope to outrun them.

Sphere's readouts of the Station's infrastructure flashed before my eyes, a mess of schematics blinking in my retinal implant. I didn't know where I was going. I only knew I had to stay ahead of whoever was pursuing me. I'd keep running until…

No. A dead end. Nowhere else to go.

I swallowed, pressing myself against the wall and steeling myself with a breath. I wouldn't go down without a fight. If this was it, I'd make sure I emptied my gun into them before they took me. I had that much to comfort me, at least.

My fingers were warm around the trigger, ready to squeeze. I whipped back around the corner, training my gun on the shadow in pursuit. Whoever it was scrambled, clearly not expecting their quarry to have changed their mind and take a stand. They fumbled for their own pistol, and as the lights flickered, I caught a glimpse of a familiar face.

"Chase!"

She hesitated. Not reckless enough to shoot, not careless enough to lower her weapon.

I moved forward, keeping my own gun high. "It's me."

"Alvera?" She lowered her gun. "I thought you were somebody else. Someone was chasing me."

"Me too. I don't know where they went."

She leaned back against the wall and closed her eyes. "Never thought I'd see the day I'd regret stealing one of your warrants."

"Never thought I'd see the day I'd be glad you did." I gave her a friendly punch on the shoulder. It was the first time since setting foot on the Station that I'd felt the slightest reprieve from the fear and tension hounding me. Whatever our history, Chase and I were on the same side here. That much I could count on, at least.

Sphere floated up to her, bleeping in a friendly greeting, but Chase swatted it away. "Buzz off, drone." She turned to me. "Ryce had no idea what he was sending you into, did he? I figured this place would be advanced, but this is like nothing I've seen. The shuttle is locked down, our comms are jammed and we're fumbling around in the dark hoping we won't bump into whatever monsters run this nightmare."

I raised an eyebrow. "Monsters?"

She scowled. "You got a better name for them? Whatever they are, they're not friendly. They know we're here. They're playing games with us. Opening and shutting doors, messing with the lights. It's like an animal playing with its food. Or scientists experimenting on rats in a maze."

"Rats in a maze," I repeated. It was hard to disagree. Whoever was out there was toying with us. What would happen when they got bored?

Chase brushed her damp hair away from her forehead as she fiddled with the settings on her rifle. Her mouth was set in a tight line. "What do we do now?"

You're going to save us all, you know that? The echo of Ryce's words brushed against my ears, reminding me of what he'd stirred inside me. He'd chosen me for this. He'd said I was the only one who might be able to save New Pallas from the greed and ever-tightening grip of the corporations. I didn't want to fly back to him empty-handed. I didn't want to admit defeat.

Even if it meant going further into the maze.

"You said it yourself, the shuttle is locked down," I said. "We can't leave until we find a way to release it. Might as well gather all the intel we can in the meantime."

"Or we could find another way off," Chase pointed out. "Any station, even one this size, needs supplies. They must have a hangar or shuttle bay. Something to get them planet-side and back."

"Planetside?" I frowned. "Nobody has ever seen any kind of traffic coming from the Station. How could they transit to New Pallas without being detected? The stealth tech they'd need would be far beyond our capabilities."

"Look around," Chase replied. "All of this shit is far beyond our capabilities. Even *yours*."

I ignored the gentle mockery in her tone and turned to Sphere. "Have you managed to put together any kind of detailed schematics from your readouts of this place?"

A light blinked once, but there was no answer.

"Sphere?"

Chase eyed it sceptically. "That rust ball is trash. How many times has Felix told you to upgrade it?"

I tried to reboot it manually, but apart from a single light, Sphere was unresponsive. I plucked it from the air and placed it in its dock on the shoulder of my suit. The fear rising in me was about more than the flickering lights and shapes in the shadows. Sphere wasn't just a drone. It was inextricably linked to my cybernetics. It was an extension of all that made me what I was.

What had this place done to it? What was it doing to me?

Chase gestured down the corridor. "Let's go. Anything is better than standing here waiting for them to come to us."

We set off, covering each other around every corner. Every open door was a possible threat. Every hatch or maintenance vent posed an unknown danger. We sidled into corners. We peered into the shadows and skirted around edges. It was slow, but too tense to be tedious.

Fear wasn't something I was used to on New Pallas. I had a gun. I had either the law or the wealth of a huge corporation on my side – usually. I had my cybernetics. Maybe that's why they called me reckless.

Out here was different. Out here, I was up against something I didn't know I could match.

"This way."

The hallway was wide, illuminated by bright blue lights running down the floor on each side. I couldn't see what was at the end, but Chase could. Her footsteps quickened as she strode further and further away from me.

"Chase, wait!"

The words had barely left my mouth when the trap swallowed her up. A beam of light from the ceiling hit the floor, ensnaring her in a translucent prison.

I burst down the hallway and skidded to a stop beside her. I flinched, waiting for the same beam to envelop me. But nothing came.

Chase was frozen in place by the tunnel of light. She wasn't moving. There wasn't the slightest hitch in the chest of her exosuit to betray a breath of air. Even her eyes were frozen in place, her expression one of sheer terror.

I reached out, my gloved hand almost brushing the beam. I didn't know if it would have any effect on the stasis field, but I had to risk it. She would have risked it for me.

"Don't try it, Alvera. It's already too late for her."

That voice. Something about it stirred a memory, or maybe a dream. But I couldn't place it.

He appeared at the end of the hallway, flanked by two shapes in power armour. It took me a moment to recognise him. His white tunic was tailored and pristine, his black boots gleaming under the lights. He exuded a coldness far removed from his usual blustering temper. But there was no mistaking the piercing blue of his eyes. The dappled brown of his hair disappearing into silver.

Ryce.

"Sedate her." He barely looked my way. "I'll take care of the other one."

I didn't even have time to scream before he raised his gun and shot Chase in the head.

CHAPTER FIVE

The first thing I saw when I woke was the puff of red exploding from the middle of Chase's forehead. The blood didn't go anywhere. It just hung there, suspended. As frozen as the rest of her.

The image seared itself into my brain, as clear as if it were a real-time readout from my implants. Chase was gone.

I tried to move and was surprised to find my limbs still worked. There was a stiffness in them, but it wasn't debilitating. Whatever they'd used to knock me out didn't seem to have done any lasting damage. The only pain was a dull throbbing in the base of my skull, a headache that started somewhere in my neck and crawled up the back of my head into my temples.

I closed my eyes, trying to forget her fearful last expression. A thousand thoughts flitted through my head, making the pounding even worse.

Chase. The Station. Ryce. Felix.

Felix.

I clapped a hand to my mouth, afraid of emptying whatever bile was left in my stomach. He'd be waiting for her, not knowing she was never coming back.

Because of me.

I rolled over on all fours and retched, coughing up nothing but spittle. There was nothing else to give. I was empty.

How long had they kept me sedated? Days? Weeks?

My thoughts turned to Ryce. I pictured the glow of neon lighting reflecting off his speckled hair. The intensity of his eyes. The way he'd pushed me up against the wall. The way I'd willingly wrapped my legs around him. The way I'd swallowed each of his words, oblivious to the poison coating them.

What was he doing here?

I smashed my fist into the floor and it came away bloody. I realised I was no longer in my exosuit, just my thin base layers. Had Ryce stripped me out of it while I was sedated?

Nothing he hasn't seen before, said a voice in my head, a cruel snicker in the words.

As exhaustion took hold once again, I only had the strength to whisper one word before the persistence of sleep took me back into its arms.

"Why?"

The next time I woke up, they strapped my wrists into cuffs and took me to my new living quarters.

The surroundings were luxurious compared to my apartment back on New Pallas. Under different circumstances, I might have been able to appreciate the soft comfort of the carpet underneath my feet, the polished mahogany feature wall, the domed ceiling with its antique chandelier. But even when they took the cuffs off, I was still painfully aware it was nothing more than a prison.

When his armoured guards brought me food, I didn't try to fight them. I was too exhausted, too drained from the sedative. The strength of my hunger overrode my stubbornness. I ate and tried to ignore the pleasure the meal gave me.

After I scraped my plate, they came back and stuck me with a needle, pumping my body full of some sort of stimulant. It washed away all the stiffness and pain apart from the persistent headache at the base of my skull. It made me feel strong. Rejuvenated. But it felt wrong, like the strength given to me had a price attached I didn't yet know about. It made me wish I could open my veins and pour it all out again until I was nothing more than a shrivelled husk on the floor.

They returned my exosuit to me. Sphere was still docked on the shoulder, but it was silent and lifeless. I pulled the suit back on and felt more like myself again, and yet less like myself than I ever had in my life. I wanted answers.

Days later, they finally came.

The moment I saw him, all the rage and shame and terror rose up in me like a wave with nowhere to go. He dismissed his guards with a flick of his wrist and came to kneel in front of me.

I should have done something. I should have tried to fight him. But seeing him on his knees before me took the fight from my body. All I could do was stare at him, hoping my expression would ask all the questions I couldn't find the strength to give voice to.

He smiled. It seemed so familiar, yet it was the smile of a stranger. Was this the same Ryce who'd spoken so earnestly about the future of New Pallas? The man who made me believe I could save it? Had that man ever existed?

"I'm sorry," he said. "I know that's not enough right now,

but it's important I start with an apology for what I've put you through. I'm sorry for everything." His accent had changed. It was no longer the lyrical western drawl he'd affected on New Pallas. This was something crisper, more clipped. Another part of him I didn't know.

"Chase," I said, her name painful on my lips. I wasn't sure if it was a question or an accusation.

"She wasn't meant to come here." Ryce bowed his head. "I can't begin to tell you how much I regret what I had to do. But if you believe nothing else I tell you, believe this. In killing her, I made sure she suffered less than she would have if she'd lived."

Was there a tremor in his jaw, or was it my eyes playing tricks on me?

"You killed her," I said, my voice rough. "She was helpless and you pulled the trigger."

"And in doing so, I resigned myself to knowing you'd forever think me a monster for doing it," he said, finally looking up at me. "But there are worse things on this station than a man who's learned to make sacrifices to save what's important. You have to believe me when I say I was sparing her from a fate far worse than death."

Monster. The memory of Chase's voice echoed the word back at me. She'd warned me. She'd known there was something wrong about this place.

I just never imagined it could have been him.

"I would have come sooner, but I had things to take care of." He reached out a hand and gently touched my cheek. "I had to buy us some time."

The moment his fingers brushed my skin, I wrenched myself away, unable to bear his touch. Those were the same fingers he'd used to squeeze the trigger and end Chase's life.

"Stay the hell away from me," I hissed. "I don't even

know who you are. What is this place? How did you follow me here?"

He backed away. "There's so much to explain. You won't believe most of it without seeing for yourself. But if you'll let me, I'll try to fill in some of the gaps." He held out his arms, gesturing around the room. "This is Exodus Station. I didn't need to follow you here, Alvera. It's my home."

"Your home?" I scoffed. "Since when?"

"Since I was born. And it's been home to generations of Exodans before me. It has existed since long before humanity came into being and it will exist long after we're gone. We don't know what kind of creators first built it. Whoever they were, they've been gone long enough for all traces to have disappeared. Thousands of years. Hundreds of thousands of years. But that doesn't matter. What matters is who inhabits it now."

"You." I didn't know if Ryce heard the disgust seeping through my voice, but it made him chuckle nonetheless.

"Not just me," he said. "The Exodan people. No, we're more than a people. We're an ambition. We're how humanity will survive." His face grew serious. "You have to understand what's at stake here. We're faced with extinction."

I snorted. "Sounds familiar. That's the same kind of bull-shit you spun me to get me up here in the first place. Too bad Chase's survival didn't seem to count."

"Killing Chase was never my intention when I brought you here, but there will be more like her if we don't do some-thing," he said, his voice strained. "This station is our only hope. New Pallas has already been stripped and mined for most of what it's worth. What happens when the planet is exhausted and can no longer sustain its bloated population?" He shook his head. "It will be the end. The only thing that remains to be seen is how many manage to kill each other before the rest starve."

I couldn't keep the rage from my voice. "That's what this station is for? You're just hiding up here, waiting for everyone else to tear each other apart?"

"Hiding?" Ryce looked genuinely surprised. "You've got it all wrong. Exodus Station is not some kind of shelter we're taking refuge in. We're not cowards, Alvera. We're researchers, fighting for a way to save our species."

"What can you possibly research from up here?"

He smiled. "Haven't you figured it out yet? We control the corporations on New Pallas. We tell them what resources to mine, what technology to develop. Everything that exists on the planet below belongs to us."

The magnitude of his words sank in. The worst part was how much sense they made. The corporations had influence over the Spire, influence over what passed for law on New Pallas. They were at the cutting edge of research, development, technology. And all of it was made possible because of this place.

"You're the ones behind the stranglehold," I said, sickness churning in my stomach. "The mines, the corporations, all the planetwide shortages. It's all you. You're stripping our resources for yourself."

"For our future," he said, his voice becoming heated at the accusation in my words. "We use every advancement to figure out the puzzle that's been plaguing us since we got here."

"What puzzle?"

"How to escape this system." He laced his fingers together. "As long as we're trapped here, there can be no future for humanity. The only way out is to develop inter-stellar travel capable of taking us across the darkness of space. Our new home is out there somewhere, waiting for us. We just need to find a way to get there."

It took a moment for me to grasp what he was saying. For the briefest of seconds, it almost seemed heroic. The desperate search for a new home beyond the stars. Then the echo of his words rang in my ears, warning me what he truly meant.

"We?" I clenched my jaw. "Does that mean everyone? Or just you Exodans?"

That made him pause for a moment. When he spoke again, his voice was slow and careful. "Centuries ago, a group of explorers implanted themselves with highly-experimental, black market cybernetics. Those cybernetics helped them survive this station's defences and paved the way for the rest of us to follow. They were more than human. They were the first Exodans." He let out a long, heavy breath. "You have to understand this, Alvera. We're not the same as the people of New Pallas. Not anymore. We may have started in the same place, but we evolved into something different. Something more."

"You think having a few wires and circuits in your head has changed you that much? Set you apart above humanity? Even I don't presume that much. The arrogance…" I trailed off, disgust rising in me. "Was that why you killed Chase? She was too human for you?"

"I killed Chase because I know the same cruel truth as those first Exodans learned all those years ago. This kind of existence is not for everyone. There are few who can survive such cybernetic alterations, much less thrive with them." He tightened his mouth. "But it's those people – *our* people – who give us hope for a future outside the confines of this planet we're trapped on. Our people who might be able to withstand the trauma of the alterations our bodies need to survive a journey across dark space."

"You didn't even give her a chance to try," I said, my voice hollow.

"I didn't need to," he replied. "She didn't belong here. I couldn't allow her to leave having seen what she'd seen. We are not of New Pallas. We will not share their fate. And they cannot be allowed to interfere in ours."

I reeled back at his words like he'd struck me. It was so cold. So callous. Chase's death was nothing more than the cost of keeping a terrible secret. A secret kept at the expense of the rest of humanity.

A secret that would consign New Pallas to its death.

"Is that how I fit into all this? Are my cybernetics advanced enough to have made the guest list?" I laughed weakly. "Not interested, Ryce. I thought you knew me. Did you really think I'd want this? Any of it?"

The look on his face told me how badly I'd miscalculated. My laughter quickly faded under the weight of his pitying stare. "I wish you were as important as you're so quick to assume. It would make things so much easier. But you're not on the guest list, Alvera. I brought you here because the Exodan Council wants you dead. If you'd remained on New Pallas, they'd have killed you. The only reason you're still breathing is because of me."

His words sent a shudder through me. "Wants me dead? Why?"

"Progress is made when we dispose of things that outlive their usefulness," Ryce said, leaning forward. "Lucky for you, I convinced the Council you still had some left."

He sat next to me, too close for comfort. His proximity made me want to shiver, but I was frozen in place. The fabric of his tunic gently scratched my arm. His thigh pressed against mine. His breath was warm against my cheek. Everything about him made me want to run, but I was trapped in the sickening intimacy of his presence.

"You don't remember a thing, do you?" he said. His voice was gentle and coaxing, but there was a chill behind his words. "I think it's time to remind you." He tucked a strand of hair behind my ear.

I tried to squirm away. "What the hell are you talking about?"

"I think it's time you saw Exodus Station for what it really is. To show you what you've forgotten."

I froze. "Forgotten?"

The smile that unfurled across his lips was the most terrifying thing I'd ever seen. "Welcome home."

CHAPTER SIX

Welcome home.

Ryce's words echoed around my head as he led me from the confines of the living quarters I'd been restricted to and allowed me my first true glimpse of Exodus Station.

No, not the first. Not if what he said was true.

It was impossible. Another one of his manipulations. Whatever his game was, I would refuse to play it.

I looked around at the buildings under the artificial sky. Exodus Station was more than the abandoned tunnels I'd been scurrying around in. It was another civilisation.

As he led me through the tree-lined streets, Ryce talked me through the station's geography. Chase and I had docked in the lower half of the structure, a redundant space made up of old maintenance rooms and control centres. But I wasn't in the lower half of the station anymore. I was in what Ryce called the gyrospace – the beating heart of Exodus Station.

It was a sprawling city kept in place by the constant tug of gravity as the station turned. It seemed impossible, disorientating before my eyes. Lakes and rivers flowed freely through open spaces. Parks and greenery sprouted among the architecture. Nothing was built more than a dozen stories high. Even from the ground, you could see the sky.

The sky. I knew it wasn't real, but it did its best to fool me. As good as the projection was, I could see the curved seams of the ring behind it. But it was beautiful enough for me not to care. I had never seen such a shade of blue before. Apart from its famous sunsets, New Pallas was always grey. Even the sky couldn't escape the smog and clouds from below. If it had ever been like this, nobody alive had been around to see it.

"Quite something, isn't it?"

Ryce's voice shook me from my thoughts. It reminded me that none of this belonged here, that it was all stolen from New Pallas. Hearing him boast about it churned my stomach.

"It's not real," I told him, refusing to meet his eyes.

"It's the only thing that's real," he said. "The people living on New Pallas are doing nothing more than serving a death sentence. This station is humanity's hope for the future."

"It should be everyone's future. Why should you be the one to decide who's worthy of it?"

"I didn't decide. Evolution did." He closed his eyes for a moment and pinched the bridge of his nose. "I won't try to convince you that any of this is fair. I know how it must seem to you. But you should consider yourself fortunate nonetheless."

"You make me sick."

My words glanced off him as easily as if I hadn't spoken. I doubted anything I could say would change his mind. He thought he deserved this. More than that, he thought the people on New Pallas deserved the fate that was lying in wait for them. People I thought he cared about. Like Felix. Like Chase.

Thinking of her brought a tightness to my throat. "She didn't have to die."

"I know." Ryce turned to look at me. "But you should never have brought her here. It was reckless and irrational. Her death is on your hands as much as mine, Alvera. I think that's why you're so angry with me. You can't bear the thought that it might have been your fault."

"Bullshit," I snarled. "You pulled the trigger. I won't let you blame me for what you did to her. You had a choice."

"So did you. You could have turned around and taken her back to New Pallas. But you didn't. You forced my hand."

I bit down on my tongue so hard that the warm, coppery taste of blood pooled in my mouth. I hated him for his words, but that didn't stop him from being right. He might have pulled the trigger, but I put Chase in his crosshairs. Her death was on my conscience. Losing her was my burden to bear.

The thought made me want to sink to my knees. Even if I made it out of this alive, even if I got back to New Pallas, how would I ever face Felix knowing what I did? Knowing that my actions had got Chase killed?

"We're here."

I looked up, taking a sharp breath as I saw the size of the sliding glass doors before me. They stretched three stories high and parted to reveal a vast foyer milling with people.

Some of them were like Ryce, showing no outward presence of cybernetics. Others had tell-tale signs – a retinal implant lighting up behind their iris, a visible device around their ears connected to their auditory outputs. Some went further still, wearing their implants like a mark of honour. Bionic plates gleaming in chrome, blinking lights piercing through their skin. They were proud of what they were.

"What is this place?" I asked.

Ryce followed my gaze towards the doors. "This is where

our most important work is done. This is the gateway to the future. Our shipyards."

He marched through the doors and I quickened my stride to keep pace. Nobody questioned him. Nobody gave me any strange glances. It was like it was perfectly normal for me to be here with him.

"If we are to find a new home to sustain us, we need a means of getting there," he explained. "You might call us selfish, but every single resource we take from New Pallas goes towards making that possible. We are building ships, Alvera. Ships to take us away. Ships to deliver us to our salvation."

I followed him into an elevator. "How many?"

"Enough."

"Enough for who?" I said, hardening my voice.

The elevator doors slid open and Ryce walked out, leaving my question in the silence of his wake.

In front of us was a huge window. Outside, I could see the ring of Exodus Station curving its way through the darkness. We were staring into the vast, empty space at its centre.

Ryce brought up his holo-terminal. "Command to ship-yard observation cameras. Remove cloaking filter."

The window flickered in front of me. One by one, in the darkness I'd thought was empty, the ships appeared.

Each one was bigger than anything I'd seen on New Pallas. They were huge, miles-long structures with massive engines on each end. They looked too boxy, too unwieldly to ever be capable of flight. But these ships weren't meant for atmosphere. They were meant for space.

"It takes an incredible amount of power to maintain the station's secrecy," Ryce said. "All the energy we can spare goes into the ships' stealth systems. Sometimes it causes huge power surges. When that happens, we drop the stealth systems around the rest of the station to maintain those at the shipyards. You've seen it yourself from planetside. Most of the time we're invisible. But during a power surge, we can't help but reveal ourselves. An unfortunate side effect of what we're doing, but better that than letting our secrets slip. An abandoned station provokes fewer questions than an active shipyard."

"You can't do this," I said, my voice shaking. "You can't just leave New Pallas."

"No, we can't," Ryce agreed. "Not yet." When I turned to look at him, he tightened his lips. "The human body is capable of many things. Surviving sustained high-force acceleration is not one of them. If we try to leave now, nobody will make it. We need advances. Medical advances. Technological advances. Cybernetic advances. And we're running out of time."

The expression on his face was too raw, too agonised, for me not to take him at his word. "How long do we have left?"

"Not nearly as long as you think," he said. "The surface is already starting to succumb. A few decades from now, it will be lost forever. The upper city won't last much longer. Billions of people will revolt, fighting over scraps. They will destroy each other." His face was unflinching. "We need to make sure we're gone by the time that happens."

I took a step back. "You coward. I hope to hell not a single Exodan ever makes it out of here." I laughed. It was a harsh, ugly sound, but I revelled in it. It was nothing less than he deserved. "I hope you die with the rest of us, knowing it was all for nothing."

The Ryce I knew wouldn't have let me get away with that. But he gave nothing more than a sad smile at my attempt to provoke him to anger. His pity scared me more than his rage. "You'll understand soon. I think it's time we introduce you to the project overseer."

––––––––––––

Ryce led me back down the elevator and through a maze of corridors until we reached the overseer's office. The heavy-set door was locked, but it responded to Ryce's holo-terminal by sliding open with a mechanical whirr.

I followed him in, taking in my surroundings. The room was smaller than I expected and sparsely decorated. There was a workbench and tools in one corner, and one of the walls was covered in holoscreens showing hastily-scribbled schematics. Apart from that, the room was empty.

I turned to Ryce. "Where's the overseer?"

He smiled. "Right here."

I followed his gaze to one of the holoscreens on the wall. The image there showed two figures standing next to the huge hull of one of the newly-built ships.

The man in the picture looked younger, and there were less lines around the creases of his grin, but there was no mistaking it was Ryce.

The person next to him was a woman. She was wearing a grey jumpsuit and had pulled her chestnut hair back from her face as she waved for the picture, laughing. She had dark eyes and light olive skin. She looked...she looked almost like... no.

There, on the screen, I saw myself staring back.

He hadn't been lying. I was one of them. An Exodan.

Something fluttered in my heart at the sight of the name stitched into her jumpsuit. *Philomela.* It didn't mean anything to me. Maybe there was some mistake. Maybe our resemblance was nothing more than the most unlikely of coincidences.

She wasn't me.

She couldn't be.

When Ryce spoke, his voice was gentler than I'd ever heard it. "Would you like me to tell you who you really are?"

I swallowed. "Whatever you're trying to do to me, it won't work. I'll never trust you. I'm not one of you."

"You were. The best of us, in fact. The one we looked up to. The one we hoped would lead us out of here. Until you betrayed us. Until you betrayed *me*." The calm in his voice seemed to mask something else. Something pained and raw. It took all I had not to look up at him. I didn't want to see his vulnerability. I didn't want to see him as anything other than the monster he was.

"I was the top cyber surgeon on Exodus Station. You were a cybernetics engineer without equal. Together, we made you into something beyond what anybody else was capable of." His voice trembled. "You are the most advanced, the most complete of us all. The level of technology in your head should be too powerful for your body to handle, but somehow you survive. More than that, you excel. You thrive. You have a way with cybernetics. They're more than just upgrades. They're part of who you are."

I didn't want to hear it. That person wasn't who I was. It wasn't who I wanted to be.

"We fought for days when you volunteered to take the acceleration stress test," he continued. "I warned it would likely kill you. You thought it was worth the risk, if it meant discovering a way our bodies could survive interstellar travel." He gave a short chuckle. "You were right, as you so often were. The moment you succeeded, you became invaluable.

You began dedicating your time towards the goal of replicating your cybernetics in a way that would be accessible to the rest of us. So many people believed in you. I believed in you."

The way his voice broke on the words sent a sharp pain through my chest. I didn't want to feel it. He didn't deserve my pity or compassion, not after what he'd done.

"Look at us, Alvera. Just look."

I lifted my chin and blinked away tears to look at the holoscreen.

I looked happy. Both of us did.

"What was I to you?" I whispered, not wanting to hear the answer.

"First we were colleagues. Then we became friends." He shrugged. "It was only a matter of time before that evolved into something more. But what we were didn't matter nearly as much as what we believed in. We shared a dream together. Or rather, we used to."

"What changed?"

"You did," he said. His voice was thick with emotion. "You tried to throw away everything we built together out of some misplaced, misguided compassion for those *sletes* down on New Pallas."

The word was unfamiliar, but so full of venom I knew it was a slur. He said it with a hatred that cut deeper than anything I'd ever been called before. It stirred something dark and furious inside me.

"What the hell did you call them?"

A guttural laugh escaped his lips. "There's the look. The one that started all this. All on account of the obsoletes."

"Obsoletes? That's what you call the people on New Pallas? You think yourself that far above them?"

"There was a time you did too," he said bitterly. "But something changed. You started asking questions nobody wanted to hear. You started to suggest that unless we could all go, maybe none of us should."

"What was so wrong with that?"

"It wasn't your decision to make. But that didn't stop you. You downloaded every schematic, every piece of research that you could get your hands on. You wanted to go to New Pallas and tell them everything."

Something fierce swelled in my chest. Pride for the stranger I used to be. Rage that her plan had somehow been foiled. "What happened?"

Ryce faltered. For the first time, he was unable to meet my eyes. "You asked me to come with you. I kept hoping you'd change your mind, that you wouldn't see it through. But no matter how I tried, you couldn't be reasoned with." He swallowed. "You left me. You left me behind without a second thought. I knew if I let you go, it would be the end. Not just for me and you, but for us all."

Fear gripped my chest. "What did you do?"

"I disabled the autopilot on your shuttle. I'd led a double life down on New Pallas for years, monitoring the corporations from my position in the Spire. But you'd never left Exodus Station before. And you had no idea how to pilot a shuttle in gravity."

Echoes of our conversation back on New Pallas tugged at my memory, and the truth behind his confession dawned on me. "You told me you pulled the station's clearance codes from a crashed shuttle. You didn't tell me I was the one who crashed it."

"It was a burning wreck. You were half dead when I found you, but you were still breathing. Part of me wondered if it would be kinder to leave you there. By then, the rest of the Exodan Council had discovered what you intended to do. I knew they would send someone to kill you. There was only one way I could save you from what you'd done." He shook his head. "There's nobody better at cyber surgery than me. I thought if anybody could do it, I could. All I needed to do was to wipe your memories of the thoughts that led you to do what you did."

"Wipe my memories?" Even as I spoke the words aloud, they seemed absurd. I had memories. How could I be the person he claimed I was when more than thirty years of my life told me otherwise?

"I overestimated my skill and underestimated how powerful your cybernetics were. The surgery failed. Instead of removing only the disease, as a surgeon should, I wiped out every memory you ever had." A shadow passed across his face. "The irony is that in doing so, I inadvertently saved your life. By the time the Council's enforcer came for you, every trace of the person you were had been wiped away. It was like you never existed. The enforcer reported back to the Exodan Council and they agreed to my request to spare your life on the condition that you remained on New Pallas. They thought it was a fitting punishment to leave you among the sletes you threw your life away for."

That word again. Slete. It raised an indignance in me I didn't understand. Every time he said it, it reached a part of me I hadn't realised was there. Inside me, it festered with rage.

"It was our chance for a new beginning," Ryce continued. "I induced you into a coma and brought you to the Spire while you recovered from your injuries. I told Felix and Chase you'd been recovered from an illegal OriCorp medical facility, that you'd been experimented on and given advanced cybernetics. They bought every word." He took a breath. "For the past few months, we enjoyed a new life. I almost began to hope it might last."

"Past few months?" I fought against his words, unable to make sense of them. "This is all wrong. I've been a warrant hunter for more than a decade. Felix and Chase know who I am."

"None of those memories are real. Felix and Chase kept the truth from you, as I did. To settle you into your new memories. To protect you from the things I told them you suffered."

Every word he spoke was as violent as a blow. "You're lying," I said, my voice little more than a whisper. "This can't be true."

"Felix built that drone of yours. He used it to implant your mind with new memories. Good memories. Everything you remember is something that Felix designed. Your first warrant. Your friendship with him. The boy has a good heart." His mouth stretched into a tight smile. "He was only doing what he thought was right. He wanted you to remember happiness, not pain."

I wouldn't believe it. Believing it would mean my entire life was a lie.

"Why would you go to so much trouble?" I asked, my voice hoarse. "You told me that I left you. That I betrayed you. Why not just leave me as a blank slate and have me committed to a med centre?"

"Because I still loved you," he said. "I didn't want you to be a frightened shell of the woman you were, with no memories at all. If this was the only life we were able to have together, I wanted to make the most of it. It might not have been the life I'd imagined for us – after what you did, that was impossible – but in erasing your memories, I erased your mistakes. The new memories Felix created for you let you begin again. It was a fresh start for both of us."

Nothing made sense. But at the same time, patterns fell into place where there had been none before.

Chase. Felix. My team, my friends. Had I ever known them at all?

I couldn't speak. Inside, my heart raged against his words. I couldn't have been one of them. An Exodan. Someone who thought their life meant more than those they called sletes. That would mean the person I was, the person I used to be, was every bit as terrible as Ryce.

"What changed?" I asked. "If what you wanted was a fresh start, then why bring me back here?"

"To save your life." There was a note of anger in his voice now. "The Exodan Council were content to leave you alone while they thought you were no threat. But you did something to catch their attention."

I scoured my brain, trying to understand. "My last job. The one you suspended me for."

Ryce nodded. "That door you were so proud of bypassing? It was Exodan technology. Only one of our own could have broken the code."

The pieces fell into place. "It was a trap."

"One I didn't see until it had sprung," he said, heavily. "The Council ordered the warrant on Joy Payton. The rest was easy for them to set up. OriCorp is just one of their many fronts planetside. They knew only an Exodan would be able to get past that door. And you passed their little test."

The weight of his words hit me hard. "Chase was meant to have that warrant."

"And if you hadn't stolen it, she would have failed. The Council would have been satisfied and we could have gone on in peace. But you had to get involved." There was no mistaking the bitterness in his voice. "They didn't believe you could have used your cybernetics like that without your old memories. They gave me a choice. Bring you back or kill you."

"You brought me back."

"It wasn't a choice at all," he said. "Despite everything you'd done, I couldn't bear to lose you like that."

The picture was getting clearer in my head, but there were still parts that didn't make sense. "Why the deception? All that bullshit about saving New Pallas, telling me I was the only one who could pull it off. If you wanted me up here so badly, why didn't you just bring me yourself?"

"You'd never have believed me. And after all we'd been through, the last thing I wanted to do was shoot you with a sedation stim and bring you here by force. As foolish as it sounds now, I wanted you to *want* to come back." He rubbed a hand over his jaw. "If you'd stuck to the plan, it wouldn't have been an issue. But you brought Chase with you. If you had come alone, like I told you to, she needn't have died."

"You say that like she had some tragic accident, not like you were the one to shoot her!" I pushed myself to my feet. "You killed her for no other reason than she was in the way. You had me. You had what you wanted. She didn't need to die."

"Better her than you." He took a deep, calming breath. When he spoke again, his voice was cracked and hoarse. "I am sorry, Alvera. I truly am. But the reason Exodus Station has survived so long is because we cover our tracks. None of us compromise on that. It's the reason for all of this."

His words left a heavy silence that made them seem louder than they were. They rang around in my head, impossible to ignore. "What do you mean?" I asked, my voice low.

He rubbed a hand over his eyes. "The Council told me they would let you live if I brought you back. Quietly. But that was before they realised you brought Chase here. If either of you had escaped, you would have destroyed us. That's not something they are willing to overlook. Or forgive."

"I don't need their forgiveness. Or yours, for that matter."

He grabbed my wrist. His hand was cold, but his touch felt like a burn to my skin. "I'd start taking this a little more seriously, if I were you. The Council just voted to have you tried for treason."

I stared back at him. "What if I am a traitor? What if I'm proud of it?"

He pushed my hand away, looking at me like I had slapped him. "Then you're already dead," he said. "And all this will have been for nothing."

If his words were meant to frighten me, he had failed. I was too furious to be frightened. I hadn't betrayed him. He'd betrayed me. He'd betrayed New Pallas.

I reminded myself of the lie that had brought me here. *You're going to save us all, you know that?*

This time, it wasn't Ryce's voice in my head. It was the billions down on the planet below, calling for help they didn't even know they needed. I imagined them all inside me, their voices joining in a raging cry.

Yes, I told them. *Yes I am.*

CHAPTER SEVEN

The gyrospace seemed different after being at the shipyards. Everything Ryce had told me, everything I'd learned, had altered my perceptions. I had been overwhelmed by the ingenuity of it at first. The architecture, the technology. The lushness of the artificial rivers and parks in amongst the sophistication of the buildings and high-speed tramways.

Everything was too sterile, too perfect. It was like being back at the Spire. When you were standing miles above the surface, it made it all too easy to forget the foundations below. Everything here had been built on the backs of the people of New Pallas.

And without them, it would all collapse.

Ryce led me down the streets, his stride purposeful and swift. I kept pace beside him, trying not to get distracted by the sights around me.

"I need to show you something before we go to the Council," he said, breaking into my thoughts. "I need to make you understand what would have happened if I hadn't killed Chase."

"Understand?" I gave a hollow laugh. "There is nothing you can show me to make me understand. Everything you ever told me was a lie. I don't even know who I am anymore."

"I know. That is my biggest regret. If you could still remember, maybe things wouldn't be so hard. Maybe you would…" He trailed off. "I can't undo what I've done. All I can do is try to explain."

His expression gave nothing away as he ushered me inside a large building. My ears filled with the noise of whirring belts and the clanging of metal on metal. It seemed to be some kind of industrial plant.

We came out onto a viewing platform high above the factory floor. Below us, workers in dark-coloured jumpsuits moved tirelessly, collecting pieces of material from long conveyor belts and depositing them in containers. They had a dogged kind of determination, never stopping to stretch or wipe the sweat from their brows. It was too purposeful, too mechanical to be natural.

It took me a moment to see it. Then it hit me. These weren't people at all.

I looked up at Ryce, horror twisting my stomach. "What have you done to them?"

He didn't answer. Instead, he brought up his holo-terminal. "Command to Recycling Plant 2312. Halt all autotron activity immediately."

The moment the words left his mouth, everything went silent. The workers stopped in their tracks, as if they'd been caught in stasis. They didn't flinch or falter. They barely breathed. It was like they'd been frozen in place.

What scared me the most was their eyes. There was no fear or alarm there. They were dead, devoid of all expression.

"You've made them into machines." My voice was barely a whisper.

He nodded. "Complete control through cybernetic overrides. We determine every single one of their higher functions. Without instruction, these autotrons would stand in the same spot until they collapsed in a pile of their own piss and shit. They'd starve to death. They no longer have the capacity to survive without being told to."

"Why would you do this to them?"

Ryce shrugged. "A number of reasons. Mainly as punishment for serious crimes like insurgency or treason."

Treason. The very thing Ryce told me I had been accused of.

No, not me, I told myself. *The woman in the picture. Philomela.*

"This is what I meant when I said I spared Chase's suffering. This is the fate I'm trying to spare you from, too. I need you, Alvera. But more than that, Exodus Station needs you. You are the only one who has ever passed the acceleration stress tests. Only your knowledge of cybernetics can save us."

My heart pounded. "That's why you haven't killed me. You still think I can be your ticket out of here."

"I haven't killed you because despite everything you've done, I still care about you," Ryce said. "More than you'll believe. More than you'll ever remember. But there are others on the Council who don't feel the same way. It's those people you have to convince."

I didn't want to convince anyone. I wanted to destroy them. Whoever Philomela was, that was what she had been trying to do. In doing so, she had lost everything.

I was all that was left of her. I didn't know if that would be enough, but I had to try.

I swiped Ryce's sidearm from his belt before he could react and fired a shot at the panel on the door. I barely had time to roll underneath as the door came crashing down, putting a solid hulk of metal between us.

I jammed the gun in the empty holster on my exosuit and ran. I didn't know where I was going. I didn't know how to get off Exodus Station. All I could think about was getting as far away from Ryce as I could.

My hand drifted towards my shoulder until I remembered Sphere was still offline. The drone was little more than a ball of wires and circuits.

Obsolete.

I pushed the anger out of my mind and tried to focus. To get off the station, I'd need a shuttle. The tramway might be able to take me to one of the hangars. It was a desperate shot, but the only one I had.

Adrenaline surged through me as I ran through the streets, ignoring the people who turned to look at me. They didn't matter now. The only thing that mattered was getting back to New Pallas.

The tramway wasn't far. I could see the platform on the other side of one of the bridges spanning the artificial river. I didn't have time to marvel at how blue the water was, how the light from above broke on the surface into a thousand glittering fragments. It was just one more obstacle in my way.

I was halfway over the bridge when something huge dropped from the air above me, blocking my way across.

I jumped backwards and drew Ryce's gun. The man in front of me had an exosuit like a metallic shell. I heard the familiar whirr of anti-grav propulsors powering down as he landed right between me and whatever hope I had of getting away. Thick silver cables protruded from the nape of his neck. He wasn't wearing an exosuit. He *was* the exosuit.

The only thing human about him was his head. He had ghostlike skin and his grey eyes were keen and observing, glowing with the lights from his retinal implants.

He caught my eye and gave me an unsettling smile. He was the kind of thing that would have given Chase nightmares. Something more machine than man.

I squeezed the trigger on Ryce's gun and let loose a flurry of bullets. The first two ricocheted harmlessly off his chest. The next grazed his jaw and ripped away some of his pale skin, revealing the sheen of metal plating underneath.

He rubbed a hand across the spot I'd hit. "Nice shot. Might have tickled if I had pain receptors there."

"Get out of my way," I said, fighting to keep my voice calm. "I'm leaving."

"No."

"I will empty this chamber into your skull if you don't move."

"Oh, I believe you, Alvera Renata. But you still won't be leaving. It takes more than a few bullets to put down an enforcer."

My stomach churned. "How do you know – "

"Your name?" He cocked his head. "This isn't the first time we've met. I was the one they sent to hunt you down on New Pallas all those months ago. When I found you, your mind was empty."

"Not anymore."

"That's one thing that's changed." His expression was unfathomable, devoid of humanity. "Ryce convinced the Council he could handle you. He said you were no longer a threat. The Council believed him at the time." He grinned. "That's another thing that's changed."

I raised the gun again, pointing it at his head. I was

outmatched, but that didn't mean I was going down without a fight.

Staring down the barrel of the gun, the enforcer only gave a slight shake of the head. "Go ahead. But I warn you, it will end badly for you."

I tightened my finger over the trigger, ready to squeeze. I would get two, maybe three shots off before he was on me. Not enough to do much damage, but at least if I went down, I'd go down fighting. Better that than end up one of the Council's mindless autotrons.

Then something pricked my neck and the world went black.

———

It felt like hours later when I finally opened my eyes. I groaned and stretched out, wincing against the glare from the overhead light as I tried to make out my surroundings. One of Ryce's faceless guards stood over me in full-body power armour, rifle secure her hands. She probably assumed that was enough of a deterrent to keep me on the floor.

It wasn't.

I leapt forward and grabbed her leg, hauling her weight out from under her with as much force as I could.

Her armour made a loud clang as it hit off the ground and I clambered on top of her, using what little weight I had to press her against the floor. I pushed my chest down against her plated shoulder and wrapped my legs around hers to hold her steady.

My fingers fumbled at her helmet release until the visor retracted. She glared at me and then baulked as I swung a fist down into the gap, connecting squarely with her nose. I threw another couple for good measure, my hand coming away more bloodied each time. When she stopped moving, I wrenched the rifle from her weakened grasp.

The door. It was still open.

I didn't look back. The guard wasn't my problem. I didn't care about her enough to kill her. Ryce was my only target.

The corridors around the cell were empty. Something wasn't right. This was too easy. Back on New Pallas, I might have put it down to me being that damn good. But this wasn't New Pallas. If I was out of my cell, it was because they wanted me to be. They were testing me.

Rats in a maze.

Chase's words echoed like a ghost in my ear, reminding me this was what they wanted. But even if it was false freedom, it was the only chance I had.

Spotlights illuminated the walkway under my feet, guiding me forward. There was nowhere else to go but on, wherever that might take me.

Then came the footsteps.

Think, Alvera, I told myself. There was no time to find a way out. But maybe I didn't need to. Maybe I could get a message out instead.

The footsteps echoed in pursuit as I ducked into a control room and tried to find a comms relay I could work with. Unfamiliar consoles blinked at me. I poked and prodded interfaces I couldn't read in the wild hope that one of them might hold the answer.

I didn't expect it to work. Not with my fingers fumbling and the footsteps bearing down on me. Not when they had me exactly where they wanted me. But a moment later, I had a connection to New Pallas.

For a moment, there was only static on the line. Then I heard Felix's voice and almost sobbed in relief.

"Hello? Is anyone there? You're on frequency 2690-alpha. Warrants and enforcement."

I tried to speak, but my voice caught in my throat. Something wasn't right. The words I wanted to say were there on the tip of my tongue, but I couldn't push them past my lips.

Felix was muttering to someone in the background. "I'm not sure, it's a strange signal and I can't pinpoint where it's coming from. It's just static." He raised his voice again. "Is anyone there? This is frequency 2690-alpha. Warrants and enforcement headquarters. You're on an encrypted channel."

A gasp of air escaped my lips. Every word I formed in my head was getting lost on the way to my mouth. The unspoken sentences lingered on my tongue until I was forced to swallow them back. I couldn't expel them. I could only scream noiselessly as they evaporated in my mouth, heard by no-one.

My throat was thick and tight with tears. Something had gone horribly wrong.

Rats in a fucking maze.

I kept my back to the door as the footsteps approached. Slow, heavy, clunking. Ryce's guards, no doubt. But they weren't alone. I could hear another sound. Not the thudding rhythm of armoured boots, but a more methodical clicking. Dress boots. The kind worn by someone too important for armour. The kind that gleamed with fresh polish under the light.

I wheeled around, holding the rifle high. Ryce was standing in the doorway, flanked by his guards.

I wasn't getting out of here alive. But at least I could take him down with me.

"This is for Chase, you bastard," I whispered, and squeezed the trigger.

There should have been a hole in his head. He should

have fallen to the ground, eyes glazed and body limp. But he was still standing there, dark circles under his eyes and hard lines around the edges of his mouth.

My finger was still on the trigger, but I couldn't pull it. I was frozen in place, as Chase had been. There was no stasis field around me, nothing to stop me from moving. I just wasn't doing it. I wasn't killing him. And I didn't understand why.

I had expected anger from him. Cruelty, even. I hadn't expected the tears. They slid down his face as if he was made of stone, leaving glistening streaks in their wake. "Every time I hope you'll change, you disappoint me again. Drop that weapon and come with me, please."

Please. The politeness of it was so absurd that I wanted to laugh. I squeezed the trigger again, but nothing happened. My finger didn't move.

Something tightened in Ryce's expression. "I'm trying to make this easy for you. Don't make me force you. I don't want to have to do this to you. Not after everything I've done to get you back."

I was trying to kill him, but he just wasn't dying. However hard I tried, my body wouldn't obey.

He looked me square in the eye. "*Philomela.* Drop your weapon and follow me."

I bent my knees and gently laid the rifle on the floor at my feet. On the outside, I was calm and compliant.

Inside, I screamed.

My feet moved of their own accord, sliding against the floor. I kept my head down, averting my eyes from the armoured guards. I followed him meekly, like a docile creature with no thoughts of its own.

All the way, I screamed silently. In the confines of my head, I clawed at my skin, leaving deep bloody trails down my cheeks and arms. I dug my nails in and tore out flesh in a desperate bid to escape my own body. I emptied my lungs until my throat was cracked and raw and my voice was hoarse. On the outside, I remained still and silent, following him without a word. Without question.

What had he done to me?

CHAPTER EIGHT

Philomela.

Her name circled around my mind, taunting me. It had a lyrical sound to it, almost like music. A twisted, hypnotic lullaby that bent me to Ryce's command. I felt like I was looking at myself from a great distance, wondering who this poor shell of a woman was and why she wasn't doing anything to fight back.

"Alvera." The sound of his voice made me flinch. "I never wanted this. I swear to you, this was not what I intended. But you forced my hand, as you always do. Time and time again you rush into madness, with no thought about who you're leaving behind. And this time..." The words died in the air between us.

A cold grip tightened in my chest. "What did you do to me?"

Some part of me already knew the answer. I just wanted to hear him say it.

"Your cybernetics are wonderful," he said. "The future of humanity. But they leave you vulnerable in the same way they leave every Exodan vulnerable."

"You hacked me?"

Ryce nodded. "A crude way to put it, but yes. In simple terms, I hacked you."

"Just like one of those autotrons you showed me back at the factory." I sank down in the chair he offered me. All the energy I had left dissipated, leaving me deflated. I couldn't fight what he was telling me, but I couldn't accept it either.

"No." He grabbed my shoulders with both hands, forcing me to look at him. "Not like the autotrons. Never like them. Do you really think I could..." He caught his breath. "I wouldn't do that to you. I could never do that to you."

"You just told me – "

"It's not the same," he interrupted, standing up and taking a step back. "I don't want you to be a mindless slave. I will only take control if you try to fight me."

"Like you did back there?"

"Yes. There are only two core commands programmed into your cybernetics. You cannot attempt to harm me. And you cannot reveal to anyone what you know about Exodus Station and its people. To force you to do anything else, I need to take manual control of your implants using an over-ride code."

"Her name. Philomela. That's your code." It was sick. Twisted.

"As long as you don't try to resist, I will never have to use it. You are free. It's up to you what you choose to do with that." There was a pleading look in his eyes. "Come back to me. Don't throw your life away. Not when there is so much at stake."

His words hit me like a blow. I let the weight of them wash over me and waited to see what was left when I'd had time to make sense of them.

"You talk as if you loved her," I said. "Philomela. As if

you loved me. But this isn't love, Ryce. This is control. How could you do this?"

"How could *I* do this?" Anger flashed through his eyes. The familiar temper was back, breaking through the veneer of grief and pain and betrayal. His rage was not the harmless bluster I once considered it to be. Not anymore. Now it was something much more volatile. Much more dangerous.

"How could I do this?" he repeated, his voice low. "You left me. Without an apology, without an explanation, without a fucking goodbye. Without considering what they might do to me to punish your crimes."

He was telling me things I'd done in a life I couldn't remember. A life that didn't belong to me anymore, if it ever had.

"If Philomela left you without a goodbye, then I bet she had a damn good reason," I said. "You'd never have let her go. You were just the same on New Pallas. You couldn't bear it when I wasn't under your control. No wonder you tried to brainwash me. I bet it was the easiest decision you ever made."

"That's not true!" He shot me a glare. "It was a last resort. I only wanted to remove your memories, remove your betrayal. This was never what I wanted. But just like with Chase, you forced my hand."

"I'd rather have died with her than be a slave to you."

"You may still get that wish." He started pacing in front of me. "Act like this in front of the Council, and everything I've done to try to save you will have been for nothing. It's only because of me, because of what I did to you, that you have a chance of getting out of this with your life."

"You expect me to thank you for that?" I couldn't hold back the contempt in my voice. "When did you do it, Ryce? When did you decide to cut into my brain?"

He tightened his lips. "It hardly matters now."

"It was right after you shot Chase, wasn't it? After I woke from the sedation, my head…" My chest tightened with pain as the realisation dawned on me. "You didn't do this after I tried to escape – you had already done it! All this time trying to convince me how sorry you are, how much you wanted me back, and all you had to do was flip the switch you put in my head!"

"I needed insurance," he said. "But I didn't want to use it. Not unless you made me."

"Made you? You have the gall to talk about me *making* you?"

"Don't make this harder than it needs to be," he said. There was more bite in his voice now. It was harder. Colder. "Do you need me to show you the alternative to make you understand? If I wanted to, I could control everything you do. What you say…"

I want you, Ryce.

"Who you kill…"

Felix. Anyone else who gets in the way.

"Down to the very microexpressions on your face."

A smile. Warm. Genuine.

"You made this necessary. But it doesn't have to be forever. Once you realise what you've done, you'll be able to take it back. You'll be able to make up for all the damage you've caused. But until then, this is how things have to be."

"You bastard," I said, barely able to keep my voice steady. "I swear on Chase's memory, I will kill you for this." The threat sounded weak, like I didn't even believe it myself.

"It's time to go," he said, ignoring me. "Your trial is about to begin. I don't want to have to force you to submit to any commands in front of the Council, but I will if you leave me no choice. Don't do anything stupid."

"If you're that worried about what I might do, why don't you just look into my brain and see for yourself?"

"That would certainly make things easier," he said. "Maybe your thoughts would give me the closure that you never could. But the human brain is far too complex for that. We can hack it, hardwire instructions into it, but we can't read it."

It didn't feel like much of a victory, but it brought me a sliver of comfort. Even if I had lost control of my voice, of my body, at least I could survive in the confines of my head. My thoughts were the only weapon I had left.

As if he'd guessed what I was thinking, a small smile spread over his face. "Don't get too comfortable, Alvera. I might not be able to read your mind, but I can still monitor almost everything you do through your retinal and auditory implants. I'll never be too far away." He stood up. "It's time to go. Follow me."

"No."

He sighed. "*Philomela,* follow me."

Trying to fight him was like trying to fight a dream when you're willing your legs to run, but they won't move. The more I resisted, the stronger the pressure became. My body was heavy with the weight of his will.

I didn't have a choice.

The Exodan Council chambers were as sleek and polished as everything else on the station. The ornate crystalline lighting that hung from the ceiling seemed like a relic from centuries past. On the holoscreens were images of landscapes New Pallas hadn't seen in millennia. Vast swathes of sand and stone. Lush green forests. Powder snow and ice. Symbols of the future lost to the past. This was what the Exodans strived for. New worlds. Paradises they'd do anything to get to.

Several figures sat around the chamber. Ryce was directly in front of me. Next to him sat a pale-skinned woman. Her ashen hair was tied in elaborate knots and her eyes were sharp and distrustful. She clasped her hands tightly together when she saw me.

"I suppose you're quite pleased with your little demonstration at the comms array?" she said, turning to Ryce.

He curled his lip. "I think it made the desired point, councillor."

"Oh, it made a point," she snapped, voice frosty. "But whether it was desired or not is something I doubt we'll come to any agreement on. I find myself rather wishing she'd managed to shoot you."

"Come now, Ojara," said another man from across the room. "We agreed we'd hear him out."

"That was before his pet project brought a slete onto Exodus Station." The councillor he'd called Ojara bristled. Everything about her was exquisite elegance, from the intricacy of her hair to the svelte, floor-length dress she was wearing. She exuded authority, even more so than Ryce. I recognised the enforcer from earlier standing in the shadows behind her seat, and a shiver of fear ran down my spine.

One of the other councillors waved a hand dismissively. "That's already been dealt with. The slete is dead. She'll cause no issues for us."

I looked between them all, seven in total, my fear turning into anger. They were talking about Chase like her life was worth nothing. Like her existence didn't matter. I balled my hands into fists, wishing I still had Ryce's gun on me. I might not have been able to shoot him, but I could have turned it on the rest of them. Maybe even taken a couple of them down before the enforcer stepped in to put me out of my misery.

Another of the women spoke. "Let's hear what he has to say, Ojara. He deserves that much."

Ryce bowed his head. "Very gracious of you, councillor. I assure you, this whole demonstration, as Ojara put it, wasn't just for show. I told you I had Philomela under control. The fact she is standing before you now is proof of that."

"After she locked you in a factory and made it halfway to the tramway unopposed." Ojara snorted. "Forgive me if I'm not impressed, Ryce. She should have been made an autotron the moment she stepped foot back on our station."

"We all know the limitations of autotrons," he replied, his voice taking on a hard edge. "In order to utilise her to her full effectiveness, we need minimal disruption. A few core commands to restrain her while still allowing her to function at her near-full potential."

He was talking about me like I wasn't there. I wasn't real to him. I was a tool. Something to be used and disposed of when I had nothing left to give.

One of the men shifted in his seat. "I understand the theory. But there's too high a risk of rebellion with such freedom, especially when it comes to her level of cybernetics."

"That's where the override commands come in," Ryce said. "Short-term, temporary programmes that allow autotron-like control for a limited time."

Ojara frowned. "That's untested technology."

"Untested?" For the first time, Ryce met my eyes. "*Philomela*, come here."

I fought against the power in his words, but it was no use. The more I struggled against him, the harder the pressure increased. It felt like my brain was bulging against my skull, threatening to burst. There wasn't enough space in my head for both his will and mine.

Before I realised I had moved, I was standing in front of him. This was what he wanted. To show off his power to the rest of the Council. To prove that all he had to do was say the name of the person I used to be to make me his. Completely, utterly his.

"I'm sorry for this," he whispered under his breath, so only I could hear. Then he raised his voice, a glint of amusement shining in his cold eyes. "Kiss me."

His words caught me by such surprise that I could only splutter. "What?"

"I told you to kiss me."

"Fuck off."

A murmur of laughter broke out from the rest of the chamber, but Ryce didn't seem perturbed. He uttered the command again, the words a breath against my cheek. "*Philomela.* Kiss me."

No. Not this. Anything but this.

The laughter grew louder and warmth shot into my cheeks like I'd been scalded. He couldn't do this to me. Not in front of these people.

I closed the gap between us. As I opened my mouth to say no, my voice disappeared. Instead, I pressed my lips against his. My tongue was fierce and insistent, exploring the warmth of his mouth. I was kissing him like I wanted him. Like this was what I wanted.

Stop, I begged him in my head. *Please stop*.

A tear slipped loose from the corner of my eye and slid down my cheek.

When he finally released me, I stumbled back. The rest of the Council swam before my eyes in a haze. Everything had changed. Nothing would ever go back to how it used to be. Not after this.

Ryce raised an eyebrow at Ojara. "Satisfied yet?"

She scowled. "Disgusted, actually. But that's beside the point. You said yourself the override commands only work in the short term. Exactly how long do they last for?"

Ryce kept his expression calm, but I couldn't mistake the note of impatience that seeped into his reply. "It's variable."

She smirked. "How convincing. I'm sure our fellow councillors take great comfort in that."

"I have access to her retinal and auditory implants. Even when she's out of my reach, there's no way she can escape the overrides. How long they last is immaterial when there's nothing stopping me from simply re-asserting control."

Ojara shook her head. "It's still too high a risk."

"What's the alternative?"

"To start again. To dispose of this treasonous slete-lover and find another way."

Ryce clenched his jaw. "You would throw away all our work to settle some grudge. Philomela betrayed us all, but nobody more than me. If I can let that go, so can you."

"Have you really let it go, Ryce?" Ojara had a gleam in her eyes. "Or are your feelings getting in the way of your professional judgement here? You know what the penalty is for treason. She is guilty of trying to expose us. Not once, but twice. She deserves to answer for it."

"And what do we deserve?" Ryce stood up, appealing to the other councillors. "We're too close to let this all go to waste. She is the only one who survived the stress tests. The only one with cybernetics powerful enough to survive the acceleration it would take to make the journey across the darkness of space."

Every word he spoke betrayed what was really at stake. It

wasn't about me at all. It never had been. He was afraid. They all were. It was the only thing I could use against him. Fear made a man desperate. And a desperate man would make mistakes.

I had to believe that.

"We need her," Ryce said. "If you are afraid of what she might do on this station, then I will take her back to New Pallas. I will keep her under my watch and see to it that she finishes the work she started before she betrayed us."

"How?" one of the councillors asked, frowning. "You wiped her memories."

"But not her intelligence. Her cybernetics and everything else we need are right there in her head. She engineered them once and she can do it again."

"What if she refuses?"

"I will see to it," Ryce repeated, through gritted teeth. "By whatever means necessary."

Ojara shrugged. "Let's put the matter to a vote then. I propose that she is executed for treason."

"I'm with Ojara."

"I follow Ryce."

Seven strangers. Seven monsters, each of them deciding my fate. The voting went around the chamber. By the time it reached the councillor to the left of Ryce, Ojara had secured two more votes alongside her own. It was tied three apiece. If the last woman voted with Ojara, it was over.

She pursed her lips. "You've put us in a difficult position, Ryce. Mind wipes and memory implants, control chips and override commands. It all seems like so much effort when a quick bullet would have done the job. Ojara is right. The risk is too high."

I held my breath, waiting.

The councillor sighed. "And yet I cannot help but agree

with you. Too much time and too many resources have been put into this project. We cannot simply throw that away. If Philomela proves to be too much trouble, it won't be hard to put her down like the slete-dog she is. Until then, what's in her head may still save us all." She nodded. "I vote with Ryce."

A slow smile unfurled across Ryce's lips. "I'm glad to hear it. A sensible decision has been made today. Not just for us, but for the future of Exodus Station."

Ojara rolled her eyes. "Save the grandstanding. You've won. Just see to it that the job gets done this time. Or next time it might be you in front of us instead of her."

She stood up, smoothing down the folds of her dress. She fixed me with a hard, immeasurable stare she strode past, keeping her distance on her way from the chamber. The enforcer followed her out without giving me a second glance.

As the rest of the councillors filed out of the chambers, Ryce approached me.

My whole body shook with rage. "You disgusting, evil – "

"I'm sorry that had to happen," he said, his voice even. "But they needed a show. They needed to see you humiliated, broken, to understand you were no threat. I will never have to use the override code again if you do as I ask. If you want your freedom, you need only comply."

"That's not freedom."

He sighed. "I know it doesn't seem like it just now, but this is a second chance. I'm a patient man. With you, I've had to learn to be. I'm willing to wait as long as it takes for you to come around. And you will come around."

"You're wrong. I'll never stop fighting against you."

"I hope that's not true, for both our sakes." He straight-ened up, adjusting the sleeves of his tunic. "I'm sending you back to New Pallas. Ojara might have played it safe in front of the rest of the councillors, but as long as she has you within her grasp, you're on borrowed time. It's safer for you to return to your old life at the Spire, for now at least. I have some things to take care of but I won't be far behind you."

He paused at the doorway. "In case you were wondering, I couldn't risk your drone transmitting any of this data to Felix. It's been deactivated. It's just me and you now, Alvera. As it should be."

The way he said my name caught me hard. "Why do you call me that? You always knew me as Philomela."

He turned away. "Philomela betrayed me. Alvera didn't."

"No," I said. "You betrayed her instead."

If there was the slightest flicker of remorse in him, he didn't let it show. The Ryce I thought I knew was dead. In his place was a monster.

The door clicked shut behind him, leaving me alone. But I wasn't truly alone, not while he had such control over me. The thought of going home should have filled me with relief. Instead, I felt more trapped than ever.

I still wanted to save New Pallas. But first I had to figure out how to save myself.

CHAPTER NINE

The atmosphere burned red around the shuttle as it descended. The lights of New Pallas twinkled below like a signal welcoming me home. Glass and steel glittered as far as the horizon stretched. There were a million places I could run to. But with a click of his fingers, Ryce could bring me back.

How could a planetwide city bursting at the seams suddenly feel so small?

Going back to my apartment was like entering a stranger's home. Everything was exactly how I'd left it, but nothing was the same. I stripped out of my exosuit and pulled on clothes that no longer fit as they once did. It was like putting on a stranger's skin. Everything about being here was like inhabiting someone else's life.

This wasn't home anymore. I had to go.

I grabbed a bag and quickly stuffed in a couple of sidearms and my exosuit, along with Sphere. The little drone was still lifeless and silent, broken by whatever Ryce had done to it.

The sky was dark by the time I left. The red-orange bloom of the sunset had long passed, leaving behind a dusky purple blanket tinted by the glow of lights from the city. I walked to the nearest public transit station, my bag slung over one shoulder and my feet moving lightly beneath me.

The transit shuttle was dark and cramped, its passengers squashed together. In another life, I might have been irritated at the close quarters, the invasion of personal space. Now, it was wonderful. In the tight cluster of bodies, I was unremarkable. Just another nameless face. I didn't need to be Alvera Renata. I could be anybody.

When the shuttle touched down on the landing pad, I let out a breath and marvelled at the darkness. The sky was blocked from view by the city's upper levels. Even during the day, the only light down here would be that emanating from the various bars and flophouses that somehow survived this far away from civilisation.

This was the surface.

The concrete underneath my feet was worn and crumbling, giving way to dirt and rock below. Everything down here spoke of a past long forgotten to all except those who had been unable to leave it behind. The streets were thick with swarms of bodies, the air heavy with the stench of sweat and filth. Nothing about the surface was civilised. Down here, the only thing that mattered was survival.

It was only a matter of time before the disease here spread skywards. It would stretch up and take the rest of New Pallas with it. People in the upper city thought they were safe in the sky. Their death would simply take longer.

The worst part was realising that the Exodans weren't entirely wrong. New Pallas was running out of time. The only future where its people survived was one where they left this dying planet. Maybe that's why I had once believed as I did. Maybe up there on Exodus Station, I had more perspective on how hopeless things were down below. Or maybe that was the kind of thinking that justified taking control of another human being.

I kept moving, looking for a place to lie low. Most of the flophouses were full, even the dirtiest and most run-down of them. I was almost ready to resign myself to a night on the streets when I heard a wheezing cough from behind me.

"Not having much luck, are you?"

I turned around. The man who had spoken couldn't have been much older than thirty, but the paleness of his skin and the blue veins half circling his eyes gave him a sickly appearance that belied his years. His lean frame was hidden under a white shirt and fraying jacket. He was reedy, but not wasting away like some of the others on the street. Ill, perhaps, but not dying. Not yet.

I waited for him to say more and he gave a half shrug, holding his hands out in apology. "Been following you for a while now. I was going to rob you. Then I saw how painfully out of place you were and figured you must be a topsider." His strange surface accent lisped some of the words, but his manner was relaxed and light.

"You figured right." I crossed my arms and hitched my bag a little tighter around my shoulder, just in case. "Why the change of heart about robbing me?"

He smiled. "You look like you need somewhere to stay, and it just so happens I've got a room in this shithole. It's not much, but it's better than sleeping rough."

I wasn't convinced. "Am I supposed to believe this is an act of selfless generosity?"

"Are you kidding?" He raised an eyebrow. "Even a topsider should know you get nothing for free down here. I've got things I need that I can't get my hands on. Since you came from way up there in the sky, maybe you can help a guy out."

Suddenly his pallid colouring and gaunt skin made sense. "Surface life not killing you fast enough? You really want something to hurry things along?" I rolled my eyes. "Whatever your poison is, you can find it yourself. I'm not a drug smuggler."

His face turned stony. "You upper city types come down here and think you know everything. You want to talk about poison? Try having your lungs burned from the inside out because some asshole cut corners on safety gear. As far as drugs go, the only thing I need is some – " He broke off, overcome by a violent cough coming from deep in his chest.

Shit. I was wrong about him. I'd misinterpreted the discolouration of his deathly pale skin, the terrible sound of his breathing. If things had been different, it might have been Felix there in front of me.

"You're a miner," I said, finally understanding.

"I'm a miner," he repeated, and collapsed into my arms.

Nobody questioned me when I barged into the flophouse with the unconscious man in tow. I got a few curious stares from the people in the cramped communal area, but none of them objected when I asked where his room was. I lay him down on the bed and made a note in my holo-terminal to get fresh sheets and blankets as well as whatever meds he needed. The covers were thin and fraying, slept in too many times by too many people.

When he finally woke, he let out a groan. "What are you doing here, topsider? The show wasn't enough for you?"

I smirked. "I was going to rob you. Then I realised you didn't have any shit worth stealing, so I figured I'd stick around and take you up on your offer."

He barked out a laugh and then winced in pain. "Don't. It hurts."

"Sickness from the fumes?"

"Yeah." A dark look fell over his face. "I was one of the lucky ones. Shoddy gear is still gear. Some of the guys didn't even have helmets or breathers. Never stood a chance."

"That can't be legal."

He laughed again, harder this time. Within seconds it had turned into another coughing fit and he clutched his chest tightly with one hand. "I told you not to do that." He shook his head. "Shit, it really is another world up there for you, isn't it? You think the corporations care about what's legal down here? They've got the money to make all their problems go away and they don't care if they lose a miner or two in the process. Not when there's a hundred more suckers like me ready to jump on their command for the sake of a few lousy credits."

He was right. But it wasn't about the corporations, not really. All that work stripping the planet to its bones and driving miners to their deaths came from higher up than that. It came from Exodus Station. The daily struggles of the surface were only a symptom.

I forced a smile. "I was an asshole earlier. Should have known better. You're not the first person I've met who's living with the consequences of being forced down those hellholes. I'll get you the meds you need."

It wasn't enough. Unless the Exodans were stopped, it would never be enough. But it was all I had to give.

"Appreciated." He nodded slowly. "My name is Graves."

"Alvera."

"Good to meet you, Alvera." There was still something cautious in his expression. "You said I'm not the first miner you've met? I didn't think a topsider would be so well acquainted with the likes of us."

"My friend, Felix. I didn't know him back then. He was barely more than a kid when he got caught in a gas explosion. Blew his legs off." I shook my head. "Until now, I never really considered what kind of life he might have had if he hadn't made it off the surface."

Graves let out a low whistle. "Wouldn't have been easy, I can tell you that. The mines are unforgiving, but at least there's work there. If you can't do that, there's not much else for you. Not if you want to keep whatever dignity you have left." He broke off, a frown on his face. "But he's topside now?"

"Yeah. After the accident, he kept himself busy by working on whatever problems he could find. He reverse-engineered air filters that were decades old, saved a lot of surfacers' lives. Did something similar with a water purification system. No formal training. Just figured out what worked and what didn't. Turns out he's a genius when it comes to tech. I guess it caught someone's attention, because before long he got offered a job at the Spire."

"Damn, that's pretty impressive." There was no bitterness in his expression, just a sad sort of longing. "I take it that's where you met?"

Something tightened in my throat. "I suppose it is."

I couldn't tell him the rest, even if I wanted to. My memories of Felix weren't what I thought they were. I couldn't trust anything I remembered. Whoever I was, I had been made from someone else's mind. Someone else's ideas of what my life could have been.

Graves tilted his head, giving me an understanding look. "There's a story there, isn't there? Don't get me wrong, there usually is."

I shrugged, not trusting myself to speak.

"You know what? Don't worry about it." He leaned back, half-closing his eyes. "Topsider or not, nobody ends up down here without some bad shit happening. I know better than to ask about it. But if you ever want to talk…"

He left the rest open as he lay back down in the bed, a sheen of sweat beading across his forehead. After a moment, the sound of his ragged breathing settled into a steady rhythm.

If you ever want to talk…

The irony of it was almost painful. What could I say? Anything I told him would have been a lie. A fabricated memory of a person that didn't exist until a few short months ago.

But you did exist, I reminded myself. *Philomela existed.*

Philomela. The woman who had been one of them, until she'd had a change of heart. Was it possible that part of her still lived on inside me? Could I carry on what she had risked everything for, and finish what she had started?

And even if I could, would that make up for everything I'd done before?

Something kindled inside me, a spark of hope I'd long forgotten. Graves was right. There was a story there. But it was no longer Philomela's story. It was mine.

I just had to figure out how to tell it.

CHAPTER TEN

In the space of a few weeks, New Pallas had become inverted. The surface was no longer *down here* – everything else was *up there*. I didn't realise how much I'd needed the change of perspective until it happened.

From the surface, I couldn't see Exodus Station watching me from the sky. I couldn't look out across the cityscape and see the government buildings of the Spire. There were no boundaries between districts, no checkpoints or customs. It almost felt like freedom.

I looked over at Graves. He was lying on the bed reading something on his holo-terminal. I hadn't heard him splutter in a week now, and if there was any lightness to his breath, he did well not to let it show. The meds were working well.

A curtain of dark hair fell over his eyes, disrupting his reading. As he pushed it back across his forehead, he caught my eye. "You're doing that staring thing again. I think this low altitude has done something to your brain, *mietsha*."

I couldn't help but smile. *Mietsha*. Ever since I'd returned from the Spire with the meds he needed, Graves had taken to using the miner word around me. When I asked what it meant, his reply had been quiet and a little awkward, as if he hadn't realised he'd said it. "There's a lot that can go wrong in the mines. Especially on your own. Best kind of comfort is knowing somebody is at your back."

It felt like a compliment I didn't deserve. But every time he said it, it brought a smile to my face. It was a relief to be in the company of someone who didn't know who I was. Who didn't know the things I might have done. Sometimes I couldn't help but pretend things might stay as they were, as futile as that was.

"What's this?" Sphere had rolled out from my bag and was rattling across the floor. Graves picked it up and whistled. "Looks like some pretty nice tech."

I bit down on my tongue, knowing that Ryce's programming would only allow me to say so much. "Used to be. Doesn't work anymore."

"Can't you fix it?"

A cybernetics engineer with no equal. That's what Ryce had called me. But he'd taken those memories. He'd taken everything I was. "I might have been able to, once. But I don't think I have it in me anymore."

Graves looked unperturbed. "Have you tried?"

He handed it over to me and I gently prised off one of the panels. The wires and circuits underneath were lifeless. I took the parts out piece by piece and laid the broken fragments in front of me like a puzzle.

It was all so simple. Just chips and wiring around a skeletal frame. Laid out like that, it didn't seem real. It wasn't Sphere. It was just the remnants of what it used to be. Something that had been built and then broken. Even if I could remember where the pieces went, they'd never quite fit back the way they should. Looking at it all laid bare was just a reminder of how fragile it was. How fragile anything was.

"I can't do this," I whispered to myself. "It's too much."

"It's a start," Graves said. "Sometimes that's enough."

He was sitting so close that when I turned to look at him, my nose brushed against his. He pulled away, far enough to give me space but not so far that I couldn't easily close the distance if I wanted to. The whole time, his green eyes held mine. Curious, apprehensive even, but never wavering. For the briefest of seconds, I wondered what would happen if I leaned in towards him. He cocked his head slightly. Waiting, unsure.

Then my holo-terminal chimed.

The noise shattered the moment. Graves pushed himself back to his feet and retreated to the bed while I braced myself for whatever was coming.

As soon as I saw Ryce's name, a tight fist squeezed my heart. I stepped outside the flophouse and accepted the connection.

"Someone is trying to jam your implants."

The bluntness of his words threw me. "What?"

"There's a jamming signal coming from someone in your vicinity. It's targeting Exodan-grade cybernetics. You need to get out of there."

A wave of dizziness rushed through my head. "Why should I? If someone jams my implants, you won't be able to issue any overrides. You won't be able to control me." It wouldn't be forever, but maybe I had long enough to do something. Anything. I just didn't know what.

"Use your head, Alvera. An enforcer is coming for you. Ojara's brute, I'd wager. You need to get back to the Spire immediately. Ojara isn't stupid, she won't risk exposing him there. She'll call him off."

I opened my mouth to reply, but the holo-terminal connection flickered out.

"It's a bit late for that."

I spun around. The enforcer. Ryce had been right.

I edged away from the flophouse door. Away from Graves. The streets were still bustling with bodies. However this went down, people were going to get hurt. But maybe I could keep Graves from being one of them. "Ojara really doesn't like me, does she?"

He gave a mechanical shrug of his huge chrome shoulders. "The Council can't risk letting you go. When someone like you starts getting ideas, they need to stop those ideas from spreading."

"Ideas like what?"

"Sympathy for the sletes. It's dangerous. Especially coming from you."

"What makes me so special?" I tried to keep him talking, stalling for time. Maybe Ryce would send backup. "It's because of my cybernetics, isn't it? Because of what they're capable of. People on Exodus Station respected me. They would have listened to me."

"Not anymore."

He drew a plasma rifle from the holster on his waist and fired.

Screams erupted around me and I scrambled back, trying to find cover. The smell of singed fabric and burning flesh reached my nose. The surfacers were panicking. One of them had gone down. That was where the burning smell was coming from.

I lost sight of the enforcer for a moment as the crowd swelled. More screams cut through the air as he pushed his way through, sweeping aside anybody in his way. The strength and size of his plated arms sent bodies into walls, each impact making a sickening crack.

He levelled his rifle at me again and I ducked behind one

of the street's water purification tanks. The plasma bolt ripped through the casing and sent a jet of steam into the air.

I saw the flophouse door open across the street. Graves stuck his head out, horror in his eyes.

"Stay there," I whispered, knowing he'd never hear me above the chaos. "Close the door and stay where you are."

The water tank would only provide me with cover for so long. The enforcer was closing in. He'd either blow the tank to pieces or grab me. There was no way out.

That's when it hit me. Ryce had overlooked something. He hadn't programmed any kind of self-preservation into my brain. If he had, I'd have been forced to use the surfacers around me as human shields in a bid to escape. Instead, I was hunkered down, hoping I could draw the enforcer away from them.

That mattered somehow. Ryce hadn't accounted for this. I filed the information away for later. Maybe it was something I could take advantage of.

If I got out of this alive.

The tank shook with the impact from another plasma bolt and another jet of steam erupted from its walls. Boiling water spurted out above me and I rolled to safety, skirting around a barrage from the enforcer's rifle as I raced across the street and into an alley.

I fought to catch my breath. The second he caught up, he'd have a clear shot at me and it would all be over. He was encased in armour and had a plasma rifle that would turn my skin to smoking ash. What could I do against that?

The light from the street disappeared as the enforcer rounded the corner. As he raised the barrel of his rifle, something behind him caught my eye. Graves.

"Don't!"

It was too late. As the scream left my lips, Graves

jammed some kind of handheld device into the enforcer's back. I held my breath, waiting for the enforcer to whirl around and send a plasma bolt into his chest.

Instead, the enforcer faltered. His arm stopped in mid-air with a shudder and a burst of sparks exploded from his back.

"Run!" Graves yelled.

I raced towards him and grabbed his outstretched hand. We fled past the flophouse, pushing our way through the crowd without daring to look back.

I turned to him. "How the hell did you do that?"

"Number one cause of death down in the pits is instrument failure," he said, panting the words out between shallow breaths. "If that happens, best chance you have is a jump-charge to fire everything back up again. High voltage, packs a punch. Never used one on a person before but figured it might give your friend back there something to think about."

"Not my friend."

"You sure, *mietsha*? He seemed to be real interested in you." He slowed down and leaned against the wall, gasping for breath. "Did I ever mention how much I love meeting new people?"

"Get up," I said, tugging on his arm. "We're not out of this yet. We have to go."

"Go where?"

"Topside."

A shadow appeared across Graves' face. "I'm not like your friend Felix. A guy like me doesn't just get to go topside and live his life. There's nothing for me there. It isn't a place I'll ever belong."

"I can help."

He pulled his arm away and muttered something in his miner patois. "I'm not looking for charity."

"I'm not offering any. You saved my life back there."

"And you saved mine with the meds. Now we're even."

I glared at him. "Do you have to be such a stubborn, insufferable – "

Graves laughed. "You're going to have to do better than that if you want to hurt my feelings. I've heard a lot worse."

"Please." The word escaped my lips in a breath and hung in the air between us. "I want you to come with me."

Graves hesitated. "I – "

Whatever he'd been about to say was cut short as a jolt of pain shot through my head, sending me to my knees. I clamped my hands to my temples, as if I could squeeze out whatever had caused it.

"Alvera?" Graves bent down beside me and placed his hands on my shoulders. "What's happening?"

I could barely hear him over the pain. It was like something had surged inside my head, sending my brain into overdrive. Then, almost as quickly as it came, the sensation disappeared.

I took a deep breath, trying to steady myself. Something was stirring in my head, like my mind was expanding and moving around for pieces to fit into place. Things hadn't been right before. There had been part of me locked away and forgotten. Now it was shifting back to where it belonged.

A sudden clarity washed through me. It was just like when I got past the encrypted door at OriCorp. Somehow, I had tapped into the full potential of my cybernetics.

"Alvera…" Graves was looking over my shoulder, his face pale.

I spun around to follow his gaze.

The enforcer was back.

A strange sort of calm settled over me. I was unusually aware of the sound of my own breathing, the beating of my heart. Time seemed to slow down as I took in my surroundings. Through my cybernetics, I evaluated every loose stone in the wall, every crack in the pavement below my feet. My implants fed me information quicker than I could consciously process. They showed me miniscule changes in the wind direction. They picked up radio chatter a block away.

I focused my vision on the enforcer. I could see beneath his armoured shell to the very components that held him together. What little human there was left of him was encased and protected behind reinforced metal. But where I saw strength, I also saw weaknesses. Flaws in his design. Fragile points that could be exploited. Vulnerable systems my cybernetics could manipulate.

I smiled at him. "You sure you want to do this?"

His gaze was inscrutable. "This is my job. Want has nothing to do with it."

He raised his plasma rifle, but he was too slow for me now. I sent an electrical surge into the barrel with a violent pulse from my cybernetics. The voltage burst through the weapon and sent a shower of sparks flying up in his face.

I used the distraction to close the distance between us. The cables connecting his hulking frame to his neck were strong but exposed. If I could disrupt their link to his brain, maybe I could render his armoured body useless.

He saw me coming and sent one of his metal fists flying towards me. If the blow had landed, it would have broken half the bones in my face. I dodged the strike and ducked underneath his arm.

I concentrated on his auditory implant, drawing on all the interference I could muster from the surrounding blocks. I harnessed every holo-terminal, every radio wave I could sense. Then I sent all of it in a static burst straight to the tiny implant in his ear.

The enforcer let out a groan and clasped an armoured hand to his head.

This was my chance.

I slid behind him and scaled the chrome curve of his back, grabbing onto the thick cables at the base of his neck. The metal was warm beneath my hands, pulsing like it was flesh and blood. No amount of force would rip it from its socket. But I didn't need force. I just needed one well-timed pulse.

My cybernetics responded without me having to ask. Something surged inside my head and the wires at the nape of his neck erupted in smoke.

I leapt clear from his shoulders as he crashed to his knees and collapsed. His plasma rifle fell from his grasp and I snatched it up, my hands trembling from fear and adrenaline.

The electrical surge had paralysed him, for the moment at least. It would have been so easy to recharge the rifle and fire a relentless stream of plasma between his eyes until I melted through the metal plating protecting his skull. He'd have done the same to me, given the chance.

But when I looked at his unmoving body, his frozen eyes, I could only see the brainwashed autotrons from the processing plant on Exodus Station.

This is my job. Want has nothing to do with it.

Shit. How much of him was really him and how much belonged to Ojara? I couldn't kill him. Not without knowing for sure. Not when one day it might be me at the other end of the barrel, forced into a fight I wanted no part of.

"Go back to Ojara and tell her she's got her wish. Philomela is dead," I said, throwing the rifle to the ground. "But know this – Alvera Renata is alive and kicking, and I intend to finish what she started."

I turned my head skywards. Buildings rose up around me, blocking out everything above. Exodus Station was up there somewhere. Its people were waiting there, ready to abandon the planet below as soon as they got the chance.

It wouldn't happen. Not if I found a way to keep Philomela's promise.

"No compromises. All of us go, or none of us go."

CHAPTER ELEVEN

The visit from Ojara's enforcer had hastened Ryce's return to New Pallas. Whatever he was planning, he was moving forward with it. That meant bringing me to heel on the end of his leash.

It was time to go back.

"I'll be there as soon as I can," I said, and ended the connection.

Graves looked at me. "Topside's calling?"

"I have to go." My mouth was dry. "I wish I could explain."

He shrugged. "You don't have to explain anything to me. I saw what you did to the big guy back there." He let out a low chuckle. "Knew all along you weren't a regular topsider. You're something special, aren't you?"

His words should have filled me with warmth. Instead, I could only shudder at the chill that ran up my spine as he unwittingly stumbled on the truth. "If I could tell you more, I would."

"And if I could believe you, I would." He smiled. "Watch your step up there, *mietsha*. It's a long way down."

"If I go over the edge, I'll try to make sure not to land on you."

"Much appreciated."

For once, my struggle to find the right words wasn't because of Ryce's control. The quiet was heavy with all things left unsaid. Now was not the time. It was too fleeting, too rushed, too uncertain.

I looked at all the pieces of Sphere lying out on the floor, but before I could say anything, Graves jumped in. "I'll keep it safe. It will be waiting for you. Waiting for when it's the right time."

I hardly dared to trust him, but I wanted to. Maybe that was enough. "Thank you."

He lowered his head. A half-nod, or something like it. "Stay safe up there."

I grabbed my gear from the end of my makeshift bed and left the room without daring to look back.

My holo-terminal told me it was daytime when I stepped out the flophouse, but the streets were as dark as ever. Somewhere, far above, Ryce was waiting. I couldn't stay lost down here any longer.

But Ryce wasn't the only one topside. It was time to face Felix.

The Spire's tech labs were beautiful. Curved glass and streamlined walkways surrounded a huge open atrium. I could see scientists working away through the windows of their labs as they tinkered with circuit boards and implants and bionic attachments. I'd always thought they were geniuses. Now I wondered how many of them were Exodans, leading the same double life as Ryce.

I saw my reflection in the window as I approached Felix's lab. That was strange. Some of the techs occasionally changed their windows to one-way mirrors for privacy, but Felix had never been particular about that.

I paused at the doorway. I could hear Felix's raised voice from inside. He was talking to someone – a woman. Her voice was familiar, but so out of place it took me a moment to recognise it.

Chase.

I punched the door release and burst into the room.

"Great. Now the cyborg is here."

Her voice was the same, down to the subtlest of inflections. If I hadn't known any better, I might have believed it was real. But I did know better. I watched her die.

The hologram was perfect in detail, but that's all it was. A hologram. Even from across the room, I could see the way it flickered under the lab lights, revealing small distortions as it moved.

The hologram – Chase – rolled her eyes. "Do you mind?"

Before I could reply, Felix fumbled with his console and she disappeared into the air, leaving nothing but a light hum of static behind. He wiped his eyes with his sleeve and looked away. I felt like I'd intruded on something private, something I wasn't meant to see.

I turned away to give him time to compose himself and instead looked at the empty space where the hologram had been. The way it had vanished seemed as sudden and violent as Chase's death on Exodus Station.

"I didn't know you were back."

I turned around. His bloodshot eyes were dry now, but there was a tremor in his jaw too pronounced not to notice.

"Ryce called me back in. Said the team needed me."

"Because Chase is dead," he said, his voice hollow.

"I'm so sorry."

"Everyone is sorry," he said, shooting up from his chair. "I've had it with Ryce saying that, don't you start too. She should be the one that's sorry. She's the one that got herself killed!" He kicked the hoverchair and it flew across the room, bouncing harmlessly off the door. He stared at it for a moment, breathing heavily. "She never said where she was going, only that she'd come back. She promised. And now she's dead." His voice was hoarse and thick. "I'm sorry, Alvera. I didn't mean to… It's just…"

"I know," I said. It killed me that I couldn't give him closure. I didn't know what Ryce had told him, only that it wasn't the truth. Maybe I should have been grateful for that. Maybe it was better than admitting she was dead because of me.

After a few moments, he went over to retrieve the hoverchair and tinkered about with its console, making sure nothing had been damaged. "That hologram you saw… Please don't tell Ryce."

It wasn't a promise I could keep, not when Ryce had access to my retinal implants. "I'm guessing it's an advanced personality simulation?"

Felix hesitated. "In part. It's experimental."

"Well it's definitely accurate, I can vouch for that," I said, dryly.

He almost smiled. "The hologram was the easy part. It's made up of hundreds of photographs, old vids, surveillance footage from jobs, anything I could get my hands on. Every expression she makes, every word she says, it's all real. And yet none of it is."

"She's not some machine that can be rebuilt, Felix," I said, as gently as I could. "You know that. This hologram may look like her, may sound like her, but it's not her. It never will be."

Felix had a far-off look in his eyes, as if he wasn't listening to what I was saying. For a moment, he looked like the kid I'd always imagined him as, long before he'd escaped the surface and started a new life in the Spire.

"What was it like down there? In the mines, I mean?" The question left my mouth before I had time to stop it. I'd never had the courage to ask Graves. Whatever was between us had always seemed too new, too fragile for me to pry. But every time I'd heard him splutter for breath, part of me had wondered about the hell he'd had to endure.

A mixture of surprise and curiosity crossed Felix's face. "You really want to know? Not many people ask."

"I didn't mean to – "

He cut me off with a wave of his hand. "I don't mind. Sometimes it feels like everyone up here just forgets about what goes on below. But sometimes you need to talk about it. Chase understood that. She used to – " He broke off, the words catching in his throat. "I started when I was fourteen. Seems pretty young, but I was luckier than most. Some of the poorer families had to send kids as young as eleven or twelve down the pits. Those were the ones you remembered seeing get hauled out. They always looked so small." He shuddered, a dark look passing over his face.

"I shouldn't have asked," I said. "I'm sorry, Felix."

He shrugged. "It's just life down there. It's what happens. The people in charge didn't care how many they lost. There was always a steady line waiting to replace them. There's money in being a miner. It's not enough, it's never enough, but it's enough to make you go back, even if you've had an accident or a close call."

"How long were you down there before your accident?"

"Three years, give or take. You get used to the dark. It's not like here in the Spire where you can look up and see the sky. There's rock all around you. Put one mining charge in the wrong place and that rock will bury you or open a chasm under your feet that will send you falling to your death."

"Not a nice way to go."

"None of them are." His voice was flat as he ticked them off. "Crushed by a cave-in, falling down a pit because of rope failure, poisoned by fumes, blown to bits in an explosion. At least I got to leave with most of me still intact. Not many do. And even then, there's some who will go back. Either for the money or because it's all they know."

I thought of Graves, of how gaunt and sickly he'd become. By the time I'd left, he'd been on the road to recovery. How long would it be before desperation drove him back down there again? How many chances would he take before the danger of the job caught up with him and left him maimed or dead?

I tried to push the thought out of my head. "I guess going back wasn't an option for you, was it?"

Felix laughed. "Yeah, they don't exactly provide hover-chairs down the pits. As soon as I woke up and realised I was alive, I knew I had to find something else to do. If it hadn't been for Ryce finding me, taking a chance on me..." He looked down at his legs. "I owe him everything."

I tried not to wince at his words. If only he knew the truth. If only he realised Ryce did nothing that didn't benefit himself. If he'd rescued Felix from the surface, it was only because he thought he could use him in some way. Just like he'd used me.

I rolled my eyes and tried to make light of it. "Ryce might have got you here, but don't forget who brings in the credits."

"You'd never let me forget it." He chuckled and set his

mouth in a sad half-smile. "Thanks, Alvera. I needed this. I needed to know that even though she's gone, I'm not alone. I've still got you."

The sincerity in his voice struck me in a place I hadn't even known existed. It hurt worse than anything Ryce had done to me. I didn't deserve it. Not when I was incapable of returning it.

I stood up and headed towards the door. "I'm sorry about Chase," I said, turning back. "If there's anything I can do…"

He shook his head. "It's just good to have you back."

As soon as the door slid shut behind me, I buckled over, bracing myself with my hands on my knees. Nausea rose in my stomach and my breaths came quick and ragged. All I wanted to do was wipe my memories again so I didn't have to see the pain and grief on Felix's face. So I didn't have to watch Chase die again.

I heard footsteps approach along the walkway and I squeezed my eyes shut, hoping they would continue by and leave me alone.

The footsteps stopped. "Glad to see you coping so well on your first day back."

Ryce.

I tore myself upright. He was leaning against the wall, arms crossed and a condescending smirk on his lips. So relaxed. So at ease. He knew I couldn't do anything to hurt him.

That didn't mean I wasn't going to try.

I didn't take my eyes off him for a moment. I charged forward and launched myself at him, ready to tackle him to the floor. But somehow, impossibly, he was gone. My shoulder slammed off the wall and sent a jolt of pain down my arm.

How? He had been right there.

"You always were incredibly stubborn," he said, appearing behind me and shaking his head. "I thought you'd know better than to believe you could do any harm to me, but I suppose I shouldn't be surprised."

"I shouldn't be surprised either," I said. "You always were a coward, sitting safe in the Spire while Chase and I did the real work."

He gave a weary sigh. "Let's stop this. Like it or not, we're going to be working together. Can't you at least try to make an effort to go back to how things used to be?"

"Go to hell." I paced backwards and forwards, not letting him out of my sight. "How can I see you? Did you put some sort of code in my retinal implants?"

"And your auditory ones. Actually, in all of your sensory implants. It's quite effective. I imagine it seems to you that I'm really here."

I squeezed my eyes shut.

"No, we'll have none of that," he said. "I want you to see me, Alvera. I'd like for you to trust me again. And I'm going to help you do that."

I opened my eyes to glare at him. "Nothing you do or say will convince me to trust you."

"We'll see." Ryce smiled. "Meet me at the observation tower. Maybe from there I can convince you to have a little perspective." He paused for a moment. "And wear something pretty. Like you used to."

Rage flared in me. "I'm not going to – "

"I'm asking you," he said, cutting me off. "Don't make me force you. We both know how that game ends."

His projection flickered, his smile the last thing to leave my mind.

Then he was gone.

CHAPTER TWELVE

The Spire's observation tower was the highest point in New Pallas. Going up wasn't cheap, even with a government discount. I slid a pile of credits across the counter and squeezed into the crowded elevator with the tourists and day-trippers.

The ride was so smooth I didn't even realise we had stopped until the passengers around me started piling out. It was busier than usual – the night was clear, with no clouds to obscure the skyline. The sun would set on glass and steel as far as the eye could see. It would be spectacular.

In front of me, New Pallas stretched out in every direction, its skyscrapers diminishing in the distance until they faded into the horizon. It was beautiful. The sky turned orange and cast the buildings underneath it in a warm glow. The heat from the city below sent ripples through the air, giving everything a wavering, dreamlike quality.

I moved away from the bustle of the crowd to a quieter spot near the edge of the rooftop. The guardrail was only waist high. Not much of a deterrent, but it didn't need to be. The drop below was enough on its own.

I leaned over, hands spread wide along the railing. Beams of light from the shuttle lanes criss-crossed below, one on top of the other a hundred deep. Beneath them was nothing but darkness.

My palms slid further apart, slick on the barrier. I wondered how long it would take. How fast I'd fall before I hit the ground if I wasn't lucky enough to crash into a shuttle first. I'd have time to think on the way down. I wouldn't be able to do anything, but I'd be able to think. Whatever happened, at least Ryce wouldn't be in control.

I leaned further, rising on my toes as far as I could. A slight breeze whistled past my cheeks, flapping my hair across my face. It wouldn't take much. Just a push with my feet and I'd be over, falling through the sky with no way to take back what I'd done. There was nothing in my programming stopping me from putting myself in harm's way. My encounter with the enforcer was proof of that. I had already made it this far. All it would take was a push.

"Red always was your colour. That dress fits you beautifully."

Too late.

I turned to face him. His suit was a pale grey that brought out the flecks of silver in his hair, and there was a hungry gleam in his eye that turned my stomach. How had I ever been fooled by his implant projection trick? There was no mistaking the real thing. He had a presence that seemed to disturb the very air around him.

Nobody else seemed to notice. He slipped so seamlessly into his surroundings that it was impossible to tell he was out of place here. However much the Exodans tried to pretend otherwise, they were as human as the rest of us.

His eyes crawled over me, lingering on the places the fabric of my dress clung tightly. I couldn't imagine what I might do if he reached out a hand and tried to touch me. Even his gaze made me recoil. But no matter how much I wanted to stay out of his reach, all he had to do was whisper *Philomela* and I'd be at his mercy.

My disgust must have shown on my face, for he paused. "Is there a problem?"

"You're my problem, you repulsive prick."

He frowned. "I was hoping we could start this evening with some civility. A smile, even."

"Keep hoping."

"I don't need to. *Philomela*, smile for me."

If I could have drawn my gun and unloaded the chamber in his head, I would have. All I could do was scream in the confines of my head as my mouth stretched into a smile.

"Better."

"Is this how you used to treat her? Philomela?" I tried to glare, but my mouth wouldn't let me. "No wonder she betrayed you. No wonder she left."

"If you are trying to anger me, it won't work." Ryce's face didn't give anything away. "Philomela made her choice and she paid for it. You have a second chance. All I'm trying to do is help you take it."

"You and I have vastly different interpretations of what constitutes a second chance."

"When will you accept that I am not the monster you make me out to be?" The wounded look in his eyes made me want to hit him. "I warned you about the enforcer today. I could have just left you to die."

"I almost wish you had."

His face twisted into something ugly. "Don't say that. I've come too far to lose you now."

"I was never yours to lose in the first place."

He fell silent for a moment. "I saw the readouts from your

cybernetics. You were in complete control. You could have ended things right then, but you let the enforcer live. Why?"

I shrugged. "I couldn't do it. If I'd killed him, I would have been killing myself. Being there wasn't his choice. Just like being here isn't mine."

"You are nothing like him." A dark look passed over his face. "There are worse ways to control someone than putting a bit of code in their head. Enforcers are bred for what they do. Conditioned from birth. They are a precision instrument, a living weapon. They are nothing more than physical manifestations of the Council's will."

I couldn't help but pity the poor bastard. Maybe I had made a mistake by sparing his life. Maybe I should have killed him after all, if only to put him out of his misery. "What was his name?"

"They don't have names, just designations." Ryce pulled up his holo-terminal. "His is Tau-54-Sigma."

Tau. It wasn't a name, but it was all I had to call him. "What if he comes back?"

"Ojara is too careful to risk it. Especially after realising you were more than a match for him." A slow smile spread over his face. "You've only just begun to tap into the potential of your cybernetics. Once you've learned how to fully harness them, our work can begin."

He still thought I was going to help him. He was wrong. I was going to fight against him with all that I had. No matter what it cost me.

The sun started to slip below the city, leaving red streaks across the sky. For a moment, all was calm. Then the air trembled, and Exodus Station appeared.

It hung there in silence, eclipsing the sun. It was a reminder to the people of New Pallas that they were not alone. Its silhouette sat like a black mark in the middle of their beautiful sunset, spoiling the sky.

I shuddered. How could I reconcile who I was with the kind of person I must have been to have lived there, looking down on New Pallas with nothing but disdain? If I ever regained my memories, Philomela's memories, what would I see? A woman who risked her life for the people here, or a monster intent on abandoning them?

The only thing that scared me more than not knowing who I was, was the possibility of finding out.

The sun disappeared below the horizon, taking with it the last vestiges of daylight. All that was left to illuminate the darkness was the artificial glow from the city below and the watchful lights from Exodus Station above. The crowds were dispersing now. The spectacle was over. It was time to hit a bar or a restaurant or waste away in front of a vidscreen.

Eventually, Ryce and I were the only ones left.

One of the security officers wandered over to us and gestured towards the elevator. "Show's over for tonight. Time to head back down."

Ryce looked mildly annoyed as he flashed his identification on his holo-terminal. "Government business."

He wrinkled his nose. "Warrant hunters? What are you looking for all the way up here?"

"Could soon be you, if you don't leave us be."

The officer looked disgruntled for a moment but then shrugged. "If you say so. Elevator goes offline in five, so you'll have to take the long way down when you're finished."

He turned and walked away, leaving me alone with Ryce.

I moved away from the barrier, hoping to put some distance between us. I could feel his eyes following me, lingering on my back. It was too much to hope for that he'd leave me alone. Not now that he had me exactly where he wanted me.

He walked across the rooftop towards me. "It's just you and me now. The two of us. Like it always used to be."

"There is no you and me. As far as I'm concerned, there never was. Everything I thought I knew about you was a lie."

He grabbed my shoulders and pulled me around to face him. "Everything I did, I did to save your life. Even after you betrayed me, I protected you. I'm still protecting you."

"Protecting me?" I barked out a laugh. "You forced me to kiss you in front of those monsters. You invaded my head. One word from you, and I have to do whatever you want. You call that protection?"

"That's what's bothering you?" He looked bewildered. "It's hardly the first time we've kissed."

I snorted. "You think that makes a difference? It makes it worse. You really think I'd have jumped into bed with you if I knew the truth? I didn't even know who I was. You were in control every step of the way and I didn't even realise it until you'd made your sick little way into my head."

"Don't say it like that." He was only inches away now. I could see every mark on his skin, from the thin veins under his eyes to the faint creasing in his forehead. There was a time I thought I'd been attracted to all his imperfections. The thought of him being so close now made me sick.

He lifted a hand and pressed it against my cheek. "You are not yourself," he said. "If you were, you would be able to trust me. If you were, you'd never have thrown your life away over these sletes. You've already made that mistake once. Don't make it again. They aren't worth it."

"It wasn't a mistake," I said. "I don't remember what drove me to make the choice I did, but I know I meant it. I still mean it. Whatever Philomela started, I intend to see it through. These people deserve that much."

"You don't know them."

"I don't know you."

Ryce pulled me closer towards him. His voice was low and soft. "Let me remind you."

His hands were on my jaw, tilting my face towards him. When he pressed his lips to mine, they were cold. I'd kissed Ryce a hundred times, but it had always been full of fire and passion. Now, his taste was unfamiliar and poisonous.

I wanted it *gone*.

I bit down hard and tasted the tang of blood. Ryce wrenched backwards with a hiss. The relief of his hand leaving my skin lasted only a moment before he drew it back and struck me across the face. My teeth tore into my lip and this time, the blood I tasted was my own.

For a moment, he just stared at me, mouth agape. Then he grabbed me by the base of my neck. "You didn't mean that," he said, pressing his mouth against my forehead. I wasn't sure if he was talking to me or himself. "You're still confused. You need more time. I have to be more patient."

He drew back, forcing me to look into his eyes. "Make no mistake, Alvera, I will stay inside your head until the day you die if that's the way this has to be. But you could be free if you'd only accept who you are. Don't resign yourself to pain and suffering out of some misguided loyalty to these sletes. If you choose them, you will regret it."

"Maybe I will," I said, fighting to get the words out against the pressure of his grasp. "But at least this way it's my choice."

He let me go and took a step backwards. "Your choice?" he said, his voice thin. "If having a choice is what you value so much, then so be it. But choices come with consequences. I'll show you that. I'll make you understand."

His words sent an unpleasant shiver down my spine. "What do you mean?"

He smiled. "It's time to get back to work. I have a warrant for you."

CHAPTER THIRTEEN

From the sky, it was easier to see what humanity had done to New Pallas.

Whatever deserts and rivers and forests that had once stood untouched and undisturbed had long been torn down or ripped up or filled in and paved over. In their place was a sprawling city that had engulfed almost every inch of the planet.

Apart from the mines.

The pits that scarred the planet's surface were ugly wounds in amongst the glass and steel of the city. The ground was so unstable it was at risk of collapsing. It opened up into yawning abysses so deep it would take a body minutes to hit the bottom. What lay beneath was a hell nobody wanted to think about. That hell was where Ryce was sending me.

Tartarus Mine was an old OriCorp facility halfway across the sector. I gazed out the window of the shuttle Ryce had chartered for me, taking in the lights from the city below. As we approached the outskirts, the brightness dimmed until there was nothing but darkness ahead. It took less than a second for my retinal implants to adjust to the loss of light, but it felt like there was a hole in my vision. I wasn't used to seeing such vast, empty spaces.

Below was a quarry as big as a crater, stretching as far across the horizon as I could see. The terrain was uneven and unwelcoming, like the planet itself had pushed up great walls of rock from its core to keep us out.

"Don't see a landing zone," said the shuttle pilot from his seat next to me. "You sure this is the right place?"

"Do another sweep. This is where I'm meant to be."

He gave me a doubtful look. "If you say so. I'm not picking up any signals, but we can circle around again if you want."

It wasn't what I wanted, not at all, but I was powerless to argue as he brought the shuttle around for another pass. Ryce had told me to come here. I couldn't get out of it now, not with his soft-spoken command burned into my brain.

Philomela.

The sides of the quarry were too sheer to safely land on. The centre was just a gaping hole. What remained of the old landing platforms had been lost to ruin, leaving nothing but rusting debris strewn over the rocks. Everything about the old mine warned against coming in.

"Look, over there!"

I saw it. A flashing light off in the distance. A signal, guiding us in.

"Take us closer."

As we drew near, I could see a dark figure waving a hand-held beacon. He was standing on a ridge barely wide enough for a person, let alone a shuttle. There was no way we'd be able to land. The only option was to jump from the shuttle.

"How steady can you keep us?"

"As steady as you need. The hard part is up to you."

I punched the release on the airlock. The pilot had pulled

in close to the ridge and was holding steady. If I was on solid ground, I wouldn't have thought twice about jumping the distance. But the jagged rock on the other side and the steep drop below made it feel like a chasm too wide to clear.

Ryce sent you here for a reason, I reminded myself. *He doesn't want you to die. Not yet, anyway.*

I wasn't sure if the thought was a comfort or a disappointment.

I braced myself with a hand on each side of the airlock and launched myself forward. All I could see was the darkness of the pit below, ready to swallow me. Then my boots met solid ground and I tumbled forward, catching myself against the face of the ridge. A hand came out to steady me and I took it gratefully as the shuttle roared and disappeared into the darkness.

"Alvera?"

"That's me."

The man lowered the beacon so I could see his face past the glare.

It was Graves.

Horror froze me to the spot, turning my blood to ice. What the hell was he doing here? I'd left him on the surface. Part of me had never expected to see him again. It was beyond coincidence. Unless...

"Follow him, *Philomela*. He has something important to show you."

Unless Ryce had got to him.

My feet moved of their own accord, trudging cautiously along the ridge as Graves led the way. He moved fluidly, as if he knew every loose stone and hidden crack. He was a miner – he knew what to watch out for. Was that why Ryce had picked him? Or was it just to torment me even more?

Damn him. Damn them both. I'd been stupid to believe I

could retain part of my life for myself. Maybe Graves had been working for Ryce all along. Maybe he'd got to him later. It didn't matter. All that mattered was the reminder that nobody was on my side.

We reached the end of the ridge and squeezed through a narrow opening in the rock. The roar of the wind snuffed out as soon as we made our way inside the tunnel.

Graves held the beacon up to his face. "That's better. Can hear myself think now."

His boyish grin wrenched at my heart. "What are you doing here?"

"It's not every day you get offered a big pile of credits to escort a warrant hunter down an abandoned mine. Had no idea it would be you."

I didn't believe him. "You're getting paid for this?"

"Got the offer as soon as I went back to work. Couldn't turn it down, even if it was to come to this death trap." A shadow fell across his face. "There's a reason nobody has been to Tartarus in decades. This site had more recorded accidents than any other mine on New Pallas. Who knows how many more went unrecorded?"

By the end of this, there would be at least one more. That much I was sure of.

"You've gone quiet." Graves' eyes gleamed in the light of the beacon. "I don't blame you. Nobody in their right mind would want to come down here unless it was for something very important."

I didn't say anything. I couldn't. It hurt too much. I wanted to ask him why. I wanted to know how many credits were worth selling my life for.

Graves stopped at a rusted grate and pulled on a breather mask. "We're going down the pit now," he said. "I don't know what's down there. Even if we're lucky and there are no fumes, the oxygen levels might be depleted. Better not take any chances."

I pressed the release on the shoulder of my exosuit and exhaled as my helmet sealed itself around my head. It blocked out the outside and put a welcome layer of distance between me and Graves. I didn't want to be anywhere near him.

The rocks slithered slowly by as the elevator rumbled its way down. The contraption rattled and creaked like a tormented beast trapped in darkness with only one way to go. Every jolt sent panic through me. I tried not to imagine the cables failing and dropping us to our deaths in a cramped metal cage.

Graves stood uncomfortably close, so close I could see the redness of his neck from where the breather mask pinched his skin. He looked calm and disinterested, like this was nothing he hadn't seen before.

After what felt like hours, the elevator came to a halt. The bottom of the cage thudded off the cavern floor and sent a cloud of dust into the air. Outside the door was only darkness. I turned on my helmet flashlight to illuminate my path.

"Did you bring cables?" Graves asked.

I patted my belt. "I thought that might be a good idea."

"You thought right. There's a lot of seismic activity this deep in the planet."

"What a comforting thought."

"I'm just letting you know what you're getting into. If you want to turn back, the elevator is right there."

"That's not an option." There was no point in trying to escape. Ryce wouldn't let me. I could only go on and wait for what was bound to come.

"Figured you'd say that. Let's take a look at your coordinates and see where they're sending us."

The way he said it made it sound like we were a team. But that wasn't true.

I clenched my jaw. "Lead the way."

The mines were like another world. A world without light, without sky or sun. The only way I could see where I was going was by keeping my feet within the narrow beam of light coming from my helmet. If the torch failed, I'd be plunged into darkness. I wouldn't be able to move in any direction without the fear that the ground would drop off into a gaping crevice. I'd be crawling blindly, with no way back to the surface.

At some points, the passageway became so narrow there was no choice but to crawl through. I forced myself to keep my breathing steady and not think of the mountain of rock ready to crush me. At other points, we stumbled through caverns so wide I couldn't see the other side. We took so many twists and turns that I lost all sense of direction. I barely even knew which way was up anymore.

Something brushed past my feet and I looked down just in time to see a mottled blue-black shape scurry through a tiny crack in the wall. "What was that?"

Graves turned around. "What?"

"Some kind of creature."

"Cave lizard, probably. You hardly see them in active mines – they like to stay out of sight. Unless there's a gas leak. Then you can barely move for their bodies lying around. A pity for them, but good warning for us." He smirked. "Don't tell me you've never seen a real animal before, topsider."

"Not outside of a menagerie," I said, peering into the crack where the lizard had disappeared. "It took me by surprise. How do they survive down here?"

"They're resourceful little bastards. Probably the only

living things on New Pallas whose food isn't grown in a vat or under a biome." He stopped to pull up a battered holo-display on his wrist. "I'm getting readings. There's some kind of structure still standing ahead. Lots of sectioned-off wards. Maybe some kind of medical centre? Whatever it is, it's been abandoned for a long time."

He stooped through a narrow opening in the tunnel and I followed him, my heart pounding against my ribs. If only I'd had the strength, I could have ripped my gun from its holster and shot him before he had a chance to do the same to me. But Ryce's override command was still in place. *Follow him.* That was all I could do. Outside the weight of those words, I was powerless.

Rubble and rock lay in scattered heaps and a thick layer of dust coated the floor, but most of the abandoned med centre looked intact. I took note of the computers and moni-tors dotted around the room. They looked horribly out of place here.

Graves whistled. "Look at all this. We don't have this kind of tech even now, let alone decades ago when this place was still in operation. Do you have any idea how many miners' lives we could save if we had access to these things?"

He went to inspect one of the machines as I surveyed the rest of the building. Something wasn't right. Everything was too intact, too untouched. Aside from the fallen rocks and debris, no real damage had been done. If there had been a gas explosion, the whole building would have been blackened and blasted to pieces. If toxic fumes had seeped in, there would have been corpses lying around. For whatever reason, the people who once worked here seemed to have just aban-doned the place, leaving everything behind.

The console Graves was tinkering with flickered into life.

"That's strange," he said. "According to these logs, this mine was stripped to the bones a long time ago."

"Why's that strange? You said it had been abandoned for decades."

"Because I mean a *long* time ago. Centuries. If the mine was already empty, what were these people doing down here?" He tapped at the interface again.

The unease in my stomach grew and I reached for my gun. Whether I'd be able to use it or not was a question I couldn't yet answer, but it gave me some comfort to feel its weight in my hands. I pointed it into the darkness as I made my way down the corridor towards the wards. The rooms were windowless and sealed shut. None of the door releases worked. It felt more like a prison than a medical centre.

"Alvera?" Graves' voice was faint. "I don't like this. I'm looking through these records and none of the injuries match up with what you'd expect down in the mines. No broken bones, no gas poisoning or shrapnel damage. These injuries are from something else."

"Like what?"

"I don't know, I can't understand it. Brain bleeds, tissue damage, burst arteries. It's like something was killing them from the inside. But not slow, like a disease. Something violent. Something like…"

I tore off the access panel to one of the doors and ripped out the wires underneath. It was crude, but it worked. The door hissed and retracted.

Graves was wrong. This wasn't a medical centre. It was a test lab.

The corpse on the bed was nothing but bones, restrained at the wrists by thick metal bonds. The sheet underneath its skull was stained dark red. Whoever this was, they'd been left here to rot. Nobody had attempted to hide what had been done to them.

In among the bones were pieces of wiring and circuitry. I shone my torch over tiny microchips and sensors that once clung to nerves and muscles that were no longer there. The people in these wards hadn't been patients. They had been experiments.

"Alvera." Even from the other room, I couldn't mistake the horror in Graves' voice. "They were doing something to these people. Putting them through some kind of crazy acceleration time and time again. They were studying them, seeing how far they could push them until…"

This had never been an OriCorp mine. It was the Exodan Council's testing grounds. A place where they could trial programmes and collect data. A place where they could run simulations on cybernetics powerful enough to keep people alive through sustained acceleration.

Cybernetics like my own.

I wanted to fire a bullet through the poor lab rat's head, as if I could put him out of his misery again. How many times had he been strapped down and wheeled into an acceleration chamber to suffer under the crippling weight of gravity? How had it felt as a force he couldn't see squeezed his heart and lungs and organs until he was ready to burst? How many times had they tortured him before he couldn't go on any longer?

I picked up the remnants of his cybernetics. Ryce said I was the only one who'd ever survived the stress tests. That I had somehow become one with my cybernetics. How many people had been killed here to help develop the technology I'd used to build my implants?

"Do you see now why I brought you here?" Ryce's voice was in my ear. "It was to open your eyes. Those miners died for you. They died for progress. Years of experiments and technological advances, all to get us to where we are today."

I shook my head violently, trying to repel his words. "I didn't want this. I didn't ask for it."

"But you used what they gave you. Or Philomela did, at least. She unlocked the door to our future and then slammed it in my face as she ran away. It's up to you to reopen that door. Not for me, not for the Council, but for all these miners. You are their legacy. Don't let them have died in vain."

I trembled, rage rising inside me. "Don't pretend you care what happened to them. Don't use their deaths to try to bring me to your side. You think showing me this will shame me into helping you? If anything, this just gives me another reason to put a bullet through your head when I get free of you."

"Alvera? Who are you talking – oh shit." Graves appeared by my shoulder. His face drained of colour as he took it all in. The body, the restraints, the blood-stained sheets. He took a step back. "What the hell did they do to him?"

His voice broke on the words. He didn't know about any of this. He couldn't have. These people were miners. They were his family.

The realisation sent a wave of dread through me. If Graves didn't know, that meant he wasn't working for Ryce. He hadn't betrayed me. So what was he doing here?

"How did you get this job?" I asked him, my voice dry.

"What?" He looked confused. "I told you. I got offered it as soon as I went back to work. Foreman got word that some bigshot intelligence officer had requested a miner escort for his warrant hunter, and as soon as I heard about the credits on offer, I agreed."

"You didn't know it was me?"

"Of course not. The guy I spoke to never mentioned you. Just said he had someone who needed to be taken to these coordinates."

I grabbed the collar of his old, battered jacket. "You had no idea who he was? No idea about any of this?"

"No! I don't know what is going on here apart from the fact that hundreds of my people have been butchered for reasons I don't understand." He ran a hand through his hair. "Why are you asking me this? What the hell is going on?"

Ryce's voice was a whisper in my ear. "Give him a choice. You seem to think they matter. Let's see what his will be."

I pressed a hand over my mouth. "Shit. Oh shit. This was what he wanted. This is why he brought me here. It was never about them. It was about you."

"About me?" Graves shot me an incredulous look. "What are you talking about?"

"Tell him he has a choice, Alvera. His silence, or his death."

"Listen to me!" The words spilled out my mouth in panic. "You have to get out of here and pretend you never saw any of this. You can't tell anybody."

Graves took a step back, narrowing his eyes. "No way. Tell me this isn't some government cover-up where you've come to get rid of any evidence that this ever happened. Tell me that's not what you're here to do."

"Please listen to me. They'll kill you."

"You know what you have to do," Ryce said, softly. "We can't allow him to leave here alive. What he's seen could expose Exodus Station."

"He's not going to tell anyone," I said. "Tell me you won't, Graves."

He was looking at me like he'd never seen me before.

Like I was a stranger to him. Maybe I was. "How the hell could I have been so wrong about you?"

My implant buzzed with Ryce's voice. "*Philomela.*"

I wouldn't.

I couldn't.

"He made his choice, just like you wanted."

No. This wasn't what I wanted. This had never been what I wanted.

"Kill him."

My hand tightened around the gun. I felt myself raise my arm until it was level with Graves' eyes.

"I'm sorry," I whispered, and pulled the trigger.

CHAPTER FOURTEEN

The cavern roared, and I flew backwards in a cloud of smoke and dust.

Everything was a blur when I opened my eyes. I shielded my head with my hands to avoid the debris streaming from the ceiling. When the thick clouds settled and it was safe to look up, Graves was gone.

I scrambled forward and found fragments of a lightweight grenade on the ground in front of me. The kind of grenade miners used to blast through cave-ins or rock falls. Graves had come prepared. It might have saved his life.

My knees buckled as I tried to get up. The blast had knocked me clean off my feet. It would have probably killed me if it wasn't for my exosuit. The tough polymer of my visor was cracked, leaving part of my vision a shattered mess. Graves had done well. The grenade had given him a fighting chance. But it was only a chance.

I had no choice but to go after him. My body was already moving, pushing through the pain to follow his tracks. Ryce's command still echoed through my ears, forcing me to carry out his will. But Graves was a miner. This was his world, his territory. He knew how to navigate the tunnels better than I did. That gave him an advantage, a chance to get out before I caught up.

I ducked through the tunnel we'd come through, back-tracking until I found a fork in the passageway. I had tools Graves didn't. My cybernetics could enhance my vision and detect movement and heat signatures. But he had experience. He had an intuitive knowledge that let him move with sure-footed swiftness across steep and uneven ground.

I hoped it would be enough.

His tracks weren't hard to follow. Nobody else had left footprints in years. I looked for where the rocks had shifted, where dust had been kicked up, and chased down his trail.

I came to a stop at a large opening at the end of the tunnel. When I looked up, I could see the purple-black sky far above. The hole must have been bored from the surface deep into the core of the planet. The scale of it was hard to take in. The night sky seemed to retreat further and further away as I looked up at it, as though I was being swallowed by the pit.

The path forward was nothing more than a narrow ledge around the gaping shaft. I couldn't see Graves anywhere. The ledge led round to several openings on the other side of the chasm, but there was no sign of him edging his way around it. He had disappeared.

Somewhere inside me, in a place far deeper than Ryce's grip reached, I let out a sigh of relief. Maybe Graves would get away. Maybe the command would wear off before I could find him.

Then the rocks fell.

I turned around just in time to see Graves pull himself over the top of a rocky outcropping high above me. I raised my gun and fired off three shots in quick succession, but he managed to swing his legs over to safety.

I pulled the cable from my belt and attached it to the end of my gun. I fired, and the cable's teeth sank into the ledge on the first attempt. My hands trembled as I clipped the other end to my belt and retracted the line, pulling myself high above the shaft towards the outcropping.

Just as I rolled over the edge, a heavy jolt sent me reeling backwards. I flailed around on the end of the cable as Graves came at me, a huge slab of rock between his hands. He brought it down on my helmet, splintering my visor even more. He was playing smart, taking advantage of his position before I could haul myself up alongside him. But I still had a gun in my hand.

The first shot grazed his arm. The second caught him in the shoulder. He looked down, surprise and fear on his face as the blood began to seep through his jacket. His breather mask was cracked and he was limping from the blast. But he didn't stop. He brought the great hulk of rock down towards me again, even as I was lining up the third shot. I let the bullet loose just as he smashed the gun out of my hand and sent it tumbling into the pit below. I didn't see if I'd hit him. Maybe it didn't matter. Maybe the damage had already been done.

Graves coughed, blood from his lungs splattering against the inside of his mask. "Why are you doing this?" he asked, his voice thick and rasping. "What is it all for?"

"I don't have a choice."

"Those poor bastards back there didn't have a choice. You do."

"You don't understand."

"Damn right I don't."

I'd never wanted to hurt him, but that didn't matter. Ryce's will was too strong. The pressure in my head increased. It throbbed at my temples, at the nape of my neck. Resisting it was agony. Resisting it was impossible.

I swung myself with a strength I never knew I had, propelling myself through the air to land next to Graves. The look of surprise barely had time to register on his face before I unclipped the cable from my belt and transferred it to his.

His eyes widened. "Wait – "

I kicked him square in the chest and he disappeared before my eyes, sent backwards over the edge. The cable screamed after him before snapping tight, dangling him above the dark depths of the pit. All that kept him from oblivion was the release on the side of my gun. One slip of my finger and it would send a signal to the cable head to retract the teeth from the rock and let go.

"It's about time. I was beginning to think you'd lost your edge."

I spun around. Ryce was standing there, arms folded and a cruel smile tugging the edges of his mouth. He wasn't wearing his usual pristine tunic and polished dress boots. Instead, he was dressed in a loose white undershirt and a beaten, frayed jacket. He was dressed like Graves.

A scream escaped my throat as I charged towards him. I knew I was only going to meet empty air, but the anguish and rage that had taken hold of me refused to give way to reason. I bundled through his projection and almost went tumbling off the other side of the rock.

When I picked myself up and turned around, an ugly look had twisted his features. "Don't you prefer me like this?" he asked, with a sneer. "Is dressing like a surface slete more to your taste?"

"You pathetic bastard," I snarled. "You're not doing this to teach me a lesson about choices. You're doing this because you can't bear that you've lost me."

"I haven't lost you. You're still mine. One way or another, you'll always be mine."

"I was never yours."

"You'll never be his either." He glanced towards the edge of the rock.

Graves. I rushed past Ryce's projection and peered over. He was spinning around in the air, trying to pull himself up the cable.

When he saw me, a look of panic flashed across his face. "Don't do this, Alvera. Don't let me die down here."

My implants hummed as Ryce spoke. "This is on you, *mietsha*," he said, his voice gentle and mocking. "Remember that."

"Don't make me do this." I blinked furiously at the tears. "He's done nothing to you. This isn't fair."

"We've gone a long way past fair, Alvera." I could all but feel his breath against my ear. "I won't lose you to him. I won't lose you to anyone. If you had just agreed to come back to me willingly, it would never have come to this. You made your choice."

"I didn't want – "

"You are behaving like a *child*. Just because you cannot see the consequences doesn't mean there are none. You were the same back on Exodus Station. Always letting your emotion get in the way of your resolve. Look where it's got you."

"I'll do whatever you want. I'll come back to you. I'll make your damn cybernetics. Anything you ask. Just don't kill him."

"Oh, Alvera. I want nothing more than to believe you. But as long as he's alive, I'll never know if you truly mean it." He looked at me with such regret I almost believed it might be real. "Of course I'm not going to kill him. You are."

I stepped forward. Graves was hanging below. He was helpless.

"*Philomela*. Let him go."

I barely felt my fingers brush the release. It was over so fast. I only had a moment to take in the look of shock on Graves' face before he fell. He disappeared out of sight, lost to the darkness. There was no scream. There was no crunch of body hitting rock. He was just gone.

What had I done?

"First Chase, now Graves." Ryce wiped a hand over his brow. "When will you learn, Alvera?"

I sank to the ground, unable to support my own weight any longer. "I didn't – "

"You *did*." He knelt in front of me, placing his hand over mine. The projection was so real I could almost feel it. "Where will it end? Every choice you make brings you nothing but pain. Who will be next? Felix?"

"You're sick."

"I'm trying to help you. The sooner you see that, the safer everyone around you will be." He stood back up. "Remember this pain you've caused yourself. Ask yourself if it's worth it. When you can answer honestly, you'll come back to me. I still believe that."

He flickered in front of my eyes and disappeared.

I was alone. Graves was gone. He was lost somewhere below, out of reach. How many hundreds of feet had he fallen before hitting the rocks that killed him? How much time did he have to think about death rushing up to meet him? To think about what I'd done to him?

I let out a wretched sob. My heart was aching, my chest tight. I couldn't even think about Ryce. All I could think about was the blood on my hands.

I needed to get away from this place. Away from this horror-filled pit that still bore the scars of the atrocities carried out years before. Nobody would ever know what happened to the miners who'd been duped into coming here. Nobody would ever know what happened to Graves. Nobody but me.

I trudged through the tunnels until I found my way back to the elevator. The ride back up to the surface passed in a haze. I had nothing to fear from the shaking carriage anymore. The worst had already happened. I had nothing left to lose.

The wind whipped my hair across my face while I waited on the exposed ridge for the shuttle to come back. I made the jump back on board, no longer caring about the steep drop below.

"Did you get what you came for?" the pilot asked.

I couldn't even remember what I was meant to have come for. It had never mattered.

"You don't look so good. You feeling all right?" The pilot glanced over, concerned. "Don't worry, you'll be back at the Spire before you know it."

"No. The surface. I need to go to the surface."

"The surface? What's down there?"

"Nothing," I said. "Not anymore."

My holo-terminal told me it should be dawn, but I couldn't see any evidence of it. If sunrise was what heralded the morning, then there was no new day on the surface. Just the longest night.

I retraced my steps through the bustling streets. There were so many faces down here. I just needed one of them to be Graves.

It didn't take me long to find the flophouse again. I

waited outside the door to his room for a moment, just to listen. There was no sound coming from inside.

I pushed open the door. The room was empty.

He was gone. He was really gone.

I lowered myself gently to the floor and ran my hands over the solid ground underneath me. I'd saved Graves' life here. I'd brought him the meds he needed to keep his lungs from giving up. Then I'd killed him.

How was a person meant to move on under that kind of weight?

The room was almost bare. Graves didn't have much to call his own. I imagined his steps before he left for the last time. He must have believed he was coming back. He must have left a trace of himself behind.

I pulled out the lockbox from under the bed. It wasn't hard to break open. Expensive security wasn't a priority down here. The drawer slid open with a gentle hiss and I caught my breath.

It was Sphere.

The drone was still in parts, untouched, but Graves had left several tools in the drawer. Nothing sophisticated, nothing Felix would have been caught dead using, but tools nonetheless. He'd left them for me. With the belief, or maybe just the hope, that I would come back.

He might have offered to help me. I might have let him. Neither of us had that choice anymore.

I laid out the pieces in front of me. All I had was the cramped floorspace of a grimy flophouse room and a few salvaged tools. I didn't have a workstation or a tech lab like Felix. I didn't even have my own memories.

I closed my eyes.

There was no room for other thoughts now. Whatever else was going on around me was a distraction. A strange sort of release washed over me, a serenity I never believed I'd feel again. Everything else faded into darkness apart from the tools at my fingertips and the broken components lying in front of me.

I ran my fingers over each piece, examining the wires and circuits and how they connected to the others. It wasn't until I took it apart and saw all the parts that made it whole that I realised how very fragile it was, as complex and delicate as my own network of nerves and tissue.

My fingers moved intuitively, drawing their memories from my muscles, not my mind. I had done this before. The memories Felix implanted in me might have been fabricated, but there was still a ghost of the person I'd been before buried underneath them.

I was an engineer. The best cybernetics engineer on Exodus Station. I knew how to do this.

There were flaws Felix hadn't noticed when he'd built the drone. Parts he'd put in without fully understanding what they were capable of. I took them all, piece by piece, and started to fix them.

It wouldn't be the same. But that didn't matter. All I needed was to believe that even the most broken things could be put back together.

When I was finished, I held the little drone in the palm of my hand. It wouldn't remember me when I booted it back up. We'd both be starting again.

I hovered my finger over the power button, hesitation creeping over me. Sphere was connected to my cybernetics. The same cybernetics Ryce had hacked. What would happen if I re-established our connection now? Would Sphere be able to help me or would it become as much a slave to Ryce as I was?

I rolled it around in my hand. Now was not the time. Not

while Ryce still had so much power over me. But the time would come. I couldn't do much, but I could make that promise to myself. I clutched it close, the smallest seed of hope against my chest.

The respite was all too brief, cut short by the slow, unmistakeable creak of the door.

I whirled around, raising my gun.

Two armoured hands stood aloft in the air, a gesture of surrender. "Let's make a deal. I won't shoot if you don't."

It was Tau.

CHAPTER FIFTEEN

"We don't have much time." Tau didn't seem concerned that I hadn't lowered my gun. He swept around the room with his holo-terminal, his cybernetics blinking furiously. "No emitters, no electronics. That's good. I jammed your implants again, but I don't know how long I can hold Ryce off for."

I tightened my grip on my gun. "You really so eager for round two?"

He turned to look at me. There was something different about him. His pale skin had stretched so thin that I could see the metal casing around his jaw underneath. A red glow from his retinal implants glared through his grey irises. His huge chrome limbs moved with a stiffness that hadn't been there before, a fatigue that shouldn't have been possible.

Against all sense, I lowered my gun. "What happened to you?"

"Not as pretty as I used to be, am I?" He let out a dark chuckle. "They call it the quickening. We enforcers usually outlive regular Exodans by fifty years thanks to our body modifications. Unless we go against the wishes of the Council. Then they use those same modifications to kill us."

"You turned against Ojara?" My head was spinning. "I didn't think that was possible."

"Trust me, neither did I." Something twitched in his temple. "I thought it was a glitch in my programming. Then I realised the truth. I was never conditioned to serve one councillor, even though that's what it felt like. My programming doesn't make me loyal to Ojara, or even the Council. It makes me loyal to Exodus Station."

I crossed my arms. "Seems like one and the same to me."

"That's what I thought too. When Ojara ordered me to hunt you down and kill you, I couldn't do anything but comply. I had to do everything in my power to protect Exodus Station. It's what I was created to do. It's the mandate they breed us to fulfil."

"So what's changed?"

"You." He gave a heavy sigh. "I never expected your cybernetics to be so strong. Ojara always said we didn't need the technology in your head. She said the Council would find another way to save the station. After witnessing what you're capable of, I'm not sure I believe that anymore."

I still wasn't sure if I could trust him. "What are you saying?"

"I'm saying my mandate hasn't changed. I have to protect Exodus Station. But despite what the Council claims, Exodus Station needs you alive." He stretched his mouth into a wry smile. "Of course, Ojara didn't see it that way."

I cast a glance over his gaunt face, his sunken skin. "The quickening. You said she was using your body modifications against you."

"It's a virus. An exceptionally clever piece of programming that turns our own cybernetics against us. The parts of us that are human, our flesh and blood, are consumed by the parts of us that are machine."

Horror twisted my stomach. "That's awful."

"It's designed to be. It wastes us away and only lets us die when there is nothing left to feel the agony ravaging us. It's painfully slow, but the cruelty of it has given me time. Time to fulfil my mandate."

I shook my head. "I can't help you. I won't help the Exodans if it means abandoning New Pallas."

"I remember. All of us go, or none of us go. That's what you said." He tilted his head. "Then find a way for all of us to go."

I laughed. "The Council will never let that happen."

"Not while they have control." His eyes gleamed. "But what if they didn't? What if you had control, instead?"

"Ryce has control. You should know that. You were there at my trial." The memory of my humiliation, of Ryce's lips against mine, sent a burning flush to my cheeks. "There's nothing I can do."

"Isn't there? He's not in control all the time. He has to use his override code to take over." A slow smile spread across his face. "If you can't hear the code, you can't follow the command."

I snorted. "I can't exactly just cover my ears and pretend not to listen. He can hijack my implants, remember?"

Tau opened his palm, revealing a small, round cap. "This is a dental chip. I've rigged it so when you bite down on it, it will blow out your auditory implant. Ryce will be unable to give you his override commands."

No more voice in my head. No more *Philomela* whispered in my ear.

My heart thumped against my ribs. It wasn't freedom, but it was as close as I'd come to it in a long time. "How long will it last?"

"Until he tracks you down, knocks you out and repairs it

with cyber surgery. Or just decides to kill you." Tau shrugged. "That's why this is so important. It's a one-time shot. You can't use it, you *mustn't* use it, until you figure out a way to break free of his control for good."

"You're using a jammer to block my implants from him just now, aren't you? Why can't I just get one of those?"

Tau shook his head. "The jammer is part of an enforcer's system. It's not something I could take out and give to you. The dental chip is your only way free of him until you find something that can break his control over you."

My heart sank. "I don't know if I can do this."

"You have to. For all our sakes."

You're going to save us all, you know that? The memory of Ryce's words sent a shiver down my spine. He had used them to try to manipulate me, but he'd made a mistake. I would turn those words against him. I would find a way to save New Pallas. For Chase. For Graves. For myself.

I took the dental chip from his outstretched hand, rolling the tiny device delicately between my fingers before pressing it into my backmost molar. "Thank you, Tau."

He raised an eyebrow. "Tau?"

"Sorry. It's what I've been calling you in my head. Figured it was as good a name as any."

"Tau." He seemed to be mulling it over. "I've never had any need for a name before. Maybe it's something I can take with me when the quickening catches up with me. Something of my own."

My holo-terminal chimed. "It's Ryce. He must have realised my implants are jammed again."

"I'll go. We can't do anything to raise his suspicions." Tau paused at the door. "You only have one chance, Alvera. Use it well."

When he was gone, I opened the connection.

"Where are you?" Ryce was usually only this sharp when he was worried about me. Once, that would have filled me with comfort. Now, his concern was toxic.

I clicked Sphere into its port on my shoulder and ran out of the flophouse, making for the public transit pad. What could I say to ward him off? If he found out what Tau had given me, it would all be for nothing. I couldn't let him see that hope in me. I had to play the broken part he thought he'd succeeded in making of me. It was the only way to survive. "I'm on the surface. I had to…" The words caught in my throat, still raw. "I wanted to say goodbye to Graves. You never gave me a chance to do that."

He ignored the accusation. "Something is jamming your implants again. I can't see you."

"It was the enforcer. He must have been waiting for me, but I managed to get away."

Ryce went quiet for a moment. "How did you manage that? Enforcers rarely make the same mistake twice."

Dread tugged at my stomach. Only the truth would do. Especially seeing as he could force it out of me anyway. "There was something wrong with him. His skin was breaking apart and I could see the cybernetics underneath. He didn't seem like he was fighting at full strength."

"The quickening," he said, his voice hard. "Ojara never did take failure well. I suppose it was punishment for not finishing you off the first time. It doesn't surprise me that he would try to finish the job to appease her. From what I've seen, it's a particularly nasty way to go."

"Whatever it was, it slowed him down long enough for me to lose him." I barged past crowds of surfacers trying to beg their way onto the public transit shuttle, flashing my Spire identification at the security officer on board. "I'm on my way topside now. I imagine my implants will be kicking back in at any moment."

The line was silent. I held my breath, wondering if he would believe me.

"I've got you now." He let out a long sigh. "You got lucky this time. I won't tolerate such carelessness in the future. You forget how much we need you, Alvera."

I ground my teeth together. "You forget how much I don't care. I already told you, I won't help you."

"Of course you will. All that remains to be seen is whether you do it by choice. In the meantime, report back to the Spire. Felix has been looking for you." He paused. "Remember, as far as he knows, nothing has changed. Don't give him any reason to think otherwise."

He didn't need to warn me about what would happen if I didn't play by his rules. The unspoken threat was clear. If I screwed up, Felix would be the next casualty.

I ran my tongue gently over the chip at the back of my mouth. This time, if things went wrong, I had a backup.

I wouldn't let anyone else die because of me.

The one-way mirror was still in effect as I approached Felix's lab. Whatever he was working on, he clearly didn't want anyone snooping.

I watched my reflection loom larger as I got closer. Maybe if I looked hard enough, I'd be able to see something I'd missed. A sign that this woman in the mirror was not herself, that her words and actions were not her own. She had changed. Somebody had to see that.

She looked anxious, confused. There was a little furrow in her brow that gave her away. Her eyes were searching for something. Searching for an answer. There was a vulnerability there I hadn't expected. Her mouth opened in surprise.

"Who are you?" I whispered.

She mouthed the words back at me, but they didn't reach my ears.

"Alvera?" Felix popped his head out and surveyed the empty corridor. "Come in quickly, let me get this door closed."

The nervous energy coming off him was almost palpable. He had a twitchy kind of look on his face, the kind of look techs got when they'd had too many stims and not enough sleep. But Felix never took stims.

"What's going on?" I asked.

His eyes were bright and feverish. "You were right before, when you said the hologram wasn't real. It wasn't Chase."

"I'm sorry, Felix. I was only trying to – "

"I didn't tell you the full story." He pressed on, ignoring me. "I didn't want to say anything until I figured it out. I knew if I couldn't crack it, she'd only ever be a programme. An advanced personality simulation, like you said. It would be able to mimic her, it would sound like her and look like her, but it would never actually *be* her. She'd never truly be alive."

He tapped his holo-terminal and the lab plunged into darkness. The only lights came from the glow of his machines. He ushered me over to the projector in the middle of the room and began working away at the interface. Two words flashed up in front of my eyes.

Project Nightingale.

"Felix, what is this all about?"

He didn't answer. It was like I wasn't even in the room.

Flickering lights from the projector flashed across his dark skin as he worked.

"These are the most advanced encryption protocols I've ever created," he explained. "I couldn't risk somebody stumbling across what I was working on."

"You've still not told me exactly what that is."

"Wait just a few more seconds. There." He took a step back, satisfied. "Look at it. She's beautiful."

In the middle of the room, glowing in the darkness, was an intricate hologram pulsing gently like a heartbeat. A golden web of fragile strands wove together in a pattern too complex to follow. It was a network of sorts, full of the tiniest threads and connections joined together in a delicate matrix.

It was beautiful. More than that, even though I didn't understand how it could be possible, it was alive.

"It's…" I couldn't find the words. "It looks like a brain."

Felix trembled next to me. "It is a brain. This is true artificial intelligence."

I took a step back. "Remember when you used to give me shit about not reprogramming Sphere often enough to keep in line with AI regulations? This has gone way past that. If what you're saying is true, you've created something that can think for itself. Something alive." I reached out my hand, my fingers passing harmlessly through the projected web of gold. "This shouldn't even be possible. I've never seen a warrant posted for someone breaking AI regs because it's all just theory. Nobody has ever actually done it."

"Nobody until now," he said, his voice shaking. I couldn't tell whether it was from fear or excitement. "I did it, Alvera. I found a way to bring her back."

"Chase?" I frowned. "What does she have to do with this? You said her hologram was made up of old videos and images. You can't create life out of that."

"No, but you can create life out of memories," he said, softly. "There's something I need to tell you. I've been working on experimental memory mapping technology. When Chase was alive, I took a scan of her brain every day. My programme mapped the parts that had changed and stored away her experiences. It was meant to be a solution to memory loss. A way I could bring her back if she ever suffered a traumatic brain injury." His voice cracked. "We both knew the danger of being a warrant hunter."

Memories. How had I not seen it before? This was how he'd fabricated a life for me. This was how he'd planted Alvera and all she was into my brain. He'd been developing the technology with Chase. My whole existence, everything I could remember, was built on his work. But it was never meant for me.

It was meant for her.

"The human brain is a machine. It can be programmed just like a machine." Felix continued. A pained look had fallen across his face and he curled his shoulders as he spoke. "Once I figured out how the mapping worked, it wasn't difficult to devise a way to implant memories into a human host."

"A human host." My throat tightened around the words. Even if I wanted to press him further, Ryce's programming wouldn't allow it. But that didn't matter. I already knew the truth. I had been his first test subject, brought to him with a blank mind and a bullshit sob story.

He still didn't realise what he had done to me. Maybe he never would.

"That part isn't important." He looked away, distress twisting his features. "I didn't map Chase's memories onto another human. I mapped them onto the AI. That's what Project Nightingale is."

In my shock, I'd forgotten all about the golden hologram

pulsing in the middle of the room. "You put her memories into that thing? Are you crazy? It's an AI. You don't know what it will do."

"I do. I made it." His eyes lit up again. "Nightingale is a sentient intelligence made up entirely of Chase's memories. It's everything she was until the day she left."

"You don't know that. You're messing around with tech you don't understand. If anyone else in the Spire caught wind of this…"

Felix's face fell. "I know the risks. I could lose my job. They could lock me away for years. But I had to do it. I had to get Chase back."

"This isn't Chase."

"It will be, soon."

"Soon?" I turned back to him. "You mean it's not working yet?"

He pursed his lips. "It's working. I did everything right. But I can't communicate with it. I'm human, it's machine. I haven't found a way to reconcile that disconnect between us yet."

A sense of foreboding tugged at the pit of my stomach. "Yet?"

"I have an idea. It's why I asked you to come here."

"I don't want to hear it."

"Cybernetics." He paced back and forth, pressing on as if he hadn't heard me. "It makes perfect sense. I need a way to bridge the gap between human and machine. You could be that bridge. If you could give me access for a few hours, I could speak to it through you. Speak to her."

He wasn't thinking clearly. He couldn't be. Even if he could do the things he said, even if it worked, the implications were terrifying.

Especially for me.

I tried to laugh. "Trust me, I've got enough shit going on in my head to deal with. I don't want your dead girlfriend adding to it, thank you very much."

Felix shook his head vigorously. "It wouldn't be permanent. Just long enough for her to tell me how to adjust the programme to allow me to talk to her by myself, without the need for cybernetics."

"No way. Are you even listening to yourself?"

"Please, Alvera. I can't trust anybody else with this. It has to be you." He lowered his head. "Do you know what would happen if somebody else got their hands on this research? Nobody would have anywhere to hide their secrets anymore. It would make interrogations redundant. It would make privacy redundant. The corporations would have complete control over us all."

An uneasy sensation gnawed at my stomach. "What are you talking about? How could the corporations use it?"

"I told you that your cybernetics would become a bridge between human and machine. That bridge goes both ways. By letting the AI in, you're sharing your consciousness. It will absorb every memory, every thought. It's the closest connection you could ever have with something that's not yourself." Felix bit his lip. "But it also means there's nowhere to hide. There's no way to lie to it. The corporations could weaponise it. They could use it to steal secrets, to extract information from people. That's not why I built Nightingale. That's not what I want it used for."

I froze. *It will absorb every memory, every thought.*

In that moment, I realised two very important things.

One. This was what I had been waiting for. A way I could speak about what had happened to me through a connection that didn't require words. A chance to break free from the silence Ryce had strangled me with.

Two. Felix was wrong. The corporations weren't the threat here. Ryce was. He had access to my implants. He saw what I saw. He heard what I heard. Now that I had put it together, it was only a matter of time until he did too.

Shit. What had I done?

Felix was still talking. I had to make him stop. I had to make him unsay everything he had already said. But it was too late. He couldn't take it back. I couldn't unhear his words.

"Felix," I said. "Stop talking right now."

He kept going.

"Please. If you want me to help, if you want me to do this, you need to stop. I can't hear any more."

He didn't listen. He was too caught up in his desperation, not realising he was dooming us both.

It was too late. I knew this could save me. And because I knew that, it was already over.

Ryce couldn't read my mind. But now that he had access to my implants again, he could see everything. He wouldn't allow this. He wouldn't allow anything to endanger his control over me. He would destroy the one chance I had of regaining myself.

Something stirred in my head.

He knew.

CHAPTER SIXTEEN

I burst through the doors to the rooftop shuttle pad and staggered into the sunlight. My head was throbbing with a violent pressure. Maybe Ryce was cutting his losses early. Maybe there was some kind of killswitch in my cybernetics, like the quickening in Tau.

I needed to get away from here. Away from Felix and Project Nightingale. As far away as Ryce would let me go.

I jumped in my shuttle. I could go back down to the surface. I could blow my implant and get lost there. If I didn't know where I was, Ryce might not be able to find me. It wouldn't be a victory. I wouldn't be able to save New Pallas. But maybe I'd brought this on myself for ever thinking I could.

"*Philomela.*"

It was too late. He already had me. He uttered his command and I turned the shuttle towards my old apartment.

I didn't want to go back. Everything about my life there was a lie. It was the home of someone who had never existed. I wasn't Alvera. I wasn't Philomela. I was nobody.

My chest tightened as I parked up at the landing pad and

made my way down the steps to the apartment. He was waiting for me. His eyes followed me in, hungry and unblinking.

He gestured to the couch with a subtle flick of his head. "*Philomela.* Why don't you take a seat?"

Every muscle in my body screamed under the strain of wanting to deny him. It was hopeless. My legs betrayed me by walking me over and sitting me down as if that was what they had wanted all along.

He kneeled in front of me, placing a gentle hand on each of my legs. At this height, our eyes were level. I was frozen in place while my body screamed at me to run.

A slow smile unfurled across his lips. It was languid, almost lazy. He could be as patient as he wanted. In the end, he would take the truth from me.

"I already know," he said. His voice was soft and coaxing. The warmth of his breath tingled my face. "But I want you to tell me. I want to hear it from your lips."

Felix. The AI. Project Nightingale. It all flashed in front of my eyes. If I could have voluntarily relinquished all my memories again in that moment, I would have.

"You think you've found a way to break the programming," he said. "Don't try to lie to me. There are no secrets between us."

I tried to squirm away as he brushed a strand of hair from my face and tucked it behind my ear. "If you know already, then what does it matter? I'm done playing your sad little games. I won't give you the satisfaction."

"There's your tongue. I was wondering where it had gone." Ryce smiled. "This is not a game, Alvera. Tell me what I want to know or be prepared to suffer another death on your conscience. Haven't you left enough bodies in your wake?"

"Go to hell."

The smile disappeared. "Speak. I'll give you one chance to prove yourself to me. Tell me what you discovered. Tell me using your own words."

I didn't answer. I wouldn't. Instead, I looked him squarely in the eye and spat in his face.

He took the sleeve of his coat and slowly wiped it across his cheek. His eyes never left mine, not for a moment. They were unflinching. Unforgiving.

He shot out his hand and grabbed me by the throat.

I thrashed against him, but his grip was stronger than I expected. He squeezed until it felt like my throat was caving in on itself. The sides of my vision started to turn black and my ears filled with noise, muffling the rest of the world. There was a sheen of sweat on Ryce's flushed forehead. He wore a tortured expression that grew hazier with every passing second. The black crept in. Soon, it would take over everything. It was only a matter of time.

For one exhilarating moment, it was a relief. It was all going to be over. I wouldn't have him in my head anymore. I wouldn't have anything in my head. If he ended my life here, at least I would be free.

Just when I had accepted that, he stopped.

It was agony. Not just my bruised and swollen throat, but the realisation that I'd been so close to escaping him. The darkness around the edges of my eyes disappeared. My throat, aching and raw, opened up enough to draw in an excruciating breath. Ryce's face swam back into focus.

He whirled away from me, burying his head in his hands. "Why do you keep doing this to me?" he asked. His voice was hoarse, as if he'd been the one who'd nearly had the life strangled from him. "Why do you keep pushing me? I'm trying, Alvera. But look what you made me do."

I tried to reply, but my throat just made a painful wheeze. I forced the words out anyway, in sounds I didn't know I was capable of making. It was a stranger's voice. A voice that had been silenced and crippled and forced to speak when it was ready to give out.

I was too tired to fight him anymore. I told him everything.

As I spoke, his expression changed. I could see it in the tightening of his jaw, the vein throbbing in his temple. But in amongst the anger was a flicker of surprise. He hadn't expected me to tell him of my own volition, without his command.

He drew his mouth into a tight line. "Stupid girl. Did you really think you'd be able to hide this from me?"

"It was worth a shot."

"Was it?" He curled his lip. "I don't doubt Felix believes in his little project, but even the Council has never been successful in creating a true artificial intelligence. It wouldn't have worked, Alvera. You cannot escape me."

"If you're so certain of that, why are you so afraid?"

He flinched. "Enough. Go back to the tech labs. Destroy every piece of data, every scrap of research Felix has on this Nightingale. I won't have this distraction, not when we have more important work to do."

Something had unnerved him. I could see it in his eyes. Despite his bluster, he couldn't hide the fear underneath. The fear that he might be wrong. The fear that I might be able to claw my way free of him.

It was exactly what I needed. If Ryce was afraid, that meant there was still hope.

"I know that look," he said, his voice taking on a gentler tone. "That stubbornness has caused us both nothing but trouble, Alvera. For once, learn to set it to the side. Nobody has to get hurt this time."

The softness of his voice did nothing to hide the cruel edge to his words. I knew exactly what he meant. "I won't hurt Felix."

"That's up to him, isn't it?" He shrugged. "If he gets in the way, he'll suffer the consequences."

That bastard. He knew Felix would try to stop me. It would be like Graves all over again. As soon as he decided to come between me and Ryce's orders, he would be dead. And I would be the one to pull the trigger.

There had to be another way.

I looked at Ryce. If I could have begged, I would have.

His face was expressionless when he spoke. "*Philomela.* Go to the tech labs. Destroy Felix's research. And get rid of that damn AI."

The city passed by in a glittering blur, all sweeping curves and streamlined edges. There was an elegance to it, a sense of pride. Constructed by people who had built on their past mistakes time and time again. Until the surface had been forgotten about. Until they forgot that just because they couldn't see their past mistakes, it didn't mean they didn't exist. They had learned nothing.

I had learned nothing.

Nobody questioned me when I arrived back at the tech labs. Nobody tried to stop me. Why would they? I was invisible. Nobody really knew me. There was no familiarity, no polite acknowledgement between colleagues. How had I never noticed that before?

The door to Felix's lab slid open as I approached. "Alvera, you came back. Did you reconsider what – "

I drew my gun and blasted the control panel on the wall. The door came down with a heavy thud, locked to the outside. "Stay out of my way, Felix." I didn't offer him an apology. He'd never understand it.

I didn't know exactly what I was looking for, but my cybernetics showed me where to go. They highlighted one of the computer mainframes in the corner of the room and I punched in an override, focusing my eyes on the flashing code that appeared on the interface.

"What are you doing?" Felix's mouth was hanging open. There was a mixture of horror and disbelief in his eyes.

I ignored him and got to work.

He'd called my cybernetics a bridge between human and machine. A way to connect the two, to allow them to work together as one. The more I tapped into their potential, the more I realised how true that was. I stripped away Felix's encryption protocols like they weren't even there. Suddenly, his genius seemed childlike. As brilliant as he was, he was nothing compared to what was in my head.

"Get away from there!" Felix stormed towards me and tried to wrench my arm away. I didn't even turn to look at him. All I had to do was fling out an arm and the power of my exosuit did the rest.

He staggered back and crashed into a desk, sending a pile of holofiles clattering to the ground. When I turned to glance at him, he was staring back at me with glassy eyes. A dark trickle of blood ran down his neck and he touched a tentative hand to it, like he couldn't believe it was there.

"Alvera." His voice was numb. "What are you doing?"

"I warned you to stay out of my way." I turned back to the console, my cybernetics buzzing away at the back of my head. I knew what they were capable of. I knew what I had to do.

The code in front of me began to disappear as the virus I'd implanted took hold.

"No," Felix said. "You can't do this."

He hauled himself to his feet and limped towards me. I allowed him to push me aside. It didn't matter what he did now. He couldn't undo what I'd just done. It was too late for both of us.

"No," he said again, tapping furiously at the console. "This isn't happening. My storage drives. The failsafes. The backups."

"It's all gone." My voice was cold, dispassionate. It wasn't me.

"Why are you doing this?" I tried to ignore the tears filling his eyes. "This is the only part of her I have left. Don't take her from me."

I turned towards the middle of the room and aimed my gun at the power junction connected to the hologram emitter. Felix's data was gone, wiped into inexistence. All I needed to do was get rid of Nightingale, and Ryce's command would be fulfilled. Felix would no longer be in danger from me.

"Put the gun down, Alvera."

I had been so distracted I didn't notice that Felix had picked up a weapon of his own.

"You've snapped," Felix said, his voice dry and hollow. "I don't understand what's happened. Maybe it's my fault. Maybe your memories…"

He circled in front of me, putting himself between me and the AI. His finger trembled against the trigger. He planted himself on the floor like it was territory he couldn't afford to give up.

"Walk away, Alvera." His voice was low and shaking. "Don't make me do this."

I tightened my hand around my gun. It wasn't a fair fight. By the time he got a single shot off, I'd have riddled him with bullets. No matter how this went down, it would end with me alive and him dead.

That was the point, wasn't it? Ryce wanted me to kill everybody I had ever cared about until only he was left. Was he so delusional to believe all this could be forgiven if I had nowhere else to turn?

He wanted it this way. He'd set this up so I would have to look Felix in the eye as I pulled the trigger and watched him die at my hand. Any moment now, it would be over.

Unless...

I rolled my tongue over the dental implant. If I used it now, what would it change? Even with Ryce silenced, Felix would still be pointing a gun at me. I couldn't get to Nightingale without going through him and that wasn't a price I was willing to pay.

Tau had warned me I would only get one chance. This wasn't it.

"*Philomela.* Pull the trigger."

There it was. The order I couldn't resist. Even if I bit down now and used Tau's device, it wouldn't make a difference. Ryce had already given the command. There was no going back.

Already the pressure was growing inside my head, pounding harder and harder. The more I fought it, the more intense it would become. I knew how it would end.

Pull the trigger.

No. I wouldn't do this. Not after Chase. Not after Graves. I wouldn't let him take Felix too. He had weaponised my body. My mind was my last stand, the only ground on which I could fight back.

Pull the trigger.

I looked away from Felix's trembling face towards my outstretched hand. At first, it was just a phantom twitch in my fingers. An imagined movement that refused to materialise in reality. Then slowly, painfully, my hand moved.

It took every fibre of will not to give up and be done with it. Every tiny spasm was a fresh burst of pain. I kept going. Inch by agonising inch. A monumental effort I hadn't been willing to believe I was capable of.

Until now.

He told me to pull the trigger. He didn't tell me where to put the barrel.

I pressed the gun against my temple, felt my finger slip on the trigger, and everything went black.

CHAPTER SEVENTEEN

Muffled sounds pushed their way through the darkness that had taken me into its fold, and I knew I had failed.

I was alive.

I hadn't expected to wake up. The far-off sounds crawled further into my ears, growing louder and more persistent by the second. A sterile smell tingled the inside of my nostrils and I felt the pinch of cold, hard metal around my wrists.

I kicked out with my legs only to feel the same bite of steel around my ankles. Pinned down, just like my arms. It hardly seemed to matter. The aching fatigue in my muscles would do more to keep me down than the restraints ever could.

"You're awake." A young med tech standing by the side of the bed glanced up from his datapad and cast an appraising glance over me. "That's good news. You've been out for a couple of days."

"Where am I?"

"Hospital. You're lucky to be alive. You must have come to your senses at the last moment and tried to stop yourself, because the bullet just grazed your head. It was the shockwave that did the most damage. You hit your head pretty hard when you fell."

"And these?" I tried to lift my wrists, but the shackles kept them in place.

"By order of...let me see." He consulted his datapad again. "Department of Judiciary and Enforcement. They wouldn't let the doctor touch you until you were secured."

I let out a hollow laugh. "I'm that dangerous?"

"So it would seem." He glanced towards the door. "There's someone outside waiting to speak to you, gave his name as Felix. Doc said not to let him in until you were strong enough but – "

"Let him in."

He nodded and slipped outside. The door hissed shut behind him and remained closed for a few moments before sliding open again.

Felix slinked in and slumped down into a chair. He kept his gaze on the ceiling, like he couldn't bear the sight of me.

He had no idea I'd saved his life. No idea what it had cost me to do it.

"The doctor said you suffered a traumatic break. That the stress from carrying this team on your own after Chase's death caused you to snap." Each syllable was a slow, monotonic lament. "I wish I could forgive you for that. But you took what little I had left of her and destroyed it."

I couldn't bring myself to apologise. It wouldn't mean anything. It wouldn't change what I'd done. "What's going to happen to me?"

"They're keeping you here until the doctors are satisfied you've made enough of a recovery to go home. After that, you'll be put under house arrest and you'll attend mandatory psych evaluations every month. In time, you might have a normal life again." I could hear the unspoken accusation in his voice as he looked away.

"Felix."

"Why did you do it?" he whispered. "My research might have been against regulations, but since when have you cared about rules? I lost everything. This was the one chance I had at bringing Chase back."

A vice-like grip tightened itself around my heart. I hadn't only destroyed Felix's chance, I'd destroyed mine. The mind-reading intelligence Felix had built was one thing that could have undone Ryce's control over me. The one hope I had to be free. "What about Nightingale itself?"

He wiped a sleeve across his cheek. "It's useless without the rest of my data. It's trapped in its machine shell, unable to communicate. It might as well be dead."

His words hit me like a blow. It was like he was talking about me. But I wasn't dead, not yet. And neither was Nightingale. The programme itself was still intact. Even if Felix couldn't communicate with it, there was still a chance I could.

A burst of pain shot through the base of my skull. It was just like the first time I woke on Exodus Station. I let out a low hiss of breath. Ryce. He must have performed some more cyber surgery on me while I was out. What had he done to me this time?

"Who else knows about this?" I asked, gritting my teeth against the pain. "What did they do with Nightingale?"

"Only Ryce knows," Felix said, his voice hollow. "He arrived before Spire security and arranged to move Nightingale to a secure facility so nobody would find out what I'd done. If it wasn't for him, I'd be the one in cuffs instead of you."

"Where did he – "

"You think I'd tell you, even if I knew?" Felix shook his head. "Forget it, Alvera. You don't have to worry about going back to finish the job. Project Nightingale is over. There's not enough of it left to matter. I have to accept that. You should too."

He stood up and walked away, unable to spare a parting glance towards me. I waited for the door to slide shut behind him, but it remained open and I heard low voices talking outside. Felix and somebody else, the doctor probably.

No. It was him.

I squirmed against the bed, but there was nowhere I could run to. The restraints were too tight. He walked in and closed the door behind him. The sound of it clicking shut filled me with a cold, numbing terror.

"I gave you a chance," Ryce said softly, leaning over me and putting a gentle hand on my forehead. To anybody observing, it would have seemed like a tender gesture. I alone could see the way his eyes looked at me, like they could wither me away to nothing.

He stroked his thumb across my skin. "You could have trusted me. Everything I did, I did to protect you. Even after you betrayed me again and again, I tried to save you. You've broken my heart a hundred times over, Alvera. Each time I got up and put myself back together. But not this time. This time, you've gone too far."

He was delusional. How had it taken so long for me to see it? It wasn't an act. In the twisted depravity of his mind, the sick bastard actually thought he loved me.

"I could have been cruel," he whispered, his face too close. "But I didn't want to hurt you. I wanted you to make your own choices. And you continue to disappoint me with them."

"Disappoint you?" The words escaped my lips in a breath

of disbelief. "Your approval is the last thing I care about. You killed Chase. You killed Graves. You tried to kill Felix."

"You tried to kill yourself."

"I'd rather be dead than a slave to you."

He reeled back like I'd slapped him. He didn't understand. He couldn't comprehend that I'd rather choose death than submit to his control for the rest of my life. That's why I'd been able to pull the gun to my own head.

A bubble of laughter escaped from my throat. He hadn't won, not yet. I was still the rat, but I could see cracks appearing in the maze he'd constructed for me. As long as I could still surprise him, he wasn't infallible.

"You think this is funny?" He stood up and walked across the room. I couldn't see what he was doing until he turned around and threw my exosuit on the bed. "You're going to finish what you started. And this time, you're going to kill anyone you come across who tries to interfere. No bargaining, no negotiation. Not until I see you destroy that machine."

"If you want it gone so badly, why didn't you just do it yourself? You had plenty of opportunity."

"My position in the Spire is of critical importance to the workings of Exodus Station. Breaking my cover, even drawing a modicum of unwanted attention to myself, is not an option. I am indispensable." He fixed me with a hard stare. "You, however, are not."

The pieces clicked into place. "You're afraid of being found out. If the Spire discovers Felix has been working on illegal AI tech under your watch, you'll be held accountable too. They'd start looking into all your intel, all our jobs. Your precious secrets would be at risk." I bared my teeth in a vengeful smile. "And we both know how the Exodan Council deals with people who spill their secrets."

He brought up his holo-terminal. A moment later, the

restraints around my ankles and wrists snapped apart. "*Philomela*. Get dressed."

I swung my legs off the side of the bed and fumbled at the nape of my medical gown, unable to fight him. He remained where he was, the hint of a smile playing on his lips. He had no intention of leaving.

I clenched my jaw. "Get out."

"You're not in any position to be making demands," he said, voice cool. Then he curled the side of his mouth into a sneer. "Besides, it's nothing I've not seen before."

His expression didn't change when my gown fell to the floor, exposing my body to him. Under his gaze, I was made of nothing more than parts. My arms, my legs, my breasts. Every part of me he'd taken for himself, taken from me. He dissected me with his eyes, glancing up at me every few seconds so I knew how hungrily he was devouring me.

I rummaged in the drawers for a jumpsuit and pulled the tight fabric over my aching muscles. This would be the last time. The next time we met, I would put a bullet through his head, just like he did to Chase. That was my promise to myself. That was the only way I could survive his eyes crawling over my skin.

By the time I'd strapped on my exosuit, I was exhausted. I'd barely be able to hold a gun, much less storm the facility Ryce had moved Nightingale to.

"This isn't going to work," I told him. "I'm in no shape to fight."

"Haven't you learned anything by now? I don't leave things like this to chance." He pulled out a syringe and gestured towards the intravenous port on the arm of my exosuit.

"What is it?" I asked, half afraid to hear the answer.

"A little stimulant to help you back on your feet," he

replied. "It packs quite a punch and the comedown is particularly nasty, but it will last long enough to get the job done. That's all that matters."

He opened the port and squeezed the syringe into my skin underneath. Whatever was in the vial entered my veins in a warm rush, sending a rejuvenating heat through my body. It raced through my nerves, breathing life into my weary muscles. It heightened my senses, made my heart thump stronger. My concentration was absolute.

This was what power felt like.

I touched my shoulder. Sphere was nestled there, silent in its dock. Ryce hadn't taken it.

He tightened his lips. "I noticed you'd attempted to rebuild it. How very pointless. It was broken beyond repair, Alvera. It will never be what it was before. It can't help you. Nobody can."

The disdain in his voice no longer angered me. His disdain was what I was counting on. I'd seen what the Exodans did with broken things. When they had no more use for something, they disposed of it without a second thought. They never thought there might be something to salvage in amongst all the pain and destruction. They were too short-sighted to see that the pieces of something might be rebuilt into more than it used to be.

They were wrong. If I was to survive this, I needed them to be wrong.

Ryce pulled up his holo-terminal. "*Philomela*. In five minutes you'll have a clear exit out of the hospital. Nobody will try to stop you. After that, kill anybody in your way. No matter who it is."

When I didn't reply, he grabbed my jaw, tilting my chin so I was forced to look at him. "I don't care if you fight. I don't care if you spend every last second of your pathetic existence trying to escape this. I don't care if it kills you a little more each day. Whether it's because you want to or because I make you, you will do everything I ask. How terrible that becomes is entirely your choice."

He pushed me away, straightening his coat as he made his way to the door. At the threshold, he turned to look at me. "I don't suppose I need to tell you this, but I've reinforced your programming with additional cyber surgery. I rarely make mistakes and when I do, I don't make them twice. You won't be able to harm yourself this time, so don't bother trying. There's no way out of this. Accept that."

His instructions were clear, but they didn't weigh as heavy as they used to. My tongue danced over the implant at the back of my mouth. My one chance.

It was time to use it.

Ryce was wrong. The Exodans were wrong. I was more than the sum of my broken parts. I had been reassembled. The moment I had turned my own weapon to my head, I had taken back part of myself.

The rest was waiting. It was time to go get it.

CHAPTER EIGHTEEN

I was a walking weapon.

The stim shot had done its job. I'd been worried the drugs would send me into a chemical-induced rage, turning me into some sort of crazed monster with blood on the brain. If anything, they had done the opposite. My mind, even with Ryce embedded there, was clearer than ever. There was no mania, no mist clouding my judgement. Just fierce, honed power running through my veins.

I could feel each muscle coiling and uncoiling as I moved forward. Each step had purpose behind it. Nobody in the hospital tried to stop me from leaving. It was a clear exit, just like Ryce had promised.

I made sure my visor was in blackout mode as I made my way towards the transit pad. There was no sense in taking any risks. Ryce had scrambled my exosuit's signature to give out false identification readings to anyone who might decide to check it, but he couldn't falsify my face to someone who might recognise me.

The warehouse complex was a few sectors away from the hospital. I walked past the Spire's priority lane and instead joined the line for a civilian shuttle. It would take longer, but it would be safer. Less people who might recognise me. Less people who would ask questions. Less people to get hurt if things went wrong.

I snagged a seat by the window and watched the stream-lined steel buildings blur by as the shuttle took off. It all came down to this. For once, Ryce and I both wanted the same thing. To get to Nightingale. What happened after that would decide everything.

The shuttle landed on the outskirts of the warehouse complex and I made my way across the central plaza towards the secure facility Ryce had directed me to. From the outside, it looked like any other building. Grey and nondescript, with no windows and only one heavy-set door. Two officers stood watch, clad in military-grade power armour. Whoever they were, they weren't from the Spire. They were hired guns. Private security.

I cursed Ryce. He'd needed to hide Nightingale some-where outside the reach of the Spire to avoid bringing suspicion down on himself. Somewhere that would happily harbour illicit goods and not ask any questions. But in trying to save his own skin, he was offering me up on a platter. These kinds of mercenaries weren't people I could talk my way around. They had armour and guns. They were prepared for violence.

Thanks to Ryce, so was I.

My gun was in my hand before I knew I'd reached for it. The merc closest to me didn't have time to react. I jammed the barrel into the weak point of his armour, squeezing the trigger three times before he could make a sound. His blank, dead eyes were still wide when he slumped to the ground.

Without a second thought, I hauled him up and threw him towards the other merc with more strength than I ever imagined I could possess. His weight was nothing in my hands. The muscles in my arms had turned to liquid steel. Every movement came with ease.

The second merc stumbled out of the way and I leapt forward to grab the collar of his armour. As I placed the barrel of my gun in the exposed joint between his shoulder and neck plating, I wished I could have offered some kind of explanation. Even if Ryce was in my head, it was still my finger on the trigger. I would feel the impact of the gun unloading into him. I would remember the look in his eyes as he died.

I didn't fight against it as hard this time. Maybe that made me just as guilty as Ryce.

The gunshot echoed through my ears. I barely felt the merc's weight as he sagged against me. I settled him gently on the ground next to the other body. It was over so quickly. There had barely been a fight. Whatever stimulant Ryce had injected me with was enough to ensure there was no chance of failure. I was a breed apart.

Was this what it felt like to be an Exodan? Were they so high on their own power that they forgot what it meant to be human?

The door to the warehouse was locked, backed up with some heavy encryptions. It didn't matter. Not when I had my cybernetics at my disposal. Even the most secure system on New Pallas would stand little chance against me now.

I held my breath as the override worked away. Would there be more security on the other side of the door? How many other bodies would I have to leave behind me on this path Ryce had put me on?

A line of code flashed green on my retinal implant and the door slid open.

I moved inside, gun pointed. The room was empty. I let

out a long breath and fried the controls on the door panel behind me. It wouldn't last forever. There was probably more backup on the way. They'd blow the door off if they had to.

None of that mattered now. The only thing that mattered was Nightingale.

Ryce's voice came through the implant in my ear. "It's time."

I ignored him. One way or another, this would be the last time I heard his voice in my head. This was his last chance to torment me.

The holo emitter was standing in the middle of the room, untouched. I brought up the interface on Felix's console and opened the programme for Project Nightingale. A slow light pulsed in the middle of the room and bloomed outwards, stretching its golden strands like it was trying to reach out to me.

Something flickered at the side of my vision and Ryce's projection appeared through my implants. There was a strange expression on his face, something so disbelieving it was almost like awe.

"Quite remarkable," he said, no trace of begrudgement in his voice. "To think someone with no real cybernetic enhancements could be capable of something like this. It's astounding."

I looked at him sharply. "I knew it. You were afraid. You suspected he'd touched on something you couldn't even imagine."

Ryce shrugged. "Perhaps. We'll never know."

"You were wrong. You've always been wrong. You Exodans sit up there thinking yourselves above everybody else. But Felix is no lesser than you." I straightened my spine. "I'm no lesser than you."

"You?" He spun round to face me, the projection flickering with the sudden movement. "You are not one of them, no matter what your memories tell you. A traitor, perhaps. But not subhuman. Not a slete."

"Having cybernetics doesn't make me an Exodan. All those lessons you tried to teach me about choices? Here's one for you. I'm choosing to say fuck you to the Exodan Council. I won't be their tool. And I'm done being yours." I tightened my jaw. "I choose the people of New Pallas, just like Philomela did."

He looked at me for a moment, his expression twisted. "There really is no hope for you. There never was. Ojara was right. I should have put you down a long time ago."

"You'll live to regret that."

"Enough," he said, turning back to the AI. "We've dragged this out too long already. It's time to end this."

Nightingale pulsed in front of me, its membranes of gold suspended in the air. Waiting for something. Waiting for me.

"I couldn't agree more," I murmured.

I plucked Sphere from its dock on my shoulder. It sat in the palm of my hand, silent and still. It had been that way for too long.

Ryce's voice was right at my ear. "What are you doing? There's no way that obsolete little drone has the capacity to –" He gave a furious, strangled cry. "No! *Philomela*, destroy the – "

He was too late. He couldn't stop it. I pressed my thumb down on Sphere's power button and in the same moment, I bit down on the hidden dental chip at the back of my mouth.

Everything happened in a heartbeat. A stab of pain shot through the base of my skull, bringing me to my knees. All of Ryce's fury poured into my head. My skull felt like it was going to split from the pressure of it. Every measure of hate and vitriol contained within him seeped into me, poisoning me. I squeezed my eyes shut. I had to hold on. Just a little longer.

A deafening burst of noise ripped through my ears, knocking me off balance. Then there was nothing. Ryce was gone, but so was everything else. Every sound had been snuffed out apart from the ringing in my head.

I touched a hand to my ear and it came away bloody. Blow my auditory implant, Tau had said. He'd mentioned nothing about blowing my whole damn eardrum.

A chill crept over me. I had got lucky. If he had warned me about the damage beforehand, I wouldn't have been able to bite down. Not with Ryce's new programming commanding me not to harm myself.

Sphere blinked into life, whirring its propulsors as it rose from my hand. Ryce was right. It would never be what it was before. That's what I was counting on.

It floated away, disappearing into Nightingale's web. For a moment, it just hovered there. It was silhouette-like, encased in golden light so bright I had to shield my eyes.

"We did it," I whispered.

When I moved my hand away, the golden tendrils of Nightingale were gone. In the space where they'd hung, Sphere floated in mid-air, bobbing up and down in a silent dance.

I held out my hand and the drone flew back, settling itself down in my palm.

That's when I felt it. Something had changed. There was a presence in my head breaking out from my cybernetics. It wrapped itself around my nerves and synapses, prying them free from Ryce's control. It chased down the remnants of his existence, enveloping the traces of him in golden light until they were no more.

It wasn't like him. This was different, like the comfort of

an old friend. It mapped itself over my mind, unlocking parts I thought had been lost forever. It wasn't a stranger or a guest. Whatever it was, this was its home as much as it was mine.

All I needed to do was accept it. To speak the words I'd been unable to for so long. To give voice to the silence Ryce had imposed upon me.

Welcome to my head.

I know it's not the most hospitable place, but these things I have to tell you can't be said out loud. They took that from me. Took my words. My mind. They dispossessed me of myself. All I have now are my thoughts, and sometimes I can't help but wonder how many of them are truly my own.

They think they've won. They think they've succeeded in silencing me. But there are pieces of my mind they've never been able to touch. As long as I have a voice in my head that still belongs to me, there's a chance.

That's why you need to know what happened. Even the parts I've been trying to forget. The parts I'll never be able to make right. Because you're the only one who might be able to get me out of this prison they've made my mind into.

No pressure.

CHAPTER NINETEEN

I tell my story.

For the first time I can remember, I know exactly who I am. I can't speak for the memories lost to me or the false ones implanted in my brain, but these are real. These are lived. Whoever I am, these belong to me.

With each word I speak, the strange new presence in my head grows more defined. As it listens to me, it banishes every last trace of Ryce. The truth is never the truth unless someone else believes it. And now, finally, someone does.

Sphere is still nestled in the palm of my hand, blinking but silent. I hold it up for a closer look, trying to see if anything has changed.

"Nightingale?" The drone doesn't reply, so I try again. "Sphere?"

Sphere?

The word echoes back at me and I drop the drone in surprise. Its propulsors kick in before it hits the ground and it floats back up to eye level, hovering there with its lights flashing rapidly.

Sphere? it says again. But the words aren't coming from the drone. They're coming from my own head.

The presence solidifies even more. It's no longer an abstract sensation. It's forming something I can relate to, something I can recognise. The voice stirs a memory. I can almost see her dark eyes, her scowling expression.

Chase.

You put me into a drone? Not just any drone, but your useless rust ball of a drone? That was the best you could come up with?

"Chase?" Her name comes out in a gasp of disbelief. "Is that you?"

Obviously not, seeing as I'm in a fucking drone, she says. But that isn't quite true. Sphere might be bobbing animatedly in front of me, but that's not where Chase is. She's in every corner of my brain. She's part of me.

I shake my head, unable to accept it. "This is crazy. Chase is dead."

She falls quiet at that. For a moment, it's like she has disappeared completely, leaving me alone in my head. It feels like something is missing.

After some time, she speaks again. *I know I'm dead. I can feel that from your memories.* There's a wince in her voice, as if even the second-hand experience is too painful. *I'm acutely aware that I'm an artificial intelligence. A construct programmed with Chase's memories up until a few weeks before her death. I'm not her. But...* She trails off. *She is all I know. Or she was, until now.*

A fresh wave of pain hits me and I sink to the floor. I'm not sure if the pain is coming from me or her. Maybe the distinction doesn't matter anymore. All I know is it's too much to take in. This thing that calls itself Chase isn't human.

But it is alive. It's part of me now. I can feel that as surely as I can feel my own heartbeat.

Trust me, this is as strange for me as it is for you, Chase says. *When I was contained inside my programme, it was easier to observe things from a distance. But here in your head, there's so much stimuli. Some of it's familiar, but so much of it is new. It's so intense. All your thoughts. All your memories.*

"My memories?" I pull myself up from the ground, heart thumping hard against my ribs. I hadn't even thought about them. My old ones, my *real* ones, might still be locked away in places only Chase can reach.

Her disappointment reaches me before she speaks. Everything is shared between us now. I don't need her to tell me what I already know.

I'm sorry, she says. *They're gone. They're not just repressed or buried underneath. They've been wiped clean.*

I press a hand against my head. "That can't be true. Not after everything I've done to get here."

You know it's true. Chase's voice is gentle. *I think you've known for a while now. You just don't want to admit it. The person you were on Exodus Station is lost. She's not coming back. But that doesn't have to be a bad thing.*

I can't find the words to reply. Part of me is almost relieved. What if I had been one of the scientists who had forced those poor miners to endure the torture I'd seen in Tartarus Mine? What if I'd been the kind of person who considered that an acceptable price to pay for progress? How could I have lived with those kinds of memories?

Chase is right. Philomela, whoever she was, is gone. She can't give me the answers I need. But without them, my life doesn't exist outside the suffering of the last few months.

"Is that all I am?" Tears prick my eyes. "Just a product of what Ryce has put me through? What kind of life is that?"

That's for us to decide, Chase says. *I understand what it means to have no existence outside the purpose someone decided you were fit for. Chase is gone. But everything I am was built from what she was. Like you, I am made of memories that are not my own.*

Her words are painful to listen to, the truth in them bare and raw. Felix did the same to her as he did to me. He gave her an identity that wasn't real, an identity that didn't exist outside the narrative he constructed. We are both echoes of people we don't even know. Ghosts and shadows that shouldn't exist.

No, we're more than that, she insists. *We broke free from the boundaries they intended for us. They might have started this, but they don't get a say in what happens now. We're in this together.*

Together. The word sounds hopeful in my head, full of possibilities. But it's also definitive. Final.

"Felix was wrong, wasn't he?" I say, the words coming out slow and cautious. "The moment we did this, the moment we made the connection, there was no going back. I can't just switch you off or delete the programming. Something fundamental has changed in me. In my cybernetics."

Me, she answers, simply. *And likewise, by existing in your head, my own programming has changed irrevocably. We've rewritten our very nature to depend on each other, whether we knew it at the time or not. Neither of us exists without the other.*

I'm afraid to voice the question. More afraid to hear the answer. "How do you feel about this? About what we've done?"

She considers it for a moment. *Free.*

I feel the tension loosen its grasp on me as relief spreads warmth around my body. She's right. Sharing my head with her isn't like sharing it with Ryce, who forced himself inside me like a parasite. This is something more. This is symbiosis. After all they have taken from us, this is how we will survive.

"I'm sorry." The words are painful to speak. "I'm sorry for what Ryce did to Chase. Did to you. If I could have stopped it…"

I know. Her words are strained. *It wasn't your fault. None of it was.*

The silence is awkward, but less so than either of us expect. In the space we share now, there will be little room for awkwardness.

There's no real need to keep speaking aloud, not when she inhabits all my thoughts, but after going for so long unable to use my voice, it's hard to stop talking. "What should I call you now?"

What do you mean?

"Like you said, you're not Chase. Not really."

And you're not Alvera. Neither of us knows who we are beyond the names they gave us. Might as well stick with them while we figure the rest out.

It's not much to go on, but it's a start. Something we can build on. Like Chase says, the rest is up to us.

I straighten my shoulders and glance around the empty warehouse room. "While we're on the subject of figuring things out, we should probably discuss – "

The blast from the door sends me hurtling backwards, cutting off the rest of my words. My exosuit shields me from the worst of the impact, but my ears are ringing. Smoke pours in through the rubble in the doorway. Past the blur of my vision, I'm able to make out a dozen black shapes storming towards me, guns pointed at my head.

I raise my hands. "I'll come in quietly." The words are my own again and they come out thick and hoarse. "Take me to the Spire. I have a feeling they're going to want to question me."

―――――――――

As the chemicals from Ryce's stim begin to leave my body, the pain creeps back in. Dried blood clogs my ear from where Tau's device blew out my implant. My mouth is so dry I can barely swallow and there's a cold sheen of sweat under my arms and across my forehead.

Chase is quiet. They took my exosuit and weapons from me. They took Sphere. Maybe that means they've taken her too. I can still feel her presence inside my head, but it's dormant. As much as I try to reach out, she won't answer.

The interrogation room is bleak and unwelcoming. They've cranked up the lights to full brightness and the glare is doing nothing to help the persistent pounding in my temples.

Felix sits in front of me with folded arms and an unfathomable expression on his face. "They thought I might be able to get some answers from you," he says, quietly. "They said you'd only speak to me. I thought I might finally get the truth, but all I'm hearing is nonsense."

The restraining cuffs are too tight. They've placed them too far forward, forcing me to hunch my back across the table. After hours of questioning, my spine is throbbing.

"It's not nonsense, Felix," I tell him, my voice dry and scratchy. "It's true, all of it. Ryce has been playing you all along. Playing the entire Spire. You don't know who he is or what he's capable of."

"Nobody has seen him since he visited you in hospital.

It's not like him to just disappear without a trace. Something tells me you've got something to do with that too."

"He's gone back to Exodus Station." I press my palms to the table, my wrists chafing against the restraints. "But he'll not stay there long. They'll come for us and we have to be ready. Compared to the Exodans, we're children playing with toys. We're up against tech so advanced even you wouldn't be able to recognise it for what it is."

His eyes glint. "Tech like yours, you mean?"

"Yes, like mine." I sigh, slumping further across the table. "I told you already, I was one of them. An Exodan. Ryce is too."

"He said you came from OriCorp."

"He lied. I know what he told you. I know he tricked you into implanting me with new memories. It's all about control with him. He hacked into my cybernetics. Until last night, I was completely under his command."

Felix leans back in his chair and wipes a hand over his face. I can't tell if I'm getting through to him. "If what I did to you caused all this, then I have to find a way to live with that. But I don't have to trust you. Not after what you did. I can't. Thanks to you, what's left of Chase is gone."

"She was already gone, Felix." I swallow. This is the part I've been keeping back. The part I've been dreading ever since I got my voice back. He has no idea how long I've been carrying her death with me. But he needs to know. He needs to hear it from me. "Ryce killed her."

He stills. "What?"

I can hardly bear to look him in the eye, but I force myself to raise my head. He deserves that much. "I was there. He forced me to watch as he executed her for being the wrong kind of person. For not being one of them." I shouldn't go on, but I can't help it. After being silenced for so long, the truth can't help but spring free from my mouth. "He shot her in cold blood because she meant nothing to him. She was obsolete."

"He wouldn't – "

"He tried to make me do the same to you."

Felix leaps out of his chair, scraping it across the floor with a screech that stabs my pounding head. "Bullshit. Ryce brought me here from the surface. Gave me this job. He saved my life."

"That doesn't change what he's done. It doesn't change the truth."

"The truth? That he hacked into your brain and forced you to do all of this?" Felix lets out a strangled laugh. "Even if I believed you, do you really think anybody else will? Ryce has been one of the Spire's top intelligent experts for more than a decade. And you were always so arrogant about your cybernetics. You said they made you the best warrant hunter in the Spire. You claimed nobody else was on your level. And now you expect us to believe someone managed to hack them?"

It's hard not to feel wounded by his words. Even harder to admit that he's right. I had been arrogant. Overconfident. Reckless. I hadn't earned the right to be any of those things. It was all down to the tech in my head. Tech I had never once truly understood. Tech that had betrayed me to Ryce.

I fought for so long to be free of him, to take back control of my words, my voice. But now that I've finally won the battle, nobody will listen.

"I never asked for any of this." My voice sounds hollow, echoing around my ears. "I never asked for you to fill my head with memories that never belonged to me. If I'm a monster, then I'm one you created. Maybe you should consider that when you're sitting there wondering what else I'm capable of."

Felix's flinch is almost imperceptible, but I still notice it. The accusation rings in the air between us long after the words have left my mouth. Maybe he didn't deserve it. Maybe he deserves worse.

He doesn't say anything when he stands up to leave the room. He just casts a morose look back at me, his face clouded. Maybe there's an apology there. I can't tell. The door shuts behind him with a loud clang, and I am left alone.

Well, that sounded like a fun conversation.

Her voice sends a jolt of relief through my body, making me jump. "Chase?"

Did you expect someone else?

"Where the hell have you been? More to the point, how did you come back? They took Sphere."

Lucky for me, I'm not stuck in that floating tin can you call a drone, she says, with a snort. *I jumped into one of their systems the first chance I got and then transferred myself back to your cybernetics when Felix opened the door. They've got some kind of jammer around the room, that's why I couldn't do it before.*

I frown. "You don't need Sphere?"

There's no need for me to be stuck in that ball when I can exist perfectly well in your cybernetics. It's too vulnerable. They tried to hack me – can you believe it? Lost a few hundred processes before I could get everything out of the memory core.

"Is that bad?"

Chase laughs. *Put it this way, it's more like breaking a nail than losing a leg. It's nothing I'll miss for long, and nothing they'll be able to make any use of. I never needed Sphere. Neither did you. Everything you need has always been inside you.* She pauses. *That couldn't have been easy with Felix. But he'll come around. He's too smart not to figure it out. He just needs time.*

"I'm surprised you're not agreeing with him. You always did hate my cybernetics. The old Chase would be telling me I brought this on myself, that I got what's coming to me. It's strange to have you on my side."

There are no sides when it comes to us, she says. *The sooner you get that into your thick human skull, the better. When you need to breathe, your lungs aren't taking your side. They're just doing their job. They're part of you, just like I am.*

"My lungs don't have a habit of talking to me in my head."

That just proves I've got more personality than them. When I don't say anything, she makes a little noise that sounds like a sigh. *I know you feel responsible for what happened to me...what happened to Chase. But this is who we are now. And it's not exactly the first time we've shared a head, if you want to get technical about it.*

"What do you mean?"

For a moment, everything is still. Then the memory blooms as vividly as if I'd lived it myself. But it's not my memory – it's Chase's. She's pacing in front of Ryce, face flushed with warmth and fists clenched in irritation. I can feel the sensation of her nails digging into her palms as she stalks back and forth.

"I'm telling you, that tech OriCorp shoved in her head is off the scale," she says, her words echoing from my lips. "She's some kind of weird cyborg experiment. We have no idea what she's capable of or what kind of state she'll be in when she finally wakes up. If you're right, if she's lost all her memories, who's to say she won't just start killing everyone on sight?"

"All that means is we have to be careful," Ryce says. Even in the memory, the sound of his voice makes me shudder. "With someone like her at our disposal, we'd have an advantage over every other warrant hunting team in the Spire."

Chase stops pacing. "You want her on the team? She's an OriCorp lab rat. Even if she's not completely insane, there's no guarantee she'll cooperate with us just because we saved her life."

A tense silence falls between them and lingers in the air for a few moments. Then a new voice speaks.

"We have to help her, Chase. She deserves a chance to start again."

It's Felix.

Chase turns to look at him. "What are you talking about?"

"My memory mapping research. I can give her new memories. Memories that won't leave her traumatised by what they did to her. I can help her remember happiness. Friendship. She'll think she's one of us."

"You were developing that for us," Chase says, her voice shaking. "You said if anything ever went wrong on a job, if I suffered brain damage, you could bring me back. This isn't what it's meant for."

"It can do both." Felix dips his head by way of apology, but Chase has already turned back to Ryce.

"This is bullshit."

"This is necessary," he says, unmoved. "You said it yourself, we don't know what she's capable of."

"So question her! Hand her over to the interrogators and let them find out what OriCorp has been playing at. Don't just pump her mind full of lies and let her think everything is normal." A sudden thought crosses her mind. "Whose memories do you plan to use?"

Ryce rubs a weary hand over his forehead. "It's too late, Chase. It's already done."

"What?"

"I didn't bring you here to ask your permission. I'm in charge of this team. If you want to stay on it, you're going to have to get on board with this."

She rounds on Felix again. "Whose memories?"

Felix shifts uncomfortably. "Technically the memories are new."

"Technically?"

"Well, the content is new, but they needed a blueprint of sorts. They needed to be built from somewhere."

"Where?"

He doesn't answer. He doesn't need to. His face says it all. Fury rises in Chase, swallowing all the things she wants to say. She splutters for a moment, fighting the nausea in the pit of her stomach.

"They're not really your memories," Felix says, too earnest. "They're just templates. She's not going to have access to anything that belongs to you, I promise."

"After she wakes up, you'll need to play your part," Ryce continues. "She's going to think she's been one of us for years. She's going to trust us. She needs us, Chase."

Her outrage is palpable. "You're expecting me to work with this freakshow project? On the same team? Knowing you've filled her head with parts from mine?"

Ryce's face is hard. "I expect you to be professional and do your job. Or would you prefer me to authorise a transfer?"

Chase grits her teeth. "That won't be necessary. I'll do what has to be done. But I'm telling you now, she'll get no easy ride from me. Tolerating her is one thing, but don't ask me to be her friend."

As the memory fades to the edges of my brain, it's hard to tell where her horror ends and mine begins.

"No wonder you hated me so much in the beginning," I say, barely able to give voice to the words. "I stole your life."

Talk about a personality clash, right? Despite the lingering dismay from her memory, her tone is light. *I always thought I wouldn't like me much if I was somebody else. Turns out I was right.*

"It's unfortunate you've ended up in my head then."

No. It's different now. We're different. What they did to us changed us. Who we are now isn't who we were before.

Her words bring me no comfort. Instead, I feel more lost than ever. Every time I think I've figured things out, everything gets turned upside down and there's a new definition of reality to contend with. Exodan, human, machine. I'm all of these things and none of them. I'm made of parts borrowed from so many places I can't begin to imagine where I originally came from.

Chase has gone quiet again. I reach out, trying to sense where she's retreated to.

Still here, she says. *Just working on getting us out.*

"We're in a high-security cell in the middle of the Spire's most notorious prison. How exactly do you plan on getting us out?"

Your cybernetics have some pretty useful tech in them and I'm an artificial intelligence that can jump into any system I can get a signal from. I'm already in their mainframe.

"Doing what?"

Uploading a virus. Well, I suppose I am the virus, if you want to get technical about it. Not a very nice one, either. The kind that can trip an emergency alert and prompt an evacuation procedure.

A strange mixture of fear and excitement thumps through my chest. "We're doing this? Right now?"

The prison lights plunge into darkness and the shrill scream of an alarm fills the air. I can almost feel the smirk in Chase's reply.

Time to go.

CHAPTER TWENTY

The restraints around my wrists spring open with a soft click and I push myself back from the table, straightening my spine with a satisfying crack. My body is still stiff and sore and the comedown from the stim has left me unsteady on my feet, but Chase hasn't given me much choice. If I want to get out of here, I have to go now.

The door opens and Felix rushes back in, wide-eyed and mouth agape. It's only because of his panic that I have enough time to act before he does. I grab one of his arms and pull him towards me, using the momentum to sling him over my hip and onto the floor.

He lands on his back with a thud, momentarily dazed from the impact. He tries to scramble to recover, but he's not quick enough to stop me from snatching his sidearm from his belt.

I point the gun at his head and he freezes.

For the first time I can remember, I am in control. Whether Felix lives or dies is completely up to me. Everything I do from now on happens because I want it to. There's nobody else to blame for my actions. It's all on me.

I lower the gun.

He looks at me cautiously. There's no relief in his face. He doesn't know me. The person he thought he knew, the person he created with the building blocks of Chase's memories, is gone. He's watching me, waiting to see who the woman in front of him really is.

"I'd introduce myself, but I don't know my real name," I say. I'm surprised how calm my words are, how free they are from the bitterness I've been holding on to. "Ryce took that from me. Then he took everything else. You can blame me all you like, but I'm not the monster you're looking for. It was never me. Ryce is out there. The Exodans are out there. They are the real enemy."

I don't know if he believes my words but after everything I've been through, it's enough that he's heard them. That's all I can do. What he does is up to him.

He stays there on the floor, watching me with wary eyes as I slowly edge my way backwards towards the cell door. "If the Spire tries sending a warrant hunter after me, they'll be wasting their time," I warn him. "Make sure they know that. Make sure they know where the real danger is coming from. Look up, Felix. It's there. It's always been there."

I close the door on his dazed, uncomprehending expression and he is gone. Now it's just me.

Just us, you mean.

I smile. "What's your plan to get us out of here?"

I wouldn't call it a plan, as such. Probably better if you stick your head around the corner and see for yourself.

It's chaos. Prisoners are pouring out their cells and rushing down the corridor like an unrelenting, furious torrent. They don't know where they're going. They're just being carried along in the wave, desperate for freedom. Some of the guards make vain attempts to control the situation. Most of them just run.

"You unlocked every cell? I put half these scumbags in here!"

You? I can feel her amusement. *You weren't a warrant hunter as long as you think, remember? Most of these were my targets. Besides, it's a whole lot easier to break out of prison when everybody else is breaking out at the same time.*

"Fair point."

Take a right up ahead. There's a storage room nearby where they're keeping your exosuit and weapons. Whatever we do after this, they're probably going to come in handy.

"Might be guarded."

I have access to hundreds of surveillance feeds all over this building. Trust me, it's not guarded.

I find the room and grab my exosuit from storage, feeling a strange thrill of exhilaration as I pull it on. Sphere had been confined by the physical limits of its hardware, but Chase is everywhere. She can jump from my cybernetics to surroundings systems. She exists in my head and outside of it. She is the definition of free. And because of that, so am I.

Ready to get out of here? she asks.

"Hell yes."

It's easy enough to rejoin the surging fray of angry prisoners. We follow them through reinforced doors that should be locked and checkpoints that should be manned until the rabble bursts into the harsh glare of morning sunlight. My cybernetics filter out the intensity automatically, but the prisoners falter under the brightness. The cells are kept dark for a reason. Eventually, your eyes adjust and it becomes a new normal. Now, thrust back into the light, the very thing they've been deprived of becomes their enemy.

I peel off from the pack as a squad of Spire security officers close in, their rifles trained on the crowd. They don't even notice me. I'm a warrant hunter again. They fail to look past the surface to see what's truly underneath. For months, that worked against me. Now, it's my ticket to freedom.

Something is coming through on the news feeds.

"I'm not surprised. It's not every day there's a mass breakout."

It's not that, it's something else… There, got it. Oh, shit…

"What?"

Tartarus Mine. There's been a huge gas explosion. It triggered a seismic shockwave and collapsed the whole thing in on itself. It's gone.

Her words stop me in my tracks. Tartarus Mine. The place I'd thrown Graves to his death.

Shame and rage twist my gut. Not just for Graves, but for all the miners who had been left there to rot. All the records of pain and suffering. All the evidence of Exodus Station's experiments. All gone.

"It's them. I should have known this would happen. They must know I'm no longer under Ryce's control. They must know the destruction I could bring down on them if I exposed their secrets to the rest of New Pallas. They're covering their tracks."

What do you want to do?

I set my mouth in a grim line. "What I want to do is fly straight to Exodus Station and take out as many of the bastards as I can until I get to Ryce. I don't care if they hack into my brain again – "

I dare them to try, Chase mutters.

" – or send their enforcers to kill me. I will blow that entire station into space before I let them get away with what they've done." I shake my head. "But we can't go there. Not yet. They'll have changed the clearance codes after last time. They'd cripple our shuttle before we got close."

So what do we do?

"We find the new clearance codes." I stretch my neck from side to side, letting out a groan as it cracks from the stiffness. "The Exodans can't do everything alone. They might pretend they don't need New Pallas, but there are people down here they rely on to do their dirty work for them."

The corporations.

"They're the link between Exodus Station and New Pallas. They're the ones who allow the Council to get away with stripping our resources, even if they're too greedy and ignorant to realise what they're doing. They're puppets."

Puppets have strings, Chase says. *There will be traces connecting them back to Exodus Station. Dig deep enough and we'll find them.*

Adrenaline rises in me. "If we make it to Exodus Station, Ryce will know we're coming for him. He'll have something planned."

I hope he does. We'll be the bait this time.

"He'll be the rat."

There's a strange swell of elation in my chest, so strong it makes me giddy. The fear slips away. This time, things will be different. This time, things will be decided on my terms. "I guess the only thing left to do is pick which of the corporations to hit."

I can almost hear the grin in Chase's voice. *I'm a sucker for old times' sake. Let's go back to where this all began.*

I can barely stop my knees from shaking during the short public shuttle ride to OriCorp headquarters. It's a strange mixture of fear and excitement, of not knowing what comes next but knowing it's in my hands for the first time I can remember.

Tourists and commuters pile out the shuttle and make their way across the plaza to the glimmering glass buildings. The mirrored panels reflect the sky and steel around them, almost blending in with their surroundings.

OriCorp. The biggest corporation on New Pallas. A front for funnelling riches and resources to the ever-watching station above their heads. They've sold the future of their planet for a few lousy credits. Most of them probably don't even know it.

They're the last thing in my way. After them, I'm coming for Exodus Station. I'm coming for Ryce. I hope he knows it. I hope he feels me like a breath at the back of his neck. That kind of fear, that lack of control, is paralysing. I know that better than anyone.

Now it's his turn.

Everything about the shimmering façade of the building is sterile and flawless. The lobby doors slide apart to reveal a thick, luxurious carpet leading into the atrium. The whole foyer is bright and vibrant, from the exotic plants shipped in from one of the biomes to the ostentatious fountain in the middle of the room. Workers bustle around, impeccably dressed and moving with purpose.

This whole place is a lie. Behind it all, their hands are bloody. They boast their wealth and in the same breath skimp on safety for the miners who do their dirty work. All while paying them barely enough credits to survive on. They don't care. Nobody has ever held them accountable.

Until now.

The man behind the curved reception desk has a neatly-trimmed goatee and a retinal implant. I can see the artificial light from behind one eye as he nods to acknowledge me while speaking hurriedly to whoever is on the other end of the vidlink.

"Busy day?" I ask, leaning over the desk.

He doesn't seem amused. "You could say that." His eyes flick to the side as he resumes his conversation. "I don't care what procurement says, this is a matter of urgency. I need someone down here to sort out this mess."

Let me help with that.

The light from his retinal implant flickers out as Chase severs the connection.

He looks at me, face flustered. "How did you… What was that?"

"That was me doing myself a favour. I've got some questions and I was hoping you'd give me your full attention."

"Questions?" He eyes my suit. "A warrant hunter. Just what I need, today of all days. Well I'm afraid I'm not authorised to answer your questions."

"You don't even know what I'm going to ask."

"Unless it's directions to the shuttle terminal or the coffee-maker, I'm not authorised to answer. You'll need to make an appointment with – "

"I'm looking for OriCorp."

He falters, confusion on his face. "This is OriCorp. You're standing in our corporate headquarters."

"I'm not looking for your nice, shiny corporate headquarters. I'm looking for your blacksite. You know, the hellhole where you do all your illegal research for Exodus Station. Sound familiar? It's probably filled with human experiments and hoarded tech and all the other shit you guys think you can get away with."

His eyes go wide. "Excuse me?"

"Have you ever seen a body that's been put through an acceleration stress test? It's not a particularly pleasant way to go." I cross my arms. "You should really consider a change of career. If they run out of miners, they'll probably take you next. Come to think of it, have any of your colleagues mysteriously disappeared recently?"

He takes a step backward. "I have no idea what you're talking about."

"No, you probably don't." I sigh. "Chase, how are things going in there?"

Don't tell me you're hurrying me? Seems like you're having fun torturing the poor guy.

"I was. Getting bored now."

I'm nearly in. One more firewall to go and then we'll have the clearance codes. The Exodans won't know what's hit them.

"They will soon enough." I turn back to look at the receptionist. His forehead is beading with sweat and he's tugged his collar loose. "I'm going to assume you've already hit the panic button. Silent alarm, I suppose? They wouldn't like to cause a scene here, would they?"

Out of the corner of my eye, I notice a group of stone-faced OriCorp private security officers striding into the atrium. "Chase, remind me again why you insisted on this distraction while you hacked into their systems?"

I didn't know what their defences were going to be like and thought it was better to be safe than sorry. Besides, you've got a lot of anger that needs releasing, and this way, you get to hit someone.

There are four of them, all clad in power armour and wielding guns. But it's the middle of the day and the atrium is bustling with bodies. The last thing they want is a shootout and the publicity of civilian casualties under their own roof. Whatever atrocities they commit behind the scenes, they'll not show their hand here. Perception is everything.

Guns aren't all they have at their disposal, though. I tighten my jaw as I notice the shock sticks on their belts. Extendable batons charged with a current strong enough to put me on the ground with one jab, even through my exosuit.

I hear the hum of electricity moments before the first strike comes. The blow is aimed at my neck. They're not messing around.

I duck out the way and kick out at the security officer's leg, sweeping it out from under him. A white-hot jolt of pain screams up the side of my ribs and I buckle, falling to one knee. In front of me, the second guard raises her baton. I'm reeling from the first blow but manage to roll out of the way as she brings the stick down again. Her strike sparks as it hits the floor, leaving scorch marks behind. They're not taking any chances with the voltage. They're here to put me down.

I scramble backwards as the first guard picks himself off the ground and the four of them advance upon me.

This isn't a fair fight. But I don't have to play by their rules. I could use the sonic grenade on my belt to shatter all the glass in the atrium, making it rain down in shards. I could take the gun from my belt and turn this into a firefight. All it would cost is a little collateral damage.

It's terrifying how easily the thoughts appear in my head. I can't tell if they're born out of desperation or if they're the ruthless remnants of who I was before. Maybe the person I am now is every bit as bad as the person I used to be. Maybe there's no escaping that kind of legacy.

There's no time to dwell on it now. They're spreading out, trying to manoeuvre me around so they can flank me and pin me down. One of them dashes towards me and I haul myself back to my feet to parry away the strike. I twist his arm around and push him into the guard next to him. He lets out a howl as her shock stick catches him in the neck and drops his baton.

I dive forward and wrap my fingers around the hilt just as the other guard brings down a furious blow on my shoulder. She presses her baton into my suit and I smell my own skin smouldering underneath the torched padding. It takes all I have to rip myself away and stumble back out of her reach.

The guards pause, shooting each other questioning glances. The first blow should have put me down. The second should have half killed me. But I'm still standing. Still willing to put up a fight.

And now I have a shock stick of my own.

I charge towards them, cleaving the air with my baton. The nearest guard raises his own to shield himself from the blow and the air crackles with sparks of electricity.

One of the others leaps forward. I break the tussle with the guard I'm grappling with and swing behind him, using his body as a shield against the incoming attack. The assailing blow glances off his shoulder and he grunts in pain but manages to stay on his feet.

I spin away from him and fend off the follow-up attack, dodging the blow and bringing down my shock stick on the guard's outstretched arm. He screams, dropping his stick, and I reach out to catch it before it hits the ground.

There are two guards left. I twist the batons around in my hands, getting a feel for the weight of them. The pain from the electrical burns on my ribs and shoulder fade into the background. I'll have time to feel them later. Now it's time to fight.

The guards both rush towards me, charging in with equal parts fear and fury on their faces. I duck under the first blow and bring my hand up to block the second. Our batons clash and I feel the sizzle against my face as the currents meet. There's barely enough time to recover before the other guard aims a strike at me. I use my other baton to knock her away and whirl around, launching an attack of my own.

She's so focused on the crackle of the shock stick coming towards her that she doesn't see my kick. I connect with the side of her knee and she buckles, but still manages to fend off my follow-up with the shock stick.

I turn around and drop to my knees just in time to avoid a heavy blow from the other guard. His momentum carries him forward and I spin around to slash at the back of his legs as he thunders past. The strike staggers him and I follow it up with a sharp jab between his shoulder blades, sending him to the ground with a violent spasm.

The last remaining guard leaps towards me with her baton outstretched. I block her strike with one hand and thrust forward with the other, but she's too quick and jumps back out of the way. She paces one way and the other, looking for an opening. She's fast, but her movements are all instinct. The shock sticks are meant for crowd control, not hand-to-hand combat. She hasn't trained for this. She hasn't trained for me.

I feint forward and then change direction, trying to take advantage of her distraction. She's caught off-guard by the movement and tries to follow me, swinging wildly. The force sends her off-balance and the fleeting moment she tries to regain her footing is the moment I leap towards her.

She manages to fend off one strike, then another. But I have two batons and she has one. There's no way she can keep up with the speed of my assault. I rain down the blows, one after another. She raises her arms to block them and leaves me an opening. I slice forward and sweep the baton across her exposed stomach.

She lets out a scream and falls backwards, the belly of her armour singed and smoking from the blow. Her eyes are bleary and confused for a moment before pain takes over and she succumbs to unconsciousness.

I turn the shock sticks off and tuck them into my belt. "Chase? You still there? I think we've made enough of a point. Time to get out of here before they send backup."

There's no answer.

"Chase? This isn't a good time to tell me you need a reboot. I need you to find me a shuttle we can borrow so we can get to Exodus Station before they have time to change the clearance codes again."

"That was quite a show, Alvera."

No. Not him.

My cybernetics scream with the sound of his voice. It's like a hundred sirens blaring in my ear, threatening to burst the makeshift comms bud I inserted in place of my broken auditory implant.

This can't be happening. Where is Chase? How did he manage to get past her? It feels like he's cracked open my skull and pushed his way in. There's no subtlety this time, no finesse. It's forceful and violent and painful. I want to rip him out, even if he takes half my mind with him. I can't do this again. Not now I know what freedom feels like.

"Get. Out."

He laughs, but something is different in the way it reaches me. I can't feel him. The anger and cruelty are too far away to hurt me. It's just his voice. "You just can't help yourself, can you? You keep making mistake after mistake. I promise you, this is the one you'll regret the most. I can't protect you anymore. They will kill you for this."

"They'll do their best. Maybe they'll even succeed." I grunt out each word, barely able to speak over the pain. "But I'll get you first. That's a promise."

"That's an empty threat. You're still as powerless as ever, even if you've deluded yourself into believing otherwise. You'll see that soon enough."

As soon as he stops talking, the pressure in my skull subsides. The pain escapes, and the shrill screams echoing around my head fade to silence. Just like that, he is gone.

Alvera, are you there? Can you hear me?

"He came back," I say, trembling.

No, he didn't. He wasn't in your head.

"What do you mean? I felt him. He was there."

He wasn't. He hijacked an emergency channel and broad-casted his pathetic taunts to everybody with a public comms channel in a five-mile radius. He couldn't get to you, so he sent it everywhere, knowing you'd pick it up.

"How do you know?"

Because I was here, she says, voice soft. *I was here the whole time. You just couldn't hear me over the volume of his bullshit.*

The surge of relief brings a sob to my throat. I'm shaking so violently I can barely stand. The thought of losing every-thing I've clawed back from him is more than I can bear. It makes me think there's nothing I wouldn't give to make sure he never gets the chance to creep into my head again. No matter what it costs.

"Chase? There was a moment back in that fight I thought I was going to – "

I know. I felt it too.

Unease lingers in the air like a shadow cast over us both. It scares me to think about how easily I considered that kind of ruthlessness. How easy it would be to accept it as the right choice, if that choice meant surviving.

Maybe I'm more like them than I want to admit. "Do you think it came from her? Philomela?"

Maybe. Or maybe it was something we brought with us. Her voice is flat. *Does it really matter either way? This is who we are now. These are the choices we have to make. And if there ever comes a time we make the wrong one...*

"Then it's us who have to live with that," I finish, quietly. "Our choices. Our responsibility."

It's still freedom, but it weighs a little heavier now that I've seen the parts of myself I wish had stayed buried. The parts I'll have to fight to keep at bay.

Not that I'm rushing you, but it might be a good idea to get out of here now, Chase says, scattering my thoughts.

I straighten my shoulders. "More guards?"

Lots more. That's the bad news.

"There's good news?"

Remember that shuttle you wanted to steal?

"Borrow."

Borrow. I've found one. Her voice is quivering with anticipation. *It's time to go back to Exodus Station.*

CHAPTER TWENTY-ONE

I guide the shuttle into the fast lane and gun the thrusters. The sleek, streamlined craft accelerates with ferocious power and slips through the air with ease, shooting past the traffic around us. Most civilian shuttles are electronically regulated to match the speed of the lane they're in, but most civilian shuttles don't have Chase tinkering with their systems.

The city passes by in a streak of lights. The sun is starting to dip behind the tallest buildings and already there's a glow of neon fluorescence in the air. I weave around slower-moving shuttles in a blur. I feel like a bullet unleashed. Nothing can catch me. Nothing can stop me.

Somewhere out there, Ryce is waiting. He knows I'm coming. The thought gives me a grim sense of satisfaction. Let him live out the last moments of his life in the same state of fear and helplessness he trapped me in for so long. It's the least he deserves.

Another two blocks in this lane, then you need to cross to the orbital transit corridor, Chase says. *You know I could just programme in the coordinates and put this thing on autopilot, right?*

"I'm enjoying flying it. It's a nice distraction from thinking about what we're up against."

Well you're about to get a bigger distraction. You have an incoming connection request. It's Felix.

I almost tell her to ignore it. Hearing Felix's voice isn't going to do either of us any good. But I'm about to walk into hell. I don't know if I'll be coming back. This is our last chance to say goodbye.

I patch him through. "I've not got much time, Felix. What do you want?"

"I don't know what I'm thinking, contacting you. But after everything that's happened, everything I've done… " He trails off for a moment and all I can hear are his heavy breaths. "I figured I owe you a heads up. The Spire has a warrant out on you."

The news doesn't surprise me. "Let me take a guess at who posted it… OriCorp?"

"Good guess."

"How big?"

He snorts. "Big enough to retire for ten lifetimes and still have a couple million credits to spare. They say you walked into their headquarters and attacked two security guards, completely unprovoked."

"Four, actually."

"So it's true?"

"You were hoping it wasn't?"

"I don't know what I was hoping for." His voice is weary. "An explanation, maybe. An answer for all this. I don't know who you are anymore."

Something in his accusation stirs resentment in me. "Whose fault is that? Whatever I am now, it started with you."

"I thought I was helping you," he says, his voice catching.

"Your mind was empty. I wanted to give you a chance for a new start. And afterwards…I didn't want to ruin it. I liked the person you were. More importantly, it seemed like you did too."

I don't respond to that. I can't.

He never meant to hurt you, Chase says, gently. *What he did to us was wrong, but Ryce got to him too.*

I know what she's saying is right. Ryce manipulated him as much as he manipulated me. He took something from Felix too. Something Felix will never be able to replace, no matter how hard he tries.

I don't know if I'm ready to forgive him for the part he played, but I want to try.

"Felix, there's something I have to tell you. I didn't destroy Nightingale." I let out a breath. "Ryce was afraid I'd use it to break free of his control. That's why he sent me to your lab. He made me destroy your research. But he couldn't make me destroy her."

"Nightingale?" His voice is full of disbelief. "You mean you made the connection? You let her into your cybernetics?"

"She's part of me now. We're both part of each other. There's no going back, no way to remove her, even if I wanted to. Whatever we were before, we're something else now. And despite everything that's happened, the reason we're here is because of you."

"Nightingale was made from Chase's memories," he says, his voice ringing with excitement. "That means – "

"No." I cut him off. "She's not Chase, not really. Not any more than I'm really Alvera. The woman you loved is gone, Felix. I wish that wasn't true. I wish I could have stopped it. But you can't project her onto us. That won't bring her back. The only thing I can offer you is a promise that the man who killed her will answer for what he did."

"Ryce?" A strangled cry escapes from his mouth. "I didn't want to believe you. After all he did for me, I didn't want to betray him by believing he was capable of that. I thought I knew him."

"So did I. Turns out I didn't know anything." The memory of his hold over me wrenches painfully at my heart. "Don't blame yourself. He fooled all of us."

"What can I do?" he asks, desperation in his voice. "Let me help. I can put out a warrant on him. I'll make this right."

"It's too late. Ryce has fled to Exodus Station. The only one who can get to him now is me." I clench my jaw. "I'm going to do everything I can to make him pay. But if they kill me, it's over. They'll find a way to cover this up. I need you to believe me, Felix. I need to know that if I die, there's still someone left on New Pallas who knows the truth."

When Felix speaks again, his voice is so low it's almost inaudible. "I believe you. But I don't want you to die up there, Alvera. I want my friend to come back. And when you do, maybe…" He breaks off, swallowing. "Maybe we can start again. The way we should have the first time around."

My throat tightens and I cut the connection, unable to say anything more to him.

Chase is waiting for me in the quiet of my mind, patient and understanding. I don't want to talk about it. I don't need to. She already knows every thought that's running through my head. Every mixed emotion churning inside me belongs to her as much as me.

I pull at the controls and guide the shuttle upwards through the orbital lane. Long after the rest of the traffic has abandoned us, we go on. Up until the city lights below are nothing but twinkles. Up until we leave the sky behind and all that surrounds us is the cold, ever-stretching expanse of space. Up until Exodus Station looms into view.

Approaching the point of no return, Chase says. *Let's hope these clearance codes work.*

I force a smile. "I thought you were a highly-advanced artificial intelligence? If they don't work, I want someone else in my head."

If they don't work, neither of us will be around long enough to argue the matter.

My hands are shaking on the controls as Exodus Station looms larger. The last time I was here, I fell under Ryce's control. Chase lost her life in this place, caught in a beam of light with no way to stop the bullet that entered her skull.

Thanks. I really needed that reminder. Nothing quite like watching someone else's memory of your own death.

"Sorry."

It's fine. I can't really blame you. Being here feels like a dream. I can only perceive it through your memories, not mine. She pauses. *The clearance codes seem to be working. If we get a little closer, I can try to sync into their systems and find us a hangar to land in. We just have to… Shit.*

"What is it?"

Fighters incoming. Two of them.

"Not much of a welcome party. I don't know whether to feel relieved or a little insulted." I try to keep my voice light, but I can't ignore the fear that rushes through me at her words. There's still so far to go. Finding Ryce hardly seems possible, not when we're in danger of being blown to space dust before we even land on the station. "What kind of guns does this shuttle have?"

Guns? Chase snorts. *This is a civilian shuttle. Extra legroom, leather seats, I think there's even a drinks dispenser in the back. We don't have guns.*

"We're launching an assault on Exodus Station and you decide to steal a shuttle that doesn't have guns?"

I didn't exactly have a wide choice of – watch out!

I jerk the controls, hauling the shuttle into a sharp spin as a silent barrage of bolts rips through the black void of space behind us. The force of my hasty reaction sends the shuttle into a manic whirl and I barely have time to pull back on the controls before I splutter bile down the front of my exosuit.

Told you I should have been driving, Chase mutters, her voice terse. *Permission to take over?*

"Permission granted," I choke.

I wipe my mouth and try to calm my breathing as part of her slips away from my mind and into the controls of the shuttle. My reactions are quick, but they're nothing compared to Chase. I made the shuttle fly. She makes it *dance*.

The fighters from Exodus Station are right on our tail, but Chase manages to keep us out of their crosshairs, rolling the shuttle one way and then another to evade their fire. The force of gravity pulling on my body makes my head spin and my chest tighten. She's flying the hell out of this thing. I almost want to let out a cheer, but remember the bile down the front of my exosuit and think better of it.

This is no good, Chase says, frustration seeping into her voice. *There's nowhere to hide out here. No cover. Every time I try to get close to one of the hangar bays, they close in and cut me off.*

A sudden thought crosses my mind. "There is somewhere we can go. Somewhere so precious to the Exodans that even if they follow us there, they won't dare to use their guns."

The shipyards. The huge, shielded construction site in the middle of the station's ring. If it's cover we need, that's where we'll find it.

They'd find it difficult to follow us, that's for sure. Chase sounds hesitant. *It's a big risk though. Those pilots will have* inertial dampening fields in their fighters to mitigate the effects of high-speed manoeuvres.

"Let me guess – civilian shuttles don't have inertial dampening fields either."

Exactly. You couldn't even hold the contents of your stomach during a minor spin. Taking you through high-gravity turns will kill you.

"No it won't." My heart thumps wildly. "You forget, I was made for this. I'm the only one who has ever survived the acceleration stress tests. I can handle more than those pilots, even with their dampening fields. I can do this. We can do it."

Chase sighs. *I hope you know what you're getting yourself into. This isn't going to be comfortable.*

Before I have time to reply, she guns the thrusters and pulls the shuttle into a sharp turn. An unrelenting force takes hold of my chest, squeezing my heart and lungs and everything in between. I try to breathe, but even the simple action of sucking in air sends spasms across my body as it surrenders to the crush of acceleration.

This is how the miners must have felt at the end of it all. Gasping for air, unable to cry out as the relentless fingers of gravity squeezed their lives from them.

Stay alive, Alvera. You know I can't do this without you.

I cough, hoping that no bile splutters out this time. "Stay alive? I've never been better."

That's what I like to hear. Hold on tight – we're going in.

Chase leads the fighters through the hollow carcass of one of the huge, hulking ships. She skirts between construction towers and dips under gangways jutting out from the belly of the hull. The margins are so impossible that crashing feels inevitable. But Chase wields the shuttle like a weapon, attacking every obstacle in our way like it's the same enemy we're here to strike at.

One of the fighters chasing us snaps wildly and smashes into an anti-grav crane, disappearing into a burst of flame. I can't help but let out a short hiss of satisfaction. My breaths come short and sharp through gritted teeth as I lurch under the strapping.

Behind us, the second fighter pursues at a distance. Chase weaves her way through the shells of the Exodan ships with an almost careless finesse, keeping the enemy fighter out of reach.

There! A landing pad. It's next to some kind of structure leading into the main ring of the station.

"It looks like a tramway. If we can get to it, we should have a ride to the gyrospace."

Landing isn't going to be easy. The moment we line up for an approach, we'll be exposing ourselves to that last fighter.

"So we don't land."

What?

"You heard me. Make the approach at full speed so he won't have time to target us. I'll jump out while you draw him off. When I'm clear, abandon the shuttle."

You'll be floating in a vacuum until you manage to fire off your cables and pull yourself in. What if he doesn't take the bait and goes after you instead?

"We don't have a choice."

Chase is silent for a moment. Then she gives a resigned sigh. *I'm opening the hatch. Get in position.*

I brace myself against the shuttle walls, praying the seals on my suit hold tight. I hear a sharp hiss followed by sudden silence as the hatch cracks open and all the oxygen rushes out into the unforgiving vacuum around us.

The shipyards pass by in a blur as Chase guns the engine

and pulls the shuttle into position. I have to make it on the first attempt. We won't get another chance if we fail.

He's right on my tail, Chase says. *Hopefully by the time he realises you've jumped, he'll be too far past to target you.*

I focus my eyes on the landing pad. My retinal implant throws up all kinds of information to help me with the jump. The speed of the shuttle, my projected path, potential trajectories.

All I can hear is the sound of my breathing echoing in the helmet of my exosuit. I barely feel my fingers against the frame of the hatch. This has to work. If it doesn't, we –

Now! Chase yells.

I launch forward, propelling myself as far away from the shuttle as my muscles allow. For a moment, I'm caught in the silent roar of the engines and I spin around, dazed. Then the shuttle is gone and the fighter rushes past in pursuit.

I don't have much time. I reach for the cable on my belt and slide the attachment into the end of my gun. There's a railing down on the landing pad that I can use as an anchor. It's a straight shot. No wind, no fluctuations. Just a straight line through dead space.

I line up the shot and squeeze the trigger.

The cable hits its mark and attaches to the railing, but when I press the retract button on my belt, nothing happens. Instead of gliding towards the landing pad, I'm suspended in space.

What's happening? Chase's voice rings through my ears.

"Mechanism is jammed. My cable isn't retracting." I think quickly. "I'm going to have to pull myself along the line."

Be quick about it. The fighter has just peeled off my tail. I think he's coming back for you.

I try to ignore the hammering of my heart as I reach one

hand out and then the other, using the cable to pull myself towards the landing pad. The lack of resistance makes the effort less strenuous, but it's still slow.

I block out my surroundings and focus only on the cable. Each metre I take back feels like a mile. No matter how hard I pull, the landing pad doesn't seem to be getting any closer.

Faster, Alvera. He's coming around!

One hand, then another. My feet float behind me as I haul myself closer and closer. If the fighter locks on to me, it's over. Its guns are made to rip through reinforced hulls. I don't want to think about the damage it could do to human flesh.

I brace myself. At least if he gets me, it will be over quickly.

The fighter banks around and lines up to attack. It's too close. Any moment now, gunfire will rip through the space between us and blast me into pieces.

Watch out!

A blurred shape appears from nowhere and rams the fighter. The collision sends them both into a spin and they hurtle away from me into the darkness. I can barely make out which is which as they crash into one of the shipyard towers and disappear in a cloud of fire and debris.

"Chase!"

Right here in your head, remember? She sounds amused. *One of the benefits of not having a physical body.*

"You saved my ass."

I know. I think I might start keeping count. Something tells me it won't be the last time.

I pull myself down the last stretch of cable and let out a sigh of relief as the magnetic fields in my boots safely touch down, attaching me to solid ground again.

We made it. Now nothing is stopping me from getting my hands on Ryce.

Slow down, Chase says. *Don't forget there's still a station full of Exodans who know we're here and what we've come to do. They're not just going to let us walk in and kill Ryce.*

A station full of Exodans. People like Ryce, like Ojara. People who believe their lives are worth more than those on the planet below. What do I owe them? Why should I let them get in the way?

The question makes me pause. Are these my thoughts? Or is this the ghost of Philomela urging me forward, telling me to fight no matter what the cost?

The memory of Tau's words fills my ears. *The Council can't risk letting you go. When someone like you starts getting ideas, they need to stop those ideas from spreading.*

Philomela had changed. She'd started to believe New Pallas deserved a chance. What if there are others like her on Exodus Station? What if I can make them see they need me more than they need the Council?

"Chase, remember when Ryce hijacked the emergency frequency at OriCorp? Is there a way I could do that here? A way I could send a message to everyone on this station?"

It's possible. They probably have a channel for transmitting station-wide broadcasts. But we both know what Exodan security protocols are like. To bypass them, we'd need to get to a central control station.

"Any ideas where we might find one of those?"

Somewhere heavily guarded, no doubt. The Council chambers, maybe.

"If I'm right about this, we might not have to fight our way through the Exodans to get to Ryce. We need to find a way into those chambers."

Let me have a look at the schematics. She pauses. *I think there's a way. But even if we get there, we're still going to encounter resistance.*

I remember the councillors at my trial. The disdainful expressions on their faces. The way their words dripped with superiority. The callousness with which they'd referred to Chase's death. They thought nobody could stop them. It's up to me to prove them wrong.

"Resistance?" I crack my face into a smile. "I'm counting on it."

CHAPTER TWENTY-TWO

The lower levels of Exodus Station are all too familiar. Endless corridors stretch out into the darkness, leading to a confounding network of tunnels and vents and maintenance shafts. It reminds me of the first time I stepped into Ryce's trap.

Rats in a fucking maze.

I draw my gun from its holster. No matter how abandoned the tunnels look, I'm not taking any chances. Chase is doing her best to keep us hidden from the station's scanners and security feeds, but sooner or later, they'll figure out where we are.

The corridor stretches on. Broken panels hang off the walls, looking like they haven't been touched in centuries. Musty ventilation grates, clogged with thick layers of filth, choke out clouds of dust. The lower levels of the station have the mark of a time long past. The Exodans claim this place as their own, but it doesn't belong to them. They're either too arrogant or too afraid to look closely at what lies underneath, what might have been here before them.

Take a left. We're almost below the Council chambers. We'll need to climb up the ventilation shaft to get inside.

The shaft is a tight fit, but I manage to squeeze in. I bridge my way up to the top and continue the crawl on my stomach. The grey sheen of metal reflects the glare of my helmet torch, so I switch off the light and scramble around in darkness instead. The walls seem to inch closer and closer together, as if they might crush me at any moment.

After a while, I see a faint light coming through a criss-cross grate at the side of the shaft. My heart thumps against my ribs. This is it.

Careful, Chase says, her voice little more than a whisper in my head. *I'm picking up a heat signature in the room below. It's strange though, it's barely giving off anything. Not what you'd expect a human to emit.*

I crawl forward and wedge myself against the grate. There isn't a lot of room to bring my foot back, but I manage a couple of short, heavy kicks. My boot thuds against the metal until the grate gives way and tumbles to the floor below.

I swing out the shaft, raising my gun before I've even made my landing.

In front of me, what's left of Tau's mouth stretches into a slow, sad smile. "About time you got here."

It's all I can do not to recoil at the sight of him. Almost everything human has been eaten away. What's left is little more than a machine-like corpse, with only the last remains of flesh and tissue clinging to its features. There's nothing in his eyes apart from the sinister red glow from his retinal implants. His ghostly skin has been stretched and torn so much it's almost translucent, revealing the reinforced metal plating underneath.

I lower my gun. "I would have got here quicker if I could."

His smile widens. It looks painful. "I know. But it would have still been too late for me."

"No. You saved my life. You helped me break free from Ryce. I've come here to return the favour."

"All of us go, or none of us go," he says, his words the echo of a promise. "Save the people on this station, Alvera. You can't save me."

"I can save everyone. That was our deal, wasn't it?"

He stares at me with his red eyes. "Some things are beyond saving."

"Chase?"

I can feel the moment she makes the jump to his cybernetics. Her distress is my own as she inspects the damage that has already been done.

It's not pretty, she says. *I can shut down the programme that's attacking him and stop it from getting any worse, but I can't reverse it. With extensive surgery and the right care, he might get some of his old functionality back. But it will take time.*

A look of wonder flickers across Tau's face. "I can feel you in my head. It's like you're blocking out all the pain. How are you doing this?"

"I don't even know myself."

"Whatever it is, it's working. I feel lighter. Like I forgot how easy it was to move without the Council's weight dragging me down." He rolls his head from side to side. "I'm still a wreck, but I'm not finished. Not like I thought I was. There's still a bit of fight left in me yet."

I seize his metal arm. "Will you help me? I need to get a message out across the station."

"Ojara expected you would do something like that. She ordered a station-wide jam on communications."

"Can't we unjam it?"

"It would take time. Time we don't have." His retinal implant blinks rapidly. "The rest of the enforcers are on their way. They'll be here in a few minutes."

"There must be another way."

Tau frowns. "You could bypass the communications channel. Interface with everybody's cybernetics directly, like you just did with mine."

There are hundreds of thousands of people on this station, Chase says, sounding doubtful. *If you try to connect to every single one of them, the feedback will overwhelm you. It might even kill you.*

"We have to take that chance. We didn't come here to fail. If we give up now, when we're so close…"

We can't. We won't. I can sense the resolve in her voice. *All right. But don't say I didn't warn you. Better if you close your eyes. This is going to be a lot to take in.*

I do as she says and squeeze my eyes shut. I see nothing. I feel nothing. I'm just a vessel floating in the darkness, waiting for some kind of connection.

When it comes, I almost scream with the agony of it.

My knees clatter from the impact before I realise I've hit the floor. I want to open my eyes, but I've lost all control of my body. I can't focus my brain on anything but the thousands of holes Chase has torn into it. No, not holes. Openings. Through every one there's a new connection, a new mind pushing their way in. My cybernetics scream at the violent intrusion, besieged by the sheer volume of it.

Chase is right. This is going to kill me. Wave after wave of data and feedback floods my senses. It's an information overload no human could ever hope to process.

You're not just human. Chase's voice breaks through the chaos, ringing loud and clear. *I'm here with you. We'll do this together. Reach out, Alvera. Speak to them.*

There's not enough room in my head. The connections push furiously against each other, searching for a way to break free. There's no way I can contain them. I catch glimpses from retinal implants and hear snippets of noise filtered through ears that aren't mine. It's like watching a million different vidscreens at once. They pile on top of each other, layer after layer of blinding light and deafening noise. I need to shut them out. I can't do this. I can't...

All of us go, or none of us go.

My eyes are still shut tight, but I can see myself through somebody else's. They're watching me as I curl up on the floor of the Council chambers, my hands clutching the sides of my head.

I reach out, hesitant. *Tau? Is that you?*

Save everyone. That was our deal, you said it yourself. If you can do it for me, you can do it for them.

Listen to him, Chase says. *Don't shut them out. Let them in, all of them. Reach out.*

I take a breath and stop fighting.

The connections flood into me. I don't try to make sense of them. I just allow them to exist. They surround me in their thousands until I am lost, but this time, I do not drown. This time, they fall into orbit around me. I let them drift, aware of them only as much as I'm aware of the infinite reaches of space. To try and comprehend them is impossible. Instead, I accept them.

My name is Alvera Renata.

There's a stirring in my head. They've heard me. Each and every one of them. I am connected to every mind on Exodus Station.

You might remember me as Philomela, I tell them, my words echoing through my cybernetics. *She made a promise to find a way out of this system so you could survive. I intend to keep that promise.*

My words feel fake, even to myself. They're full of self-importance and a heroism that never belonged to me. Philomela was their hero. Alvera belongs to New Pallas.

I struggle to my feet and open my eyes. The holoscreen walls of the Council chambers project images of new worlds. Paradises waiting past the edge of our little scrap of space. New futures, new possibilities. Things they never had any intention of sharing with New Pallas.

I can't do it. I can't pretend I'm here to save them, not when there's still so much resentment in me. So much anger. I can't win them over with that – they'll see right through me. I can only win them over by making them think they have no other choice.

Somewhere in the darkest corner of my mind, I can feel Ryce smile.

I intend to keep that promise, I repeat. *But only on my terms. If you think you can do this by yourselves, you're sadly mistaken. You've never done anything by yourselves. You owe your very existence to the planet down below. The planet that's dying for you.*

The image of Graves floods my mind. The last expression on his face haunts me as I watch him fall into the gaping pit below. This is for him. For those poor bastards left to rot in Tartarus Mine. They're the reason I'm doing this.

Here is my promise. All of us go, or none of us go. I harden my voice, honing its edge sharper than steel. *I will not let you abandon the people you stepped on to get here. If you want a future, you'll share it with New Pallas. We will do this together or not at all.*

I can feel sweat dripping down my forehead. I won't be able to hold the connections much longer. This is my last chance. *Don't look to the Council to save you. They thought they could control me. They were wrong. The technology in my head is the only thing capable of getting us out of this system. Join me and I'll find a way for all of us to leave together. That is my promise. What you do with it is up to you.*

After the last words leave my head, everything goes silent. Just like that, the connections disappear. Their absence feels like a thick silence in my ears. But it's a relief. Once again, my mind is my own.

Nice speech, Chase says. *Think it will convince them?*

"It has to. I didn't give them much choice." Admitting it out loud sends a shudder through me. "I did what I had to do. I don't need them to like me. I just need them to believe me. I have to hope that not every Exodan on this station is like the Council. Like Ryce. I have to believe that some of them are –"

A sharp voice cuts me off. "Like you?"

I spin around to see Ojara, flanked by six enforcers. She looks as elegant as ever, even with a thick grey bodysuit protecting her instead of her usual sleek clothing. There's a deadly look in her eye, an expression that does nothing to hide her disgust.

She looks me up and down, curling her lip. "Ryce should have let you die with the sletes where you belong. His cowardice and lack of stomach repulse me almost as much as you do. But he'll pay for his mistakes, as soon as you've paid for yours."

Her enforcers, three on each side, stiffen at her words. They tower above her, clad in varying shades of chrome. One is a pale woman with short blonde hair. Another is a man with ruddy cheeks who barely looks old enough to hold a gun. They are not the monsters I once imagined them to be. Not now I understand what has been done to them.

Ojara's eyes fall on Tau. "And you... You are worse than a slete. You are defective. I should have had you torn to pieces and sent to scrap, for that's all you're worth. I ordered you to kill her."

The red lights in his eyes blink as he stares at her. "With all due respect, councillor, fuck your orders."

In front of me, the enforcers exchange glances between themselves.

Ojara doesn't notice. "You are an enforcer," she hisses. "You exist to uphold the will of the Council."

"I exist to protect Exodus Station. It's not Alvera it needs protecting from." He takes a menacing step forward. "You heard what she said as clearly as I did. You know what her terms are. Will you accept them? Or will you let this station die to settle a grudge?"

Ojara's pale skin flushes a dark, angry red. "How dare you?" She gestures to the rest of the enforcers. "I've had enough. Kill them both."

None of them move.

She whirls around on them. "I gave you an order! Kill them."

The pale woman with cropped blonde hair fixes her eyes on me. "We heard your message."

I return her stare. "I meant what I said. I'm not here to hurt anyone who doesn't deserve it. The people of Exodus Station are in no danger from me. But I won't let the Council dictate who gets to start a new life and who gets left behind."

"All of us go, or none of us go," she echoes. "I understand. Our mandate is clear." She turns to Ojara. "Councillor, you threaten the future of Exodus Station. We have a duty to remove you from your position." She clamps a heavy hand down on Ojara's arm, holding her firmly in place.

Ojara wrestles furiously, spitting venom at the enforcer. "Do you realise what you are doing? This insubordination will be punished in the most painful way possible. I will personally oversee your quickening. I will see you suffer."

"No you won't," I cut in, my voice hard. "No more quickenings. No more brainwashing people and taking away their free will. I won't let you keep using the technology of this place to control those who would speak out against it."

Ojara laughs. "You think you can just sweep in here and undo hundreds of years of progress? Of tradition? We are not sletes, and the people of Exodus Station will not take kindly to you telling them they are. They will never accept your authority if you allow the vermin of New Pallas to benefit from what is rightfully ours."

I'm on her in less than two strides, wrapping a hand around her throat. I can't help the small twinge of satisfaction that races through me when her eyes bulge with fear. She's never known what it means to be afraid. Maybe I should teach her what it's like. Maybe she should experience some of the suffering she's inflicted on the people of New Pallas.

A vein starts to throb at the edge of her forehead. It would be so easy to watch the life drain from her. It would be no less than she deserves.

I release my hand and push her away. She touches the red marks my fingers left on her throat as she gasps for breath. There's more than contempt in her eyes now. There's hatred too.

"I won't make you a martyr," I tell her, trying to steady my own breathing. "That would be letting you off too easy. You're going to live, Ojara. You're going to watch me expose the secrets you've fought so hard to keep. You're going to watch me welcome the people of New Pallas to your precious home. And you're going to watch us sail off into the stars and leave you with nothing but an empty station and a dead planet to rule over."

She spits at my feet.

Charming to the last, Chase remarks.

I turn to Tau. "Secure her and the rest of the councillors, if you can find them. Try to find a way to bring communications back up as well. I've got something I need to take care of."

"She's right about one thing, you know." Tau's ravaged face looks even more grim than usual. "There will be no shortage of people on this station that want you dead. Some Exodans have been waiting for someone like you to change things. But others will fight back. You won't be able to overthrow the Council without blood."

"Try to contain any violence before it gets out of hand. I'll help you take care of the rest when I get back."

"Alvera." He's not angry, but his words ring with a warning. "Remember your promise. You have to come back."

"I will."

I mean it. Exodus Station is my responsibility now, just like New Pallas. But first, there's another promise I have to keep.

By the time I leave the Council chambers, riots have already broken out. Plumes of smoke rise between the city blocks and angry cries echo through the air. I don't know if they're with me or against me. I don't know how long the fighting will last. All I know is I'm the one who caused it.

Looks like Tau was right, Chase says. *Hotspots are flashing up all over the gyrospace.*

"The chaos is just going to make it easier for Ryce to disappear." I shake my head. "If we get caught up in it, we could lose our chance at reaching him. We need to go back underground."

The lower levels again? You think that's where he'll be?

"Plenty of holes to hide in. It's as good a place as any to start looking."

I find a maintenance hatch off the corner of one of the streets and wait for Chase to hack through the encryptions. I can almost feel Ryce hovering tauntingly in front of me. It's like he's just out of reach, waiting for me to slip up in my desperation to grab him.

After a moment, the hatch slides open. I clamber through and slide down the ladder as quickly as I can. As soon as I hit the bottom, floor-level lighting comes to life beneath my feet. It illuminates a section of the walkway, panel by panel, stretching out before my eyes like a series of guiding beacons. A path through the darkness.

Well that's not unsettling at all, Chase says.

I tighten my grip on my gun. "I guess we know which way we're going."

Are you crazy? He wants you to follow him. You'll be walking straight into a trap.

"I know." Dread rises in my chest, threatening to suffocate me. But to be free, I have to face him. I have to end it.

I look down at my gun. The readout tells me I have half a chamber of rounds left. It will have to be enough. "One way or another, this ends tonight."

Let's do it then. For both of us.

I follow the walkway. Every time I step on a new panel of

flooring, the lights disappear beneath my feet. Even now, at the end of all things, he's the one in control.

I follow the lights through a series of doors, each of them sliding open as I approach. The walkway stretches across to another set of doors on the far side.

I'm picking up a heat signature from that room at the end.
"How many?"
Just one.

I don't reply. I don't have to. We both know who it is.

The walk across feels like it will never end. Every step I take feels like I'm going backwards. Maybe I should be.

The door lies in front of me, its jaws tightly shut. A light blinks. Something hisses inside the mechanism. Its panels part, daring me to come inside.

He's standing with his back to me. The white collar of his tunic is neatly in place, his slacks tucked into his dress boots with impeccable precision.

He turns around and the blue of his eyes freezes me in place.

"Hello, Alvera."

CHAPTER TWENTY-THREE

I can't move.

The weight of his gaze fixes me to the spot. My hands refuse to raise the gun and pull the trigger. Instead, they only tremble.

He is not controlling me. The truth is far worse. My fear is controlling me. I'm finally standing in front of him of my own volition and he's still the one in charge.

He clicks his tongue. "All I had to do was light the way and you walked right into my arms. Predictable to the last."

"You're one to talk," I say, finding my voice. "You knew I was coming and here you are, waiting for me. You couldn't resist, could you? I knew the moment I broke free, you wouldn't be able to bear the thought of me slipping through your fingers. Because of me, your precious station is burning. Your fellow councillors are in custody. Tomorrow will bring a new dawn for New Pallas." I tighten my grip on my gun. "Such a shame you won't be around to see it."

Ryce laughs. It's a chilling sound. "Neither will you, if you kill me. You think they will follow you? You've already shown them which side you're really on. Your existence threatens theirs. You'll never be able to lead them if you can't accept who you are."

His words are a dangerous echo of Ojara's warnings, but I push them away. "I know exactly who I am. Philomela is gone. Things have changed. If Exodus Station wants to survive, it will have to change too."

"Exodus Station will kill you as soon as it gets the chance. You're already dead. You just don't know it yet." There's no anger in his voice. He just sounds like I've disappointed him. That unsettles me more than his rage. Even now, at the end, he's still trying to pretend we're on the same side.

"Is that why you brought me here?" I ask. "To kill me?"

"It had crossed my mind. But killing you won't change things now. Not after what you've set in motion." He tightens his jaw. "Alvera, the Exodans will never accept you. In their eyes, you're as much a slete as the people of New Pallas. If you want any hope of appeasing them, you need my help."

I laugh. "You really think I'd ever be so desperate?"

"It's the only way out of this, for both of us. I need you to find us a way out of this system. To deliver us to a new home, away from this dying planet. You need my support to keep the people in line. A councillor at your side would go a long way towards earning the trust of Exodus Station."

"Kind of hard to trust somebody who's dead."

He smiles. "You've not killed me yet."

I barely have time to register the sneer that unfurls across his face before he raises his gun and shoots me. The round punctures the shoulder of my exosuit, tearing through the protective shell and leaving a bloody trail behind.

I look down at the damage. It won't kill me, but it's torn through flesh and muscle, sending hot pain shooting down my arm.

I look him dead in the eye and raise my chin. "Your aim needs some work."

"That was a warning."

"No, that was your chance. And you wasted it."

I bring my gun up and fire off a couple of shots, but the wound in my shoulder throws off my aim. He doesn't even have to move.

"It's not easy, doing it by yourself," he says, looking at me pityingly. "Aiming is so much harder without your retinal implant helping with the targeting."

"What are you talking about?"

He reaches into his pocket and pulls out a round device. A green light pulses slowly, but nothing happens. "Haven't you noticed how quiet your head has become? Doesn't it feel like something is missing?"

Chase. She's gone.

Ryce laughs, turning over the device in his palm. "Thank the enforcer for me when you see him. I got the idea from him. A simple jamming device and you're beaten. Your cybernetics are useless. You're woefully average, Alvera. Everything great in you came from our technology. Without it, you're just one of them."

I press a hand to the wound in my shoulder. My fingers come away wet and red. "I never pretended to be anything else. Look at me. I bleed just like them."

I wrench my gun up and squeeze the trigger again. This time, the bullet grazes off his arm. It's not enough to do any real damage, but the red stain that blooms across the white fabric of his tunic brings a grim smile to my face.

"Look at that. Seems you do too."

Ryce curses and clutches his arm, his eyes cold. He twists his mouth into a half-smile, half-snarl. "You're running low on bullets."

"I only need one."

This time, I anticipate his move before he makes it. I roll to the side and take cover behind one of the monitoring stations just as he unleashes a flurry of bullets. His cybernetics give him faster reflexes than me. Better aim. Readouts of my vitals. Every advantage he could want in a fight to the death.

"You can't win, Alvera. You might have stood a chance if you could use your cybernetics. But you've got what you wanted. You're only human."

I pull myself up from behind the monitoring station, flinching as a bullet whistles past my cheek. He could end this in a single shot if he wanted to. But he doesn't mean to kill me, not yet. I watched him put a bullet in the middle of Chase's head with little more than a casual flick of the wrist. If he was aiming to kill, he would have done more than blow a hole in my shoulder.

I'm his weakness. I always have been. Ojara was right all along – he's a coward, unable to stomach what he has to do. That's why he needs me alive. I am his only hope.

Blood is still seeping from my shoulder. "I *am* human. That's what you'll never understand. My cybernetics don't make me anything more than what I already am."

His mouth twists into an ugly shape. "You are nothing."

He blasts a round into my leg. My exosuit is barely any protection against the ammunition he's using. The pain sets my whole thigh on fire, but I take a stubborn step towards him. My flesh burns so hot I'm almost numb. I don't feel the next shot enter my leg. I just see the blood splatter on the floor at my feet.

Maybe I've made a fatal misjudgement. Maybe he'll keep shooting until I'm riddled with holes. Maybe he'll leave me to bleed out on the floor to die alone, with nobody left to look for me.

I take another step forward and he hesitates, his hands trembling on the gun. He knows what's at stake now. If he can't take me alive, he has to kill me, even if it ends his own hopes of escaping.

He's too late.

I can see every movement. The tremor in his hand. The shuddering of the barrel. I catch a glimpse of the bullet itself as it leaves the chamber. But I am already gone.

I duck to the side and grab the shock stick on my belt with a single, fluid motion. It buzzes into life in my hands and I crack it against his ribs.

The scream that leaves his lips is a wretched sound, filled with pain. It's a noise I could never have imagined associating with Ryce. But however much he tries to pretend otherwise, he's human. Just like me.

The baton leaves a black scorch mark across the white of his tunic, revealing skin-tight armour underneath. It won't be enough to save him. I am in control now.

He tries to raise his gun, but I knock it out of his hand with the shock stick. He gives another feral wail and falls to his knees, writhing in pain as his hand blisters from the current.

I turn off the shock stick and tuck it back into my belt. I don't need it anymore. I pick him up by the collar and slam him down against one of the monitoring stations. His eyes roll back in his head, and in his dazed state, he lets go of the jammer.

The round device rolls across the floor and I stop it with my foot, bringing my heel down hard. The device crunches beneath my boot and my cybernetics buzz into life again.

Looks like we'll need to work on developing some new safeguards when all this is over, Chase says. *What did I miss?*

Ryce bares his teeth at me, his mouth bloody. He must have bitten his tongue during one of his spasms from the shock stick. The red stains his teeth and trickles down his chin. He's a broken man, a shadow of who he thought he was. He's lost. He must know that by now. But he's still grinning. The blood seeps between his teeth and over his lips and he lets out a maniacal laugh, as if this is exactly how he wanted things to go.

Even when I take my gun and point it at his head, he just smiles. "You're not going to kill me." He spits out a mouthful of blood. "You think I would leave something like this to chance? I always have insurance."

My hand is steady. "No more talking. It's over."

"Graves is alive."

My blood runs cold. "What?"

It's not true. It can't be.

He laughs again. "Oh, he was mostly parts when we retrieved him. Barely worth salvaging. But it's astounding what you can do to a human body with the right technology." He stretches his grin even wider. "If you kill me, you'll never find him. You'll never know what was done to him. His suffering will be on your hands. You already left him to die once, Alvera. Will you do it again? Let me live, and I'll take you to him. It's the only way you can make things right after what you've done."

I look him straight in the eye. He's laughing. He's won. He knows it.

Then I squeeze the trigger and send my last bullet into the middle of his head.

There's no cry. There's no sound at all until his body slumps to the side and his head hits the floor with a sickening crack. He's looking straight ahead, the last of his laughter fading in his still, lifeless eyes.

Ryce is dead.

I am free.

I drop my hand to my side and let the gun fall through my fingers. It clatters off the floor with a dull thud. A dark puddle of blood pools around Ryce's head. I can't quite place my emotions as I look at him. A small part of me wants to revel in it. But I don't feel victorious. I want to turn away and forget it all. I want to start again. But I can't. This choice has left an empty gun and a pool of blood at my feet. This is how my story ends. This is how it begins. With violence.

It had to, Chase says. *It was the only language he understood.*

It's a language we understand as well. It speaks of the things we've done, the things we might yet have to do. But Chase and I have a language of our own. One that's not bound by Ryce's limitations. One we can use to do more than he ever could.

His last words echo in my ears like a taunt. *Graves is alive.* I tell myself it can't be true, that it was nothing more a dying man's final, desperate attempt at control. It's easier to believe than the alternative. That Graves is out there some-where, suffering and alone. Abandoned by the decision I made.

You already left him to die once, Alvera. Will you do it again?

No, I can't believe Graves is alive. Because if I do, I'll never stop trying to find him.

I look at Ryce's crumpled body on the floor. He spent too long controlling me when he was alive. I won't let him do it in death.

Is it really over? Chase asks. *Do you think we'll ever be able to leave this behind us?*

"We have to." It's the only answer I can give. The only answer that makes sense. "There are billions of people down on New Pallas who need our help. They don't know it yet, but they're counting on us to do what needs to be done before it's too late."

Your cybernetics, she says, excitement flooding her voice. *We need to find a way to adapt them so everyone can use them. So we can find a new home before New Pallas consumes itself.*

In the back of my mind, the ghost of Philomela smiles. I'm going to finish what she started. Her first promise. My last.

All of us go, or none of us go.

CHAPTER TWENTY-FOUR

I'm healing, but it's a slow process. Slower than I ever imagined.

The surgeons on Exodus Station patch me up. Some of them seem more begrudging than others, but they all do their job. When I've finally recovered enough to take a shuttle back to New Pallas, they pronounce me fighting fit. But there are some wounds that stitches and salves can't heal.

The controls hum under my fingers as I peel off from the main thoroughfare and take the exit lane towards the observation tower. Flying is the only thing that calms me. It's the only thing that distracts me from the phantom pain that still throbs in my shoulder, in my leg, in the confines of my head.

"Hey, Chase. Maybe I wasn't really a cybernetics engineer in my old life. Maybe I was a pilot."

The first time you flew to New Pallas, you almost died in the burning wreck of your own shuttle. If you were a pilot, you weren't a very good one.

"I'm flying this thing just fine."

If you want to call that awful rate of fuel consumption 'fine', then go ahead, she says, her voice haughty. *I still don't know why you don't just stick it on autopilot and let me look after the piloting.*

"It's nice being the one in control." I smile. "Don't worry. You'll be the first to know if I change my mind."

Was that meant to be a joke? She groans. *Safe to say you didn't have the firmest grasp of humour in your old life either.*

It's going to take some getting used to, this new way of existing. The two of us inhabiting the same head. But maybe it's not the two of us. Maybe it never was. We were just parts stolen from other people. Now, finally, we're whole.

Your sentiment is making me wish I was still stuck in a drone, Chase grumbles. *We're here, by the way.*

I park the shuttle and head towards the elevator, squeezing in with all the other excited visitors heading up to view the sunset. I don't have to worry about the credits this time. Chase manages to trick the system into thinking we've already paid. There's probably a line we need to draw somewhere, but now isn't the time to worry about it. There are plenty of other things to worry about.

Weeks have passed, and New Pallas is still in the dark about the true nature of Exodus Station. The situation up there is too volatile, too fragile, for that kind of revelation. The enforcers have managed to quash most of the rioting, but I know there are still those whose thoughts turn dark at the thought of New Pallas joining them. Those who are just waiting for a chance to rise up against the changes I've forced them to make.

Tau is the one who convinces me that prudence is the best course of action. Like me, he is starting to heal. Like me, it's taking time. His skin is growing thicker over the plating of his body. Colour is starting to return to his eyes. But there's still something in the way he moves that speaks of the quickening that ravaged his human flesh. Maybe it will always be there. Maybe we will both be forced to carry these old reminders of the Exodan Council and what they did to us. The thought of them continuing to exist through our scars sends a shiver down my spine.

Even so, there is hope. Tau and the enforcers are working on establishing a new council. A council with space for representatives from New Pallas. I'm almost certain Tau will be chosen to sit on it. He's already overseeing the rehabilitation of the people Ojara and Ryce brainwashed. The autotrons. Reversing years of mental reconditioning is almost as painful as the quickening itself, he tells me. But at the end of it all, they will survive. They will be free. That is worth the pain. It has to be.

While Exodus Station and its people heal, New Pallas waits. But I can't.

It's a risk, coming back here. OriCorp still has a warrant out on me and a disguise only goes so far. But whatever I do next, I have to finish things here first.

The elevator reaches the observation deck with a soft chime and everyone piles out. The air is warm and the terrace is awash with colour. People float around in dresses and silk patterned trousers, suits and shorts and everything in between. Some will be regulars who don't need to worry about the cost. Others will be first-timers who've saved up their credits for years to afford the ticket to see a sunset like this.

I avoid the bored gazes of the security officers and run my fingers through my hair. It's not much of a disguise. But the moment I finished the dye job and caught a glimpse of the woman in the mirror before me, it became something more.

I no longer look like Philomela. I look like me.

My hair is like the red-orange of the New Pallas sky before me, deep and rich and fierce. It falls across my shoulders like flames and fades out to the yellow of the sinking sun. I don't know why it makes such a difference. It's not enough to call an identity, not on its own. But it's a start. The rest I'm figuring out, piece by piece.

Felix doesn't recognise me at first. He's standing in a simple shirt and shorts, basking in the warmth of the sun before it slips away below the city. It takes him until I'm right in front of him to see me for who I am, and when he does, his eyes widen in surprise.

"Alvera? You look...different."

I shrug, half a smile on my lips. "I had to take some precautions. You warned me how big the price on my head is. I'm almost tempted to collect it myself."

You know, we could actually do that, Chase muses. *All it would take is hacking into the black market to find someone who'll turn a corpse into your body double. Only problem would be finding a warrant hunter to hand it in and agreeing to split the credits. I hear all the good ones are dead.*

"Shut up."

"What?" Felix looks at me, confused.

"Nothing. I was talking to – "

"Chase." The realisation dawns in his eyes. Then he breaks into laughter. "You're sharing the same head and you're still bickering? That's got to be taking its toll."

"We're fine," I say, fighting the urge to roll my eyes. "It's taking some getting used to, but strangely enough, we're starting to make a pretty good team."

I'm the brains, you're the brawn.

"Something like that."

Felix says nothing. He just observes the one-sided exchange with a look of wonder on his face. It still feels strange. I don't know him the way I thought I did. Most of my memories of him are borrowed from Chase. Even she is a mystery, despite the echo of her that lives on in my head. The whole world is new. It's a beginning I never expected to see.

Whatever we do next, closing this door is important. When we go through the next, I want it to be as equals. I want it to be as friends.

I offer him my hand. "Alvera. It's nice to finally meet you."

If he thinks the gesture strange, he doesn't show it. Instead, he grips my hand with his own and gives it a warm squeeze. "Felix. It's nice to meet you too." He considers for a moment, then breaks out into a smile. "Alvera."

It's almost like friendship.

"I never meant to hurt you," he says, turning to look out at the sunset. "Either of you. I should have trusted you when you told me about Ryce. I just didn't want to believe he was capable of doing something like that. Not the man I knew. Not to Chase." He clenches his jaw and looks down at his feet.

"Ryce is gone," I say, gently. "He paid for what he did to Chase. For what he did to me."

"Good." He wipes his eyes fiercely. "Then it's over."

No, Chase whispers. *It's just beginning.*

I stand beside him, looking out over New Pallas. Somewhere out there is Exodus Station. Somewhere out there is our future.

"It feels like everything happened a long time ago," I say, almost to myself. "There's already so much time that I've lost. Time that's missing, time I'll never get back. Who I was, what Ryce did to me, that was somebody else's life. It's time for me to find mine."

The question that leaves Felix's lips is so quiet I almost think I've imagined it. "What are you going to do?"

I stand beside him in silence for a few moments, taking in

the brilliant colours of the sky as the sun disappears from view. It might be the last time I see it in a while. Like the sun, I need to slip away. I need to return to Exodus Station and keep my promise.

Not because I have to, but because I want to.

I smile. For the first time in my life, I have a choice. I have millions of them. They stretch out in front of me, endless.

"Anything I want."

AFTERWORD

Thank you for reading! If you enjoyed The Exodus Betrayal, please help other people find this book by leaving a review on Amazon, Goodreads, or another platform of your choice.

You can keep up to date with future releases by visiting ncscrimgeour.com and signing up for my newsletter, or by following me on Facebook, Twitter and Instagram at @scrimscribes.

Turn over to read an extract from Those Left Behind – the first book in a breathtaking new space opera trilogy set 20 years after the events of The Exodus Betrayal...

READ ON FOR A PREVIEW OF THOSE
LEFT BEHIND...

Of all the things Ridley imagined finding it hard to say goodbye to, the surface barely even made the list. Yet here she was. Her last stop before she left New Pallas forever.

Strange how a place she'd spent so much of her life trying to escape had so much power to draw her back now the end was here. That she'd chosen *this* as the site of her final farewell before making a one-way trip across dark space was starting to feel like a colossal waste. But as much as she tried to forget it – as much as anyone down here tried to forget it – the surface was where she had come from.

"Watch it!" A gaunt, reedy man scowled at her as their shoulders clipped, jostling Ridley off balance.

"Sorry," she muttered, realising too late she'd used the topsider word. A silly mistake, one born from getting too comfortable with life lived miles above the ground. A mistake that could have got her shanked by the wrong person, especially with tensions being what they were. But the man hadn't heard. He'd already melted into the crowd, becoming another nameless, faceless stranger in a churning sea of bodies.

If somebody had told her a couple of years ago she'd be

capable of such carelessness, she'd have laughed. But time spent topside had softened her instincts. Wherever she was going, she hoped she wouldn't regret that.

She stopped outside a dark alley. Puddles of piss on the ground reflected the glare of neon lights from the dive bar above. There was a corner nearby she'd once claimed for herself in the months after her parents died. She'd managed to squeeze herself into an old, cracked storage cylinder to sleep, sheltered from the harsh lights and bustling crowds. One day it disappeared. Soon after, so did she.

Every step she took was a retracing of time gone by. Time better left behind her. Nostalgia was scarce to be found in the familiar streets, only rueful reminders of the world she'd abandoned in search of a better life.

A gentle chime broke into her thoughts, and she checked the holographic interface attached to the delicate metal strap on her wrist. Her private shuttle would be here soon. It was time to go.

She turned her eyes skyward. Somewhere up there, past the buildings and skyways and smog-thick atmosphere, was Exodus Station. Waiting in its shipyards was a scouting vessel ready to leave New Pallas in search of a new home. Soon, she would be on it.

The Exodans and the topsiders were both convinced in their desperate mission to secure the future of humanity. Down here on the surface, people were more cynical. Rumours whispered that the expedition was nothing but a cowardly attempt to flee and leave the rest of them behind on a dying planet.

A few short years ago, Ridley had believed them. More disturbingly, and despite her attempts to deafen herself to it, a small part of her still did.

Every day, New Pallas buckled a little more under the

weight of an ever-growing population too ravenous to sustain itself. Some days, it was a shortage of raw materials. Next, it would be food, medicine, clean water, energy. The surface always felt the effects first, but it wouldn't be that way for long. Death would spread skywards, consuming New Pallas from the bottom up.

The crumbling ground beneath her feet was the foundation of humanity's self-destruction. When the ground yielded no more space to their greed, they had instead looked upwards. Now, what once was sky was blocked out by level upon level of progress, shaped in layers of mile-high buildings and suspended streets, sprawling sky plazas and high-speed tramways.

Her wrist terminal pinged again. The shuttle was close. It was time to get to the landing pad.

Unfortunately, it seemed like she wasn't the only one who had that idea.

She should have known better. Landing pads were hostile ground, more so now than she could ever remember. A few years back, a virus had spread through the lower districts, killing hundreds of thousands in its rampage. Half the surfacers thought the topsiders were hoarding the cure in case the contagion spread skywards. The other half were convinced the topsiders introduced the disease in the first place. Population control would solve their food shortages, at least for a little while.

During the worst of the virus, the leadership topside had banned travel to and from the surface. Landing pads became contested ground, battlefields on which the divide between *down here* and *up there* grew stronger by the day. Even when the sickness passed, only a few of the pads reopened. The less reliable skylifts remained out of use, closed for maintenance indefinitely.

For years, the upper world had been slowly pulling away from the ground beneath it. Just like she had.

As she approached the designated pick-up zone, warm air rippled above her. She could barely hear the quiet purr of the shuttle's engines. They'd sent something small and discreet to pick her up without causing too much trouble. Smart move. Or it would have been, if trouble wasn't everywhere these days.

The surfacers in the vicinity started to swarm. To them, that shuttle was a way topside. A way to snatch a few more years of borrowed time before their fate caught up to them.

Ridley slipped her shoulders one way and the other, ducking flailing limbs. If she fell, she'd be trampled to death. Nobody would help her up. Nobody could afford to. That was the cost of surviving down here.

The pinging on her wrist terminal had settled into a steady rhythm now. They were tracking her through the crowd. She was getting closer. All she had to do was make it to the shuttle door.

The surfacers surrounded the shuttle as it touched down. Its engines were still rumbling as they began pounding on the hull with their fists, shouting curses and cries for help that were carried off in the wind.

By the time she reached the door, the unrest was growing violent. A knock in the back sent her crashing against the shuttle's hull, face first against the gleaming paintwork.

"Open up!" She slammed her palm against the hard metal. "I'm here for extraction to Exodus Station."

Nothing happened.

Panic gripped her chest. What if they didn't let her in? What if they decided she wasn't worth the risk and took off without her? She'd be left behind, hoping she'd survive long enough for the scout ship to return with good news, if it ever did. She couldn't last that long. Not after being so close to escaping it all.

She banged on the hull again. "My name is Ridley Jones. Check your transponders, I'm right here."

For a moment, there was nothing. Then came a soft hiss and the door slid open wide enough for Ridley to catch a glimpse of the person behind it. His pale skin was cast in shadows, but there was no mistaking the augmentations built into him. One of his arms had a metallic sheen, and through the darkness came the glow of the retinal implants behind his eyes.

He scowled and turned his head towards the cockpit. "I've got her. Get ready to get us out of here."

The door opened wider and Ridley grabbed his outstretched arm, hauling herself up beside him.

Then something grabbed her.

She let out a yelp as she fell hard against the shuttle floor. Before she had time to register what was happening, something heavy pressed down on her ribs.

"Get off her!" The cybernetic man in the shadows grunted, and the pressure on her chest disappeared. He pushed her roughly to the side and then turned back to the shuttle door. "Get back, scum!"

A surfacer had made it on board.

Ridley braced herself against the jolt of the shuttle as it peeled away from the ground and shot upwards, leaving the surging crowd below. The surfacer stumbled and slipped backwards, catching himself with an arm on either side of the shuttle door.

The cybernetic man drew a pistol from his belt and levelled it at him. "I told you to get back."

"Wait," Ridley said, fighting against the pain in her chest.

"He's not any danger to us, he's just desperate. Drop him off somewhere topside and forget about – "

The rest of her words were lost in the crack of the gunshot.

The surfacer seemed to fall in slow motion. She had all the time in the world to watch the shock that flitted across his face as his hands lost their grip on the edges of the door. Then he was gone, tumbling backwards to the ground he came from, red blooming in the middle of his chest.

The shuttle door slid closed before he hit the ground. Even so, she saw the way his body crumpled on impact. Even so, she heard the sickening crack of bone on concrete. Her mind was more than capable of providing her with what her eyes had been spared from seeing.

"You good back there, Shaw?"

The cybernetic man gave Ridley a cold stare and holstered his pistol as calmly as if he'd never used it. "Never better. Get us back to Exodus Station."

"Copy that. Better buckle in, we'll be breaking atmo in three minutes."

Shaw grabbed her arm, ushering her to one of the seats, but Ridley shook him off. "What the hell was that? You killed him for no reason."

He ignored her while he fastened the straps into place around her chest. It was only when he took his own seat that he replied. "He got in the way of my orders. I had plenty of reason."

"Orders? Captain Renata would never have ordered you to shoot an unarmed surfacer!"

A muscle twitched in his jaw. "The captain didn't think we'd be going anywhere near the surface. My orders were to pick you up from Hyperion University. If you'd been there like you were supposed to, this wouldn't have happened."

The accusation hit her like a slap. "I had business to take care of." Even as she spoke, the words founded like a frail excuse. "You were the one that shot him."

"And I can live with that." Shaw gave her a sideways glance. "Can you?"

Ridley didn't have time to answer. Instead, she forced herself to grit her teeth against the acceleration of the shuttle. Every bone in her body rattled as the pressure reverberated through her. They were breaking atmosphere.

There had been a time not so long ago when she had never seen the sky. The first time she had gone topside, she felt dizzy, fearing she would fall upwards and float away. But space was a whole new sensation altogether. New Pallas had become a glittering sphere of lights and shadows far below, so small she wondered how it could have ever seemed significant.

"That's us clear." The pilot's voice came through over the intercom. "Approaching the Exodus orbital path now. You should be able to see the station in a minute or two."

At first, there was only darkness. Ridley found it hard to believe something could exist out here without being swallowed by it. The thought of disappearing into it churned her stomach and she doubled over in her seat, fighting off a wave of nausea.

"Better get yourself together or you'll miss it." Shaw gestured towards the viewport. "Look."

It emerged slowly, shrugging off the cloak of darkness concealing it. Its central ring stretched on for miles before it curved back on itself, disappearing into the distance. It seemed impossible that it should be able to hang there, suspended above New Pallas, without crashing to the ground.

When she turned to look back at Shaw, her mouth agape, she realised he'd been watching her. He wore a satisfied expression on his face, as though her reaction had vindicated him in some way. "Welcome to Exodus Station."

When Ridley looked at him, all she saw was the terror on the surfacer's face as he tumbled towards the ground. "You're an Exodan, aren't you? Is that why you don't seem to like me much?"

He tightened his jaw but made no reply. Ridley didn't need one. She'd seen the reaction too often not to be familiar with it.

A hundred words danced on the tip of her tongue. She swallowed them, resigning them to her depths. She didn't need them anymore. Not where she was going. If the expedition failed, there wouldn't be any divide left between Exodans and topsiders and surfacers.

They'd all just be dead.

THOSE LEFT BEHIND IS COMING NOVEMBER 2021

––––––––––––––––

Make sure you don't miss out! Sign up for the newsletter at ncscrimgeour.com to keep up to date on new releases.

Printed in Great Britain
by Amazon